✻STAND
A LONE
NOVEL

"JAMES A. MOORE IS ~~SOMEONE TO~~
—Be~~~~

"A GRAND STORYT~~~~
HIS OWN WIT~~~~
—*Midwe*~~~~

"THE ONLY HORROR AUTHOR OUT THERE
WHO'S ALREADY WRITING AT THE LEVEL
OF THE MODERN GREATS."
—Garrett Peck

Praise for

DEEPER

"A FAST READ THAT WILL KEEP YOU GOING UNTIL
YOU FINISH IT...Some folks are comparing Moore to King
and Koontz, but to me he is an American original." —*Baryon*

"INSTANTLY AND TOTALLY CAPTIVATING...a book
that a reader is not going to want to put down until it's finished.
While...there's plenty of action, excitement and terror, Moore
does more. [He] creates very real, three-dimensional characters...[and] some of the most compelling and frightening
monsters and supernatural creatures it has been my pleasure to
encounter in recent years. *Deeper* is simply a blast to read. You
will kick yourselves if you pass this one by." —*FearZone.com*

"JAMES A. MOORE HAS GIVEN US A COMBINA-
TION OF CTHULHU MYTHOS AND GHOST STORY
IN *DEEPER*...a captivating story with an excellent blend
of mystery and adventure that will keep even jaded readers
entertained...a great read." —*Monster Librarian*

"MOORE'S TRIBUTE TO ONE OF HORROR'S MASTERS,
H. P. LOVECRAFT. At the risk of offending HPL purists, Moore
is the superior stylist. One of Moore's hallmarks is the depth of
character given to the players in his tales, and *Deeper* is no exception...nearly perfect novel of horror, one that can stand proudly
alongside its inspiration." —*Horror World Book Reviews*

continued...

Praise for

BLOOD RED

"FAST-MOVING with a good mix of sex, gore and laughs...Moore knows how to keep the pages turning and the blood running. Sad, introspective vampires in powdered wigs need not apply."
—*Page Horrific*

"*BLOOD RED* DOES WHAT ALL THE BEST VAMPIRE NOVELS DO; it...digs for blood beneath the skin."
—*The Agony Column*

"OFFERS PLENTY OF...HORROR CHILLS leavened with flashes of humor."
—*Publishers Weekly*

"THE COMPARISONS TO VINTAGE STEPHEN KING ARE JUSTIFIED. Brutal and scary, *Blood Red* has restored my faith, not only in the vampire subgenre, but in horror as a whole."
—Kealan Patrick Burke

"THERE IS SO MUCH TO ENJOY ABOUT *BLOOD RED*. Moore is powerfully descriptive."
—*Baryon*

"MOORE HAS WOVEN TOGETHER THE BEST THREADS OF VAMPIRE LORE with lust, power and brutality...Grab this treat, turn off the phone and enjoy a refreshingly inventive take on the vampire tale."
—*Monsters and Critics*

Praise for

SERENITY FALLS

and the Serenity Falls trilogy:
WRIT IN BLOOD, THE PACK, and DARK CARNIVAL

"QUITE POSSIBLY THE BEST HORROR NOVEL SINCE *SALEM'S LOT.* [It] will grab you and horrify you while maintaining a death grip on your interest throughout. This is the ultimate page-turner...Fully fleshed, well-developed characters. Immerse them in a great plot and superb action where the

menace and mystery increase with each paragraph and you have a truly important novel. James A. Moore's *Serenity Falls* shows some of the strength of a young Stephen King, some of the flavor of the current Bentley Little and a dash of the wit and perverseness of Dean Koontz. In the end, *Serenity Falls* is a major accomplishment in the horror field. Read it and you will echo my praise."
—*Baryon*

"INTENSIFYING TERROR."
—*The Best Reviews*

"A TREMENDOUS HORROR STORY WORTHY OF THE MASTERS. James A. Moore is perhaps the most talented writer of this genre to date."
—*Midwest Book Review*

"A SPRAWLING EPIC…Moore creates and develops a whole population's worth of memorable characters…This is easily the best horror novel to appear this year. It's more ambitious than the last three novels you've read put together. If there's any justice in the world, James A. Moore will be the genre's next superstar. He's the only horror author out there who's already writing at the level of the modern greats. The name James A. Moore will soon be spoken in the same reverent tones we now speak of King, Straub and Koontz. Count on it."
—*Garrett Peck*

"YOU'RE GOING TO GET YOUR MONEY'S WORTH WITH THIS ONE, in terms of both quality and quantity. You'll become immersed very quickly, and once caught up in the story, you'll find it difficult to put the book away until you've finished it."
—*San Francisco Chronicle*

"BRINGS TO MIND EARLY STEPHEN KING—think of it as *Dawson's Creek* as written by King. In *Serenity Falls*, James A. Moore has written a novel where all hell breaks loose—literally. His descriptions of small town quirks and foibles hit the mark on all cylinders…a great horror novel."
—James Argendeli, CNN Headline News

Titles by James A. Moore

DEEPER
BLOOD RED

Serenity Falls Trilogy

WRIT IN BLOOD
THE PACK
DARK CARNIVAL

DEEPER

JAMES A. MOORE

BERKLEY BOOKS, NEW YORK

THE BERKLEY PUBLISHING GROUP
Published by the Penguin Group
Penguin Group (USA) Inc.
375 Hudson Street, New York, New York 10014, USA
Penguin Group (Canada), 90 Eglinton Avenue East, Suite 700, Toronto, Ontario M4P 2Y3, Canada
(a division of Pearson Penguin Canada Inc.)
Penguin Books Ltd., 80 Strand, London WC2R 0RL, England
Penguin Group Ireland, 25 St. Stephen's Green, Dublin 2, Ireland (a division of Penguin Books Ltd.)
Penguin Group (Australia), 250 Camberwell Road, Camberwell, Victoria 3124, Australia
(a division of Pearson Australia Group Pty. Ltd.)
Penguin Books India Pvt. Ltd., 11 Community Centre, Panchsheel Park, New Delhi—110 017, India
Penguin Group (NZ), 67 Apollo Drive, Rosedale, North Shore 0632, New Zealand
(a division of Pearson New Zealand Ltd.)
Penguin Books (South Africa) (Pty.) Ltd., 24 Sturdee Avenue, Rosebank, Johannesburg 2196,
South Africa

Penguin Books Ltd., Registered Offices: 80 Strand, London WC2R 0RL, England

This is a work of fiction. Names, characters, places, and incidents either are the product of the author's imagination or are used fictitiously, and any resemblance to actual persons, living or dead, business establishments, events, or locales is entirely coincidental. The publisher does not have any control over and does not assume any responsibility for author or third-party websites or their content.

DEEPER

A Berkley Book / published by arrangement with the author

PRINTING HISTORY
Necessary Evil Press hardcover edition published 2007
Berkley mass-market edition / May 2009

Copyright © 2007 by James A. Moore.
Cover illustration by Cliff Nielsen.
Cover design by George Long.
Interior text design by Kristin del Rosario.

All rights reserved.
No part of this book may be reproduced, scanned, or distributed in any printed or electronic form without permission. Please do not participate in or encourage piracy of copyrighted materials in violation of the author's rights. Purchase only authorized editions.
For information, address: The Berkley Publishing Group,
a division of Penguin Group (USA) Inc.,
375 Hudson Street, New York, New York 10014.

ISBN: 978-0-425-22821-0

BERKLEY®
Berkley Books are published by The Berkley Publishing Group,
a division of Penguin Group (USA) Inc.,
375 Hudson Street, New York, New York 10014.
BERKLEY® is a registered trademark of Penguin Group (USA) Inc.
The "B" design is a trademark of Penguin Group (USA) Inc.

PRINTED IN THE UNITED STATES OF AMERICA

10 9 8 7 6 5 4 3 2 1

If you purchased this book without a cover, you should be aware that this book is stolen property. It was reported as "unsold and destroyed" to the publisher, and neither the author nor the publisher has received any payment for this "stripped book."

This one is for Lee Thomas, Chris and Connie Golden, my sister Ro, for remembering my love of certain old films and, of course, my wife, Bonnie Moore.

A heartfelt and profound thank-you to Mike McCarty, an excellent writer and special effects artist with KNB Special Effects, for all of his technical assistance on *Deeper*. Several scenes in the novel required information on diving and I have never done any diving deeper than the local swimming hole. Believe me, the book wouldn't have worked without his help!

A huge thanks to Alan M. Clark. Alan, you're the best!

Special thanks also go out to Brian Keene, Jeff Strand, Kelli Dunlap and Tom Piccirilli for their insight. Thanks, guys!

Thanks to Don Koish, not only for deciding to publish *Deeper*, but for his insightful input and the numerous discussions we've had about all things in the genre and life in general. You're one of the best, my friend. Thanks also to Kelly Perry, who manages to keep me on track with my storytelling, and to Leigh Haig, who was forced to endure countless rereads in an effort to find every flaw in the manuscript!

ONE

My grandfather used to tell me that the oceans knew all the secrets the world had to offer. He said the biggest problem was that no one ever seemed to know how to listen for those secrets.

That stuck with me over the years. I've never been a man of science. I've never had the patience to go through all of the studies and tests that are required to be a proper man of science, but I have always paid attention to what the oceanographers and weather people had to say about the world that lurks below the water's surface.

It's a damned big world under there, and even with everything we've learned about the seas, there are a million more mysteries to be solved. For me the notion of actually solving them is laughable. I just like to contemplate them from time to time when I've had a few too many drinks and I'm looking out over the harbor.

My name is Joseph Alexander Bierden. Most people just call me Joe. I've lived in the same place for most of my life and I haven't been in much of a hurry to get anywhere else. I like the sea and I like the town of Bowden's Point. It's no Black Stone Bay, but it'll do in a pinch.

Anyone who's ever been to a seaside town knows the drill. There are people who live there year-round and there are people who come to visit. I'm one of the year-round residents. I make most of my money during the summer months, when there are plenty of people who need to hire a boat, mostly for fishing and sometimes just to have a party where the neighbors aren't going to complain about the noise. I have three boats all told. One old wreck called the *Marianne Winston*—after an old girlfriend who dumped me not long after I bought it—is used by me when I feel like actually going out for a little crabbing. I have a twenty-foot galleon, called *Lisa's Hope,* I use for smaller parties and I have a sixty-foot yacht, *Isabella's Dream,* for the parties that feel like spending a small fortune and don't mind the hefty security deposits. There have even been a few weddings performed on the *Isabella,* and a few honeymoons as well.

It's a living and the only one I really want to have. My job—I can't really call it a career, because I just don't take it seriously enough—provides me with a roof over my head, a good deal of free time to spend with my wife and kids, and allows me to work around my first love whenever I feel the need.

My first love has always been the ocean. Isabella knew that when I proposed to her, and still she accepted. I guess that's the reason I've always been faithful to her, despite the numerous temptations. Don't get me wrong. I don't think I'm anything special, but you mix the summer weather, enough alcohol, and a party on a yacht together and I've had a ridiculous number of offers.

It isn't all peaches and cream as the old saying goes. There are a lot of things that have to be taken care of during any year to ensure a comfortable living, and there have been a few times where I wasn't very proud of myself for some of the work I did. Back when I was just starting out,

I did some rather shady work bringing in bundles of drugs that I picked up offshore. If my reputation in town hadn't been as solid as it was, I might well have been caught, too. I didn't do it too often and I only ever took on the extra work when I needed the money to pay the bills and make a decent living. I stopped dealing with any part of the drug trade around the same time one of the other captains I knew wound up with a few bullet holes through his body and his head missing. It wasn't easy to get out of the business, but I managed, and the man I was picking up for was a good sport about it. If he hadn't been, I wouldn't be writing this down now.

So, yes, a few things I'm ashamed of, a few marks on my list of the seven deadly sins, but nothing extreme. Funny how that works. We can almost always justify our actions if we take the time to explain them to ourselves.

I'll let you in on a secret, though. Sometimes we don't know that what we're doing is wrong until it's too late. Sometimes the most innocent things, the safest things, can turn like a snake and bite you on the ankle, and when that happens, there's only one choice left.

You've got to try to fix what you did wrong and pray to whatever gods you might believe in that you aren't too late.

I should have known things would go wrong on that little venture. My guts were telling me that taking the job was a bad idea, but I brushed it off because the money was nice and because Belle wanted a vacation that was worth noticing.

All you can do in life is make sure you do things for all the right reasons. There's nothing else in the long run, except to hope the things you do don't come back to kick you in the jaw.

It started at the end of the busy season. I was just about ready to pull out my little crabbing boat and go lay some traps and call it done. The tourists were mostly gone and the air was starting to get its early morning winter chill. The girls wandering around in bikinis had graduated up to wearing jeans again—always a depressing thing for an old letch like me: married but not blind, you know. And God help me, there were already signs popping up for the end of summer sales and the new fall fashions in the windows of half the stores in town.

I wasn't really trolling for new business. It hadn't been the best summer ever, but it was far from the worst, and I had earned enough to keep the bills paid. Charlie Moncrief, my trusty right-hand man, was double-checking all of the nets and cables and I was polishing the brass railing on the *Isabella's Dream* when the offer came my way.

Charlie is a big man, with an easygoing smile and a permanent tan caused half by the sun and half by the wind. Even in the winter, when there's no way in hell to get the boats out for a long trip and the sun doesn't much peek its face out of the clouds, Charlie has that dark tan. And his eyes, Lord Almighty, his eyes are almost exactly the same color as the sea on a stormy day. Women seem to love them. I could spend days telling you stories about Charlie and his numerous adventures on the water and in different ports, but I will say this: he is a perfect example of what has been said about sailors for years. There's a girl in every port, and in most of them there are probably two or three. Charlie always had a way with the ladies, and could drink most men under the table without even trying.

Charlie noticed the people first, of course, because there were women involved. Four people came toward the yacht and looked at it carefully. I nodded my head and left them in peace, because most of the times when you have a small group like that, they're considering whether or not they want to rent your ship out for the day and trying to decide if the rates are fair enough. The rates are never fair enough, but most people are willing to pay them. I'll negotiate most times, and now and then I'll even let them win a good haggling argument, but only if the coffers at home have enough money to see me through a few more days.

None of them looked like the seafaring type. There was a couple who was obviously together and looked like they shouldn't have been. I guess I should describe them properly just so you can get a good picture of them. There was a stick of a man with salt-and-pepper hair, and a girl of around twenty hanging at his side. She was more handsome than pretty, and had a smile that was pure confidence and good feelings. She had more muscles than he did, and I assumed she was big into sports. Her hair was cut short so it wouldn't get in her way, and if I'd been asked by someone I would have labeled her an athlete. They both looked like they belonged on a college campus. The stick man had professor written all over him. I'm sure you know the type, the sort who only feels right in his classroom, where he's practically the king, but take the classroom away and suddenly he looks a little confused about where he is and why he's there.

The stick man spent a few minutes staring at the boat and then came closer. He walked up the causeway until he was almost on the yacht proper and then froze like a rabbit caught off guard by a human. He was dressed in a three-piece charcoal suit and looked about as comfortable as a thief in a confessional.

"Excuse me?" He looked directly at Charlie, who was busy wrapping a mooring cable back into a manageable mess.

"You looking to hire out?" Charlie said, barely looking up.

"Yes, I think. We'd like to hire your boat and services." The man looked uncomfortable about the entire affair, as if he'd rather have been sitting in a nice safe library reading the newspaper. Nothing wrong with that, mind you; just he seemed very uncomfortable with the notion of hiring out a yacht and even more uncomfortable with the idea of actually getting on one.

Charlie pointed his chin in my direction. "Need to talk with Joe over there; this is his 'boat.'" A lot of sailors will take a person to task for calling a yacht a boat or a dinghy a ship. Charlie might have liked to have done the same, but I had simple rules when it comes to dealing with any of the potential customers and those included not being an ass about nautical terms. Still, Charlie couldn't quite keep the sarcasm out of his voice. I'll answer questions if they'd like me to, but I won't correct them and I surely don't chastise them for being ignorant. I expect the same courtesy in return when it comes to doctors and lawyers. I don't understand what they do and a lot of them don't understand what I do, but there's always a common ground somewhere along the way.

The man looked over at me and smiled apologetically. I guess he figured I'd take offense at him approaching Charlie instead of me. If I'd been wearing a captain's hat, I might have. I put down my polishing rag and wiped my hands clean on my jeans before heading in his direction.

Up close he was just as skinny. It wasn't a starved puppy sort of thin, just a slight build. I knew several men with that sort of frame who could hold their own in a bar brawl. This particular gentleman wasn't one of them.

"How can I help you?" I tried to keep my voice cheerful and neutral. The girl who was with him gave him a light push to urge him onto the yacht. He didn't actually burst into flames when he set his foot on the deck, but he looked like he expected to.

"I'm Dr. Martin Ward." I nodded, because the name had been offered. "I'd like to see about hiring your boat for a rather long time."

"How long are we talking, Doctor?"

Ward thought about that for a few seconds, and while he was thinking, the girl with him spoke up. "One month. Does that sound right to you?" The first part she aimed at me, the second at Ward.

He nodded. "That sounds almost perfect." The look he sent her way was one of pure gratitude.

"A month? At this time of year?" My mind was divided right then. A big part of me was doing the great math dance and figuring how far into the black a month of extra cash would put me. A smaller, but equally vocal part was telling me that I was dealing with a completely unprepared imbecile who had no idea how bad the weather could get on the ocean when autumn was creeping in fast.

"Is this a bad time of year for boating?" He looked at me with wide eyes, like maybe he had just realized he'd made some horrible social blunder. I half expected to see him reach down to check his fly.

"Weather can be tricky, is all. Sometimes storms come out of nowhere and linger for a few days." He nodded his head and looked a little depressed. "Doesn't mean it can't be done, but if you actually want to stay on the water for a whole month, there're a lot of things to consider by way of supplies."

"Oh, no, not all the time. We'd want to sleep on land." Damned if I didn't want to pat him on the top of his head right then, like a puppy in need of a reward.

"I'm just warning you that if you want to go fishing every day, some of those days are going to be a little rough if you don't have your sea legs, and a few of them are going to be impossible."

He nodded his head enthusiastically. "Fair enough, Captain Joe. You come highly recommended; I'll trust you on any decisions about rough weather."

That brought a smile to my face. You'd be amazed how many seemingly intelligent people don't catch on that there are differences in how a storm affects the land and how it affects a ship on the ocean.

"As long as we understand each other."

"What are your rates for a monthlong expedition, Captain?" That was the girl standing next to him.

I looked at her and smiled. The smile was easy. She was pretty in a very athletic way, and reminded me just a little of the girl whose name was still stuck on my crab boat. Her hair was short, blond, and curly, and had the sort of color that only comes from being in the sun a lot.

"We can haggle out the details. It's the end of the normal season, which puts me in a mind to be a little generous."

Charlie laughed and shook his head, his damned grin spreading across his face like a flash of lightning and then staying there.

The girl looked his way and frowned slightly.

"You'll have to forgive Charlie," I said with a smile of my own. "He's not used to the idea of me being generous." I told them what my normal daily rates were, fully expecting them to turn a dozen different shades of green. The thing is, my yacht requires a lot of upkeep and I like to turn a profit, too. My summer rates have to pay for the whole year. I don't live in Florida, where I could rent out year-round. I have to make the money last.

It wasn't Ward who did the haggling, it was his sidekick. She put up a good fight, but in the end we came up with a fair and equitable deal.

"What are you planning on doing for a month out on the water?" Charlie looked past the couple and studied the mismatched pair who was still standing on the dock. I could see why he'd want to stare; I recognized their faces, but couldn't decide where I knew them from. It wasn't really any of my business as long as they weren't going to try to use the *Isabella* as a source of illegal income. Neither of them looked like they were up to anything riskier than sitting behind desks in a stuffy office and reading a lot. The guy looked about ten years older than me and forty pounds heavier, but not in a good way. The lady with him looked a good ten years younger and was probably a looker when she wasn't busy dressing like a conservative librarian.

No one answered Charlie's question right away, and that made me a little nervous, but not overly so. Still, I was happier when the girl answered.

"Dr. Ward is studying rumors about a system of underwater caves not too far from here. From everything we've heard this is the best time of year for actually gaining access to the caves."

"So you want to go diving?" Charlie looked at the girl as if she'd grown a second set of eyes and they were crossed.

"Is that a problem?"

"Not if you don't mind a little cold water..."

Here's the thing. It gets cold fast in New England, and the water reflects that chill. The Gulf Stream doesn't even consider coming up our way and the winds that come down from the Arctic Circle seem to specialize in sucking the heat out of the ocean. I've had a few occasions where I managed to get myself properly wet in late October or early November, and believe me, it's not something I ever wanted to do after the first time. Hypothermia is a real threat, and anyone who thinks a dry suit will keep you warm in that sort of chill has never gone diving into the waters off the coast of Connecticut or Massachusetts. And these people were saying they wanted to go for swims every day.

We discussed the matter for a few minutes, just so I could make sure the people who were about to pay for my Christmas vacation understood exactly what they were getting themselves into. I'm not really fond of the idea of pulling corpses out of the water, especially when the dead people in question are supposed to pay me a lot of money. I'm a businessman first when it comes to my services. They agreed to sign a waiver that excluded me and my crew from any liabilities.

They wanted to go diving, and they were bringing along fifteen college kids to help them with it. That would bring their number up to nineteen, and we added a little more haggling about the cost for feeding them all. Two meals a day minimum meant a lot more food shoved into the larder.

After that, it was just a matter of working out the details.

You ever hear that old saying about the devil being in the details? Well, I'm here to tell you that there is a lot of truth in that stupid phrase. More than I imagined when I met Dr. Ward and his cronies.

I was late coming home from the docks, but Belle was used to that. Between being a bit anal about how the yacht looked and the occasional drink with Charlie, it wasn't exactly a news flash. My wife, being far more adept at changing than I have ever been, started cooking dinner around the same time I pulled up in the driveway.

I got lucky when I met Isabella. We met in college, and had probably a dozen classes together, ranging from philosophy—a course I should never have taken—to a few English courses and even a class on marine biology.

I knew it was lust at first sight. Love came later, but when it finally showed up I decided to spend the rest of my life with her and she was good enough not to have me arrested for stalking her. She's the only woman I've ever met who could possibly put up with me, and, as an added bonus, she's a knockout.

She took one look at my face and knew something was up. The chances of me ever pulling the wool over her eyes are about the same as me growing wings.

"What did you do?" Her voice was teasing, and so was the grin on her face.

"I landed a really big fish."

"Meaning you went fishing instead of making a living? Or meaning you made some poor bastard pay you too much?" Belle stirred a collection of potatoes, meat, and onions on the stove and my stomach decided to let out a few rude noises to remind me I hadn't had much beyond breakfast to eat.

"Second choice. A nice gig. I get to run a couple of college types around and watch them freeze their privates off. Best of all, they're gonna pay me."

I wanted to reach out and hug her, but I knew the rules. The loving had to wait until she was done at the stove. She's always had a thing about open flames, and we had a piece of crap gas stove that I'd planned on having replaced for the last five or so years.

"How long a run?" She stirred her concoction again and I moved past her to grab a few plates and the flatware.

"About a month, but they want to come in every day."

"A month?" Her voice raised a few notes higher than usual, and I knew she was thinking like me, that they had to be nutcases.

"Looks like we'll have a little to sock away for a rainy day this time around."

"Well, I won't complain about it." She moved over and scraped the potatoes, onions, and sausage onto our plates, while I pulled two Michelobs from the refrigerator.

"You won't mind not having me here and under your feet every day?"

"Oh, please. Now I get to spend extra time with the milkman every day." Once the food was out of her hands and the pan was back on the stove, Isabella slid into my arms for a proper hug. There's little I love more than the feel of that woman against me, her head resting on my shoulder.

"You could come with, if you wanted."

"I might. Maybe a few days, just to get out and enjoy the last of the summer."

"Charlie would love to see you almost as much as me."

"Charlie would love to see anything female as long as it was in a bathing suit."

"True enough." I couldn't help but laugh because she was dead-on with Charlie and always had been. He was a heel as far as women went and Belle had warned him away from a few of her friends in the past.

We sat down to eat and it was decided. The job was too handsome not to take, even if the fools hiring me were in for a few cold and stormy days.

TWO

We started off four days later. I was ready the next day, but the group coming along needed more time to prepare, and there was the matter of the waivers for every one of them. Fifteen kids, all of legal age except one who needed to get permission from his parents. That took two days by itself. A yacht the size of the *Isabella's Dream* requires a few crew members, especially if you plan on going for extended trips. And that, by the way, was a rub I hadn't counted on. The people who'd hired me wanted to sleep on land, but that didn't mean they intended to sleep on the same land. While a few occasions would let me come home to Belle for my rest, the docks at Golden Cove would become my home for much of the stay.

Golden Cove is a strange little town, built by a real estate investment firm and then abandoned only days after it opened to the public. The original owners were out of the picture for the most part. Only a few of them ever even came around the place, though it had made them a fortune.

It's as pretty as a postcard, and looks like a little slice of heaven. Most times you couldn't get me to set foot in the area. There were all sorts of rumors about its past and the bad things that had happened there. So, naturally, I'd been suckered into taking a small army of people to the waters off the shore and letting them use my ship. I'd have been bitter about it if I hadn't been paid up front. Having a handsome sum of money sitting in the bank goes a long way to making me more forgiving.

Oh, and I also made damned sure that they paid me extra for the docking fees at Golden Cove. The place was built to take in money and they wanted a sizable chunk of mine for the privilege of parking my yacht.

On the brighter side, the fishing was supposed to be incredible and I had just the right collection of fishing poles to test that theory. My job was to get them where they were going safely; after that I was free to play a bit.

Anyhow, I hired on a couple of the local kids who I knew weren't quite ready for the whole college experience, and made clear to them that they would be working for their money. Davey Walker was just barely nineteen and looked like a freshman in high school, forget college. He was reed thin and short to boot, with a dark complexion and skin so smooth he probably never shaved more than once a week. But I also knew from experience that he was one hell of a good kid to have around when it came to working on engines. I didn't expect to have too much trouble along those lines, but it was nice to have an extra person around who could handle the work. As an added bonus, he could cook if Tom wasn't up to it.

Tom Summers was almost Davey's opposite, and was also his best friend. There was little they didn't do together. Tom had reddish blond hair he kept in a ponytail and freckles so intense that the only way to hide them was to tan himself deeply enough to match them. He'd been doing a good job of it, and was almost mahogany colored. Tom was also the sort of kid who needed to learn a few things about personal hygiene, but as long as he could handle the workload, I would provide him with free deodorant.

Aside from those two, it was Charlie and me to handle the work. It was enough.

We got under way early, and most of the trip down the coastline was as pleasant as could be. It only became uncomfortable when I mentioned our destination to Charlie.

The thing is, now and then I forget how much of a sailor Charlie is. He did his time in the Navy, of course, and he was practically raised on the fishing boats, but I forget that sometimes, because he doesn't usually let himself act like a superstitious clown.

He heard the name Golden Cove and jumped back like I'd slapped him in the face with a jellyfish.

"You have a good time, Joe." Just like that he was ready to hop off the side of the *Isabella* and start swimming for home.

"Oh for Christ's sake, Charlie, grow up." I didn't mean to laugh at him, but I did.

Charlie turned on me fast and jabbed a finger in my face. "You know how I feel about that place, Joe. We've talked about it a hundred times." He wasn't laughing. He was pissed off and he was frightened.

"Charlie, it's a damned town. There's nothing going on there that should have you ready to swim all the way home."

Remember that couple I told you about earlier? Well, the man who made me look like Hercules looked over when he heard my words and shook his head.

"Well, that's what some of us are here to find out, isn't it?" He managed a small smile, which looked like it didn't fit him at all.

Charlie looked at the man and then back at me, as if

somehow the man with the miserable face had just proved his point for him. Rather than give my first mate a one-fingered salute, I looked over at the stranger on my ship. "Care to explain that one?"

"Well, my wife and me, we're here to investigate claims that Golden Cove is haunted."

"Yeah? What makes you a specialist?"

He seemed a little surprised that I didn't know the answer already. "I'm Jacob Parsons, my wife is Mary Parsons. We're parapsychologists." It finally clicked where I had seen them before: on the TV at home. Belle was always watching shows about murders, unsolved murders, or real life haunted houses at night, when any sensible person would have been sleeping. I didn't mind, because I could sleep through almost anything. Now and then I watched enough of the shows that the names Jacob and Mary Parsons actually meant something to me. They were on a dozen or more specials every Halloween, and had been for at least a decade.

Charlie couldn't have looked more upset if the man talking to us had actually yanked a ghost out from behind his ear and thrown it at him. I don't like to make fun of people's beliefs, but I had about as much need of a ghost hunter as I did for a gynecologist.

My sentiments must have shown on my face, because Parsons nodded as if to say *just you wait and see, Mr. Know-it-all.* I rolled my eyes toward Charlie and shook my head.

"Charlie, do you honestly mean to tell me you're gonna let a few scary stories keep you from making a living?" He was acting like a child, so I treated him like one.

It's the best way I've ever learned to piss Charlie Moncrief off. And it worked just as well as it always does. Now, I need to explain a little something about Charlie. He is, as I already said, a ladies' man. He is also one of the best damned sailors I've ever had the pleasure to know. He can do damned near anything required to handle a boat in the roughest weather and he's as strong as an ox. To the best of my knowledge, he'd never lost a fight, either, and I'd witnessed quite a few of them back when I barhopped.

My point is this: pissing off Charlie is always a risky proposition. He stared hard at me, with the sort of look in his eyes that said he wouldn't have minded force-feeding his boot down my throat. I'm not really much into taking risks with my life, but I trusted that we were good enough friends that he'd let me slide and just be angry enough to stay on instead.

I sort of hate manipulating people, but I can do it when I have to.

I got lucky. Charlie nodded his head and walked away from me. I knew I'd have to placate him later, but at least he wasn't leaving or tossing me over the bow of my own yacht.

Jacob Parsons looked at me and shook his head sadly. "Sorry about that, Captain. I was just making conversation. I didn't mean to cause any trouble."

He was a paying client, so I indulged him. "Wasn't you. Charlie's always been afraid of anything that has a legend stuck to it."

Parsons tried to light up a cigarette, fighting the sea breeze the entire way. After a few failed tries he was puffing away, and once that task was finished, he finally answered my comment.

"He might not have been the best choice for this job, Captain. What you call Golden Cove is supposed to be a pretty intense place when it comes to ghosts and other things."

"What sort of other things?" It was a long trip and I was just bored enough to ask that sort of question. Besides, I needed to know what Charlie was going to be worrying about.

Jacob Parsons looked at me for a few seconds like he was trying to decide if he should actually mention what was on his mind. He squinted a bit when he was thinking. I got to see him squint a lot while we were together.

"You know the history of this area pretty well?"

"Well enough." I shrugged. There had been a lot of stories over the years.

"Well, Golden Cove was built on the remains of another town, and one with a nice long history of weirdness."

"Okay, go on."

"I can't think of the name of the town to save my life…Mary's the one with the good memory. Anyhow, there was talk of devil worship and other things before the town got leveled. And long before that happened, there was talk about the entire area being a sort of, I don't know, a sort of trouble spot. Nothing as bad as the Bermuda Triangle or anything, but there are a lot of old documents that talk about ships sinking off the shore there."

"Ships sink. I may not be a genius, but I've been on the ocean long enough to know that."

"Well, that may be true, Captain, but there are rumors that the ships might have been helped along." He puffed away on his cigarette like it had done something to piss him off and he was enjoying making it suffer. "They were sunk deliberately, and not just one or two, but closer to twenty."

"There's no way in hell twenty ships got scuttled without people hearing about it."

Parsons nodded his head and smiled. "And I'd have agreed with you if I hadn't read the papers. But please, believe me, nobody knows because it wasn't done all at once. Whatever was ruining those ships did it at a very slow rate, like maybe a ship every fifteen or twenty years."

I chuckled and shook my head. "I'm guessing you're not going to find a conspiracy, if that's what you're looking for. I can't exactly believe that someone trained their descen-

dants in the fine art of getting rid of ships and then hiding
the evidence."

"You misunderstand me." Mr. Parsons looked as amused
as I felt. "I don't think it's that easy. I think there might
be something up, but if so, I don't think it's a case of one
person or even a group of people wiping out these boats. I
think it might be some sort of phenomenon."

I have to admit that notion was more interesting.

"So, you're not looking for ghosts?"

"Oh, I might be, but not in this case. Well, not
exclusively."

"I don't get you."

Parsons stared at the deck for a few seconds, obviously
trying to figure out how to word what he wanted to say. I
got the impression that he didn't usually like to talk, and
that was a notion that stuck with me.

"Harry Houdini was a great escape artist, but he also made
a point of debunking a lot of the spiritualists who worked the
field while he was alive. Did you know that, Captain?"

"I think I heard about that a few times, yes . . ."

"Well, he did that because he wanted to find proof of
life after death. He did that because he was a skeptic and
he wanted to be a believer. More importantly, I think, he
wanted to stop the people who were preying on the griev-
ing survivors and make sure they couldn't make a living
out of fleecing them."

"Okay. I can see that. But what has that got to do with
Golden Cove?"

"I don't necessarily believe that anything at all is in
Golden Cove. I don't think there are monsters, and I don't
think there are ghosts or families who specialize in scut-
tling ships, Captain."

"You don't?" I was a little surprised to hear that. I had
expected someone with a little more passion for his profession, if you can see my point.

"No. But I'd like to find out for myself. I want to know what's behind the rumors, even if it's something as easy as natural gas pockets causing the ships to sink and that same gas igniting that has caused people to see strange lights late at night and the occasional ghost ship out on the water." He leaned over the railing and knocked the cherry off of his smoke, then pocketed the butt. "I want to know what it is, even if it's nothing at all."

"Do you think you'll find anything, Mr. Parsons?"

He smiled again, and shrugged his beefy shoulders. "I hope so. I'm paying a fortune for this expedition, and I'd hate to waste it on nothing more than a windburn."

"I thought you were along as a consultant."

"Oh, no, I'm footing the bill for the university. Well, Mary and I are footing it, anyway."

"What? Universities don't have the money for this sort of thing?" I was only half joking when I asked the question.

Parsons shook his head and chuckled. "Gotta buy football uniforms this year, and I bet there are a few academic endeavors they might consider, too, like a new set of encyclopedias for the library."

I liked Jacob Parsons. He wasn't the sort of person I normally hung around with, but I was glad to meet him.

"So tell me about these shipwrecks of yours, Mr. Parsons."

"It's Jacob, please." He leaned back against the railing and looked down at the water as it splashed away from the sides. I don't think he quite knew what to make of the ocean, like a man who's almost never been on it or in it, but I think he was starting to decide he liked it well enough.

"A lot of the ships that were wrecked could be put down as caused by different reasons." He shrugged as he spoke, as if apologizing. "A lot of them have never been explained. Back all the way to the Revolutionary War there have been ships going down in the area. In a two-year span, you had the HMS *Thornton,* the HMS *Independent* and the HMS *Ashbury* all sunk in the area. There was a small settlement back then, maybe a few hundred people, but there are no records that anyone in the area actually had any encounters with the ships. They just sank. No explanation given and no survivors or witnesses."

"Those were warships?"

He nodded. "All three had just come over from England and were fully loaded with supplies and soldiers."

"Well, I've seen a few nor'easters that could take down an armada, and wouldn't have a problem with the ships available back then. Solid wood construction is great on a calm day, but the people building those old rigs weren't always exactly craftsmen. All it would have taken is one rotted board. They didn't build in redundant safety features like bulwarks."

Parsons shook his head. "Nope. I checked. The weather was as clear as it is right now, and the ships came in the summer months. They sank for reasons unknown. The next group of ships that came along looking for them did some investigating, and decided to blame the people in the town. There really wasn't anything else around for miles, but I am very thorough in my research, Captain, and I can tell you for a fact that there were no rebel forces waiting in the town to sneak out and sink those ships. Most of the people in the town were still loyal to England—the captain of the HMS *Raven* said as much. He tortured fifteen of the healthiest men in town to make sure he knew what he was talking about. Then he burned down the docks in Innsmouth as punishment and went on his way. How's that for military logic?"

"Sounds like the military to me." What else could I say? The rules are different in wartime and back then the easiest way to handle an investigation was to just kill everyone who might be guilty. I think the captain of the *Raven* was being fairly nice for the times. That doesn't make it right, but it was how things were done.

Parsons looked around and finally decided to relax a bit. He reached into his jacket pocket and pulled out a small sheaf of photographs. "Look at these for a moment and tell me what you see."

I took the offered pictures and looked at them. The sun looked to be rising or going down and the buildings facing the water cast a lot of glare, but I could make out most of what was going on well enough. The scene was a beach-front and there was a celebration of some type going on. Or at least there had been. There were balloons and what looked like a dozen yachts off to the side, where a newly built dock could be seen. Mostly, it was the beach that was the focus of attention. There were people running, and a few of them were dying or dead on the shore. I could see one woman looking out at the water, her hands over her face, while right next to her a man was on his belly in the sand, and he looked to be covered in blood. I'm guessing it was real, because most of his back was exposed and I could see the remains of his shirt where it lay scattered around him. The details were a little fuzzy, as the picture wasn't in perfect focus. It looked like whoever had taken the pictures had been perfectly happy just pointing and clicking and never bothered to try for clarity.

There were several dark shapes on the sand, and a few coming out of the water, and these were what seemed to be the cause of the bloodshed. They didn't look quite right. They didn't look human, but again, the pictures were not as clear as I would have liked.

"What are those things?" I pointed to one of the dark shapes. This one looked almost like it had a tail.

"I have no earthly idea. All I know is that they aren't very friendly."

"So, what, these are pictures of a massacre taking place?"

Parsons shrugged his shoulders again. "I wish I could tell you. All I know is what I was told when I bought the *Silver Swordfish*."

I looked at Parsons and decided he just might be crazy. Everyone had heard about the *Silver Swordfish* and even thinking about it was enough to send a few shivers through me. I'd heard about it, and so had damned near everyone working the fishing lines on the eastern seaboard around the same time that the *Swordfish* showed up, but I did my best to hide my discomfort because I wanted to hear what Parsons would say.

"The *Silver Swordfish* was a pretty impressive yacht, Captain." He smiled almost apologetically as he said it, as if I might take offense that it was a better yacht than the one we were standing on. "She had just about everything you could need on a yacht, and a wet bar besides. I know the man who owned her had her insured for over two million dollars, if that tells you anything."

I nodded, because that said a great deal. If I'd had that sort of cash to spend on *Isabella's Dream*, I wouldn't have been leasing out her services.

"The day Golden Cove was supposed to open to the public was not a pretty one. The clouds were coming in and, as you saw from the pictures, the sky was almost red. What's that old saying about red skies at night? Well, the sailors might have been delighted, but I don't think anyone else was. Turns out there was one hell of a blow that night and it made the news.

"The *Silver Swordfish* was anchored off the shore of Golden Cove, near as anyone can tell. Her owner had brought her in that very morning for the celebration, and, as one of the movers and shakers with the Golden Cove project, he got the best spot. You saw the pictures. There were some notes written by whoever actually took them, but they got pretty sloppy at the end. His hands were shaking and the pages were spattered with blood and what looked like dead skin."

He shook his head and held up one hand. "I'm getting ahead of myself. The *Silver Swordfish* was there the night that whatever happened at Golden Cove happened. That is my point. The photos are evidence of that. But the *Swordfish* herself was found almost three hundred miles away, near Cape May, New Jersey. It cost me a fortune to purchase and validate the source of those pictures. I also have the original notes, but they're locked away in a safe place.

"No one knows how the yacht got there, but it did. It ended up wrapped around what's left of the old concrete ship at Cape May. The *Swordfish* didn't quite get scuttled but it came close.

"The camera containing the originals of the pictures and the notes that were found inside are all that gave any proof that anyone was on board when she went out. According to those notes, there was a concentrated attack on the land and the people there. What little I could get out of the coroners who examined the remains that were found— and there were only a few, not nearly enough to account for the people who disappeared that night—it looked like the people had been mauled by bears or attacked by sharks."

Quick geography lesson with a side of oceanography: there's a lot of rough terrain between Golden Cove and Cape May. The idea that it got there on its own is almost laughable. There's a lot of territory to cover, you see, and a million or so obstacles along the way.

"So, Captain, I don't really know a lot about the sea, but I know when something doesn't sound right to me. And the *Silver Swordfish* doesn't sit well with me when you add in what happened that night at Golden Cove. I want answers. I want to know what really happened."

The man's wife called out around the same time as he finished talking. He looked at her and moved in her direction with a quick wave of his hand. The first thought that came to my mind was that Parsons was whipped. Seems a man should finish his conversation before running off to see what his wife wants from him. Of course, I've been guilty of the same a few times.

I watched him go and thought about everything he'd just told me. There was definitely something about the story and about his determination that piqued my interest. Not that it much mattered. As I've said before, the sea holds a lot of secrets. I figured time would tell me whether or not it would reveal any of them to Jacob Parsons.

I had no idea...

THREE

I'd seen Golden Cove at a distance a few times, but never had any reason to set foot on the land there, or even to pay attention to the place. I could still remember the burned-out ruins of the previous town, a few lonesome collections of wood and rubble that had been a landmark for most of my life before the Golden Cove Company had come along and rebuilt the entire place.

Looking at it as we pulled up to the docks, I reassessed my opinion of the location. The old gray land I'd grown up with had been transformed into something that bordered on spectacular. The place that was known for being haunted when I was a kid—yes, I'd heard the stories, but had chosen to ignore them—had become everything it must have been in its heyday and more. The buildings had a sort of Hollywood Colonial charm, but accented to make it more pleasant than the realities of life back then. The houses that had been little more than pitted brick foundations when I was a child had grown into buildings that were elegant and rustic at the same time, with almost no signs of modern technology that were easily seen. I remembered reading an article about the reconstruction that explained the phone lines, the power lines and everything else were all hidden underground, the better to keep up the illusion.

I pulled my yacht into the spot dictated by the harbormaster and Charlie took care of docking us. Even from a distance I could see Dr. Ward and a dozen or so college-age kids on the wharf, watching on as we lowered the gangway. They observed the process like it was the most fascinating thing they had ever seen.

Charlie moved around with harsh, sharp motions, a sure sign that he was still furious about the place where we had stopped. I could see the relaxed expressions on most of the faces waiting to board the *Isabella*. Not a one of them looked the least bit worried.

Jacob and Mary Parsons walked down to the dock and spoke with the doctor for a moment. Parsons lit another cigarette and puffed away as the conversation continued. Charlie settled down near me and crossed his arms over his chest, looking at the crowd below.

"You still pissed off?"

"Goddamn right I am, Joe. This was never a part of the deal."

"You were there when I took the job, Charlie. They never said anything about Golden Cove and I never said a damned thing about avoiding it."

"I know that. Doesn't make me happy about the final result is all." He scowled down at the group below, as if they had somehow set out solely to ruin him.

"I can find someone else if I need to, Charlie. I won't be thrilled, but I can find someone else and you can head home with the rest of them in a day or two."

Charlie was not the sort of man who shirked his duties. I can tell you that as easily as I can tell you a good cure for a bright day is a pair of polarized sunglasses. I made the offer because I knew in advance what his answer would be.

"No. I signed on and I'm here, but Joe you better never put me in this position again." He pointed a finger at me. "And I better not hear a goddamned thing about this back in town or anywhere else. I don't make fun of people for going to church and I expect the same courtesy in return."

"That's a deal. Now put a smile on your face and go flirt with the college girls."

"It was on my planner." Charlie walked down the gangway and went about his business, which in this case was helping to load the boxes of equipment the college types had brought along with them. I called my other two out to help him and they made short work of the supplies. The college kids looked perfectly happy to let them handle all of the work, but the doctor showed an unexpected amount of backbone and ordered them to help. I guess they were all there for the extra credits or something.

Dr. Ward and his girl Friday came onto the yacht, and I had to suppress a smile. The man was dressed in shorts and a polo shirt and looked about as comfortable as a nun in a bikini. The girl with him was dressed in cutoffs and a plain white T-shirt. I could see her bathing suit under it, a one-piece black affair. I was struck again by the fact that she just didn't look like the academic type. I'd have expected her to be on the track team or maybe the women's volleyball team instead.

"Nice to see you again, Captain." The man was still meek, but he put on a better show of confidence when his students were around; even his handshake was firmer.

"Nice to see you again, too, Doctor. What are the plans for today?"

"Mostly we just want to take a little run around to the

reef out there and do some visuals and do a quick dive to get a feel for the reef. Nothing extreme."

I looked out to the reef. It could hardly be called an island, but there was a good-sized chunk of land out there, and even from where we were I could see the waves slapping against it.

"You know what that's called, right?"

The man looked at me and nodded. "The Devil's Reef."

"Judging by the waves out that way, you might want to tell your kids to be careful. It looks like there's one hell of an undertow."

"Oh, don't you worry. Diana here is a certified Dive Master and has over two hundred dives under her belt."

That explained the physique. "Just so you know, pieces of land like that normally earn their names."

Diana looked my way and smiled. She had a nice smile and the sort of easygoing demeanor that would have had a lot of men thinking she was either lesbian or flirtatious. I saw the way she looked at Charlie. I would have put money on her not liking girls that way.

"The Devil's Reef got its name from alleged activities dating back to the eighteen hundreds, Captain. There were rumors that the people around here were consorting with demons."

"And there are stories of shipwrecks that happened here, too. My guess is the reef out there had a lot to do with them." I pointed for her to see what I meant. The scabbed black reef rose prominently in a few areas, but by looking at the waves and the way they fell, you could see where a good portion of the land was just under the waterline. "There are a few spots there where the land barely even rises out of the water and the tide is just starting to come in. I can bet a few of the early wrecks happened because a lot of that reef is submerged when the tide is up."

"Well, according to what we've heard, there are some

interesting caves down below that reef, and that's what we're going to be looking into."

"You'd think a thing like that would have been studied by now."

"A few people have tried. Not many of them have returned without injuries. We aim to be very careful, Captain Joe."

"How big a set of caves are you talking about, anyway?"

"No one knows. There have been estimates given by sonar that make them seem pretty spectacular."

"Is that how you plan on mapping these things? With sonar?"

Diana nodded her head. "And other things. The sonar's just to make sure the measurements are accurate."

"Gonna be disappointed if the caves aren't there?"

"Oh, they're there. I've seen them."

"Really?"

The girl nodded her head. "I was on one of the last expeditions to try this. That's why Dr. Ward asked me to come along."

I looked in Ward's direction, but he'd already wandered off, fretting over the equipment that his students had brought on board.

"Did you see anything interesting down there?"

She looked up at me, her blue eyes seeming darker than they had a few minutes earlier. "Oh, yes. I saw things."

"Like what?"

"Let's just say there might be some truth to the stories of devils."

Before I could make another comment, she was on her way, heading to where the rest of the students and the doctor and the two ghost hunters were all gathered together.

I stayed where I was and thought about her words. She had piqued my curiosity. I also thought about Charlie and how he might wish he'd taken me up on my offer before it was all said and done.

An hour passed, maybe a little longer, and then it was time to go back out. The reef was only a little over a mile away. Not the sort of swim I was interested in making but not bad in a yacht. The waters were as tricky as I feared they'd be, with odd currents and the sort of shale outcroppings that could tear the hell out of a vessel if you got careless. I used the sonar to make good and damned sure I stayed well away from the hidden dangers. Then I dropped anchor and set myself up for a little fishing.

Seven people total got into suits while I was doing the driving, and within minutes of anchoring, they were ready to dive into the waters. I couldn't have much cared one way or the other. I was aiming to see if I could get into an argument with a bluefish.

The waters were dark and murky, the sediment around the area lifted with almost every wave, but the rumor was that the fishing was supposed to be damned good. I aimed to test that theory out for myself before the trip was done. Rocks and risks aside, if the stories were true, I might be able to take advantage of it the next time I hired out for a fishing trip that was longer than a day. Now and then you need to scout around for new ways to keep the business going.

I didn't catch anything, but I got a few nibbles.

The divers got lucky, if luck is the right word. They came up one at a time, eager to get back onto the yacht and shivering from the cold water. Charlie was good enough to have hot coffee waiting for them, and they probably would have kissed his feet right then. With the girls that had gone on the trip, he probably would have let them, too.

I set aside my gear after reeling in the empty hook. Something had taken the liberty of nibbling the food off my hook. That's the problem with little fish and a big piece of bait.

"Jan?" Diana was looking around with a frown on her face, her wet hair sticking up like a porcupine as it dried in the warm evening air. "Has anyone seen Jan?"

Another diver, this one a man with possibly the longest legs I'd ever seen, looked around and shook his head. "He was right behind me, Di."

Just when they were starting to look worried, I heard the splashes against the side of the *Isabella,* and looked over to see the last diver. He looked like he was maybe fifteen, and his face was drawn and pale. His regulator was dangling in front of him in the water and he kept reaching for the ladder to the deck but without much success.

I slipped myself over the top rung and scurried down as quickly as I could. I didn't know for sure if there was a problem, but he certainly acted like he was in pain.

The kid rolled his eyes at me and managed a half smile as I grabbed his wrist and started hauling. I wound up getting soaked in the cold waters when I had to actually lower myself below his level to hoist him up. He had a dry suit; I had a pair of shorts. I think it took a couple of hours for my testicles to return to their normal location after that splash. Even with the tank on his back, it wasn't that hard to get the kid onto the ladder and help him up to the deck. Long before we'd finished climbing, Charlie was there lifting Jan to safety. Diana ran over in a hurry, her face almost panicked, and started looking the kid over as he was escorted to a seat. Charlie didn't even bat an eye, he just started unfastening the kid's equipment and setting it aside.

"Jan! What happened?" Diana took the damp towel from her own shoulders and spun it around the kid's, her eyes still looking him over. She let out a weak moan when she saw the red running down his leg. It was about that time that I noticed my clothes dripping pink-tinged water.

Diana peeled him out of his suit before the kid could even protest and we got a good look at the source of his blood loss. Something out there had taken a chunk out of his leg, and the wound was flowing freely. I was smart enough to spend some of my winter months every year working as a paramedic. It kept me from going stir-crazy and stopped Belle from wanting to smash my head in with a frying pan for being under her feet constantly.

I pointed at Charlie and he ran into the cabin to get the medical kit. Diana was looking over the wound and I squatted next to her. "Let's see that a bit better." I tried to be gentle, but the kid winced when I touched him and let out a hiss when I lifted his calf. The wound was deep, but the cut was almost surgically clean. Still, looking at it, I couldn't help but think he was very lucky. I'd seen shark bites before, and judging by the size of the wound, if it had gotten a better grip the thing could have probably taken his leg off from just below the knee. There were angry red marks where the teeth had scraped and a few spots where the skin had broken. Mostly they were just abrasions, and not enough of a mess for him to be in serious danger of anything stronger than an infection.

"You're a lucky man, Jan. That was closer to trouble than you want to know." Diana leaned back to let Charlie hand me my kit and I pulled out a bottle of hydrogen peroxide and a bundle of gauze. None of the wounds looked deep enough to be a serious issue, so I poured the solution over his leg and watched it fizz furiously. I looked very carefully, and only saw two minor problems. I gauzed over both of those and then wrapped his calf with several layers more of the sterile cotton.

"What the hell bit him?"

"If I had to guess, I'd go with a sand shark, but a big one."

Charlie practically carried the kid inside the cabin and

laid him down on one of the three sofas built into the main part. *Isabella's Dream* is a comfy place if nothing else and the kid looked like he could use a little comfort. We had blankets on board and in no time Jan was wrapped up, lying back and resting. I knew his leg was going to look like crap as soon as the bruising finished.

I checked him over one more time, just to make sure there weren't any unpleasant surprises, and there weren't. He'd be walking again; he just wouldn't be thrilled about it.

Diana came into the room and sat next to the kid. His face lit up when he saw her. "What happened, Jan?"

"I don't know." He shrugged his thin shoulders. "I was right behind Steve, and the next thing I knew, something grabbed my leg and yanked me down. I kicked it like twelve times and it finally let go. I didn't hang around to give it another chance."

"Did you see what it was?" Her tone was off, almost excited about him getting into trouble, but I knew better than to think that was all that was involved. Her concern was obvious enough and looking at them next to each other without as much chaos, I had to guess that they were related.

He shook his head and looked absolutely miserable. "No. Maybe next time."

"Oh, no! No next time for you. I knew this was a mistake!" That clinched it. I have three big sisters and I knew the look she shot his way well enough. It's a look that says there-is-no-way-in-hell-that-I'm-risking-my-ass-for-YOU-again! Three parts anger, two parts guilt and just a little protective sibling thrown in for fun.

"Oh, come on, Diana! That could have happened to anyone." He wasn't angry; he was depressed.

The argument fell apart from there, with both of them

trying to talk over each other. I moved away and set the first-aid kit back where it belonged.

It took me a minute to realize that something was wrong with what the kid had said. He didn't say he got bitten. He said he got grabbed. And while I wasn't an expert, I'd never heard of a shark dragging someone lower into the water instead of just biting off a convenient piece of flesh.

FOUR

We ended the night's adventures after that little incident. Everyone calmed down and I took my girl back to Golden Cove and docked for the night. Most of the people on board left and went to the hotel rooms they'd prearranged. I stayed on board, and so did my crew. I had everything I needed right there, and felt no need to spend extra cash on a room when I had my own cabin. The rest of the guys took over the smaller rooms that were set aside for just that reason.

That was the plan anyway. Instead, I got Charlie knocking on my door and bringing in a bottle of tequila. Here's the thing about having a guy like Charlie on board: he already knew my habits and knew I wasn't likely to be sleeping for a few more hours.

"Wasn't a shark, Joe, and you know it." He poured us each a couple of ounces.

"Could have been." I downed my shot hard and fast and waited for the explosion to settle in my stomach.

"But you don't think it was, do you?"

Charlie looked at me long and hard, waiting for an

answer. I really didn't want to give him one, but we'd always been honest with each other, at least to the best of my knowledge.

"No. I think if a shark had decided to eat that kid, he would have been eaten." I shrugged and thought about the scrape wounds again. Really, in hindsight, he didn't have nearly enough marks to suggest shark's teeth.

Charlie left for a moment and came back with the kid's dry suit, or rather what was left of it. He slid his hand and forearm into the leg cuff of the thing and I could see the five deep slices where something had cut through the fabric and left the wounds on Jan's calf. The heavy material was sliced open by something sharp, but that didn't prove it was teeth.

"It could have been a shark, Charlie. Or it could have been him getting clumsy and careless with the rocks out there. That shale is some wickedly sharp stuff sometimes. You've seen what it can do to the underside of a boat."

"Yeah." He nodded and poured another shot for each of us just as soon as he'd slammed his previous one down. "Thing is, I've never heard of a piece of rock dragging someone down lower into the water."

"What can I say? Maybe he ran into a shark with a sense of humor. Maybe he got caught in an undertow. He looks like he's maybe fifteen, Charlie. I'm not getting the idea he has a lot of experience with diving."

"None of them looked like they had a goddamned clue, Joe."

"Diana is supposed to be good."

"Okay, I'll give you that one. But aside from her, not a one of them."

"I don't dive anymore, and I sure as hell don't dive with the sort of current we have around here. All I can say is it's a good thing I made them sign waivers."

"I don't like it, anyway. I don't like the idea of dragging these morons to the hospital every day if they screw up anymore."

"You volunteering to lead them on their dives?" It was meant as a joke.

Charlie looked thoughtful and I realized I'd probably screwed up.

"Maybe I should."

"Well, it'll keep you busy..."

We talked for a few more minutes and he decided he'd make the offer in the morning. I decided not to call him an idiot. I figured if nothing else, it might mean some extra cash in his pockets by the end of the trip and it might stop him from worrying about the old rumors of what used to be in the area.

When Charlie offered another shot, I declined. The night was young, but not young enough for me to get ripped. There was work to do in the morning.

After a few more minutes of silence, broken by a need to discuss potential problems with the yacht's maintenance, Charlie left for his cabin. I leaned back on my bed and looked out the porthole, staring at the reef off in the distance.

The sea was calm and the air was cooling down fast. Wisps of condensation were rising from the water, slowly building themselves into a proper fog.

I was thinking about Belle and missing her. I hated being away from her for any length of time. I was about to call it an early night and maybe even give her a buzz on my cell phone, but something out the porthole caught my eye. There was someone in the water, halfway between the black stones of the reef and the docks. Whoever it was looked to be struggling, maybe even drowning as he or she swam in our direction. I caught a glimpse of what might have been long hair and maybe a dress, so I decided it was a woman. I had to look twice to make sure I was seeing her; the ocean and distance can play some mean tricks on the mind.

She was there. I couldn't see her face clearly, but I could see the waves splashing around where she broke the water and I could make out her pale skin as it reflected back the moonlight. She wasn't using the graceful swimming patterns of a good swimmer. She was thrashing about, slapping the ocean instead of smoothly cutting through it.

"Charlie!" I ran for the cabin as I called to him, and when he approached I pointed at the girl in the water. He nodded his head and started raising the anchor a few moments later. I turned on the motors and set the searchlights to look for the girl. She was out there, still struggling to stay afloat, still floundering and losing her struggle.

We pulled away from the dock without incident and Charlie guided me toward where the girl was doing her best not to drown. It isn't exactly easy to go at high speeds in a sixty-foot yacht, and it's also not wise. We had to take it fairly slow in order to get closer to the girl without risking knocking her halfway to the reef. When we were close enough, Charlie took off his shoes, grabbed a life preserver and dove into the waters. I knew how cold it was going to be and I knew he'd hate himself for it later, but it was the best way to get to her before it was too late.

Charlie hit the water in a perfect dive and vanished into the blackness. He rose up a few seconds later only a few feet from where she was thrashing in the waves. His hands caught her with ease, and she stopped her struggles, apparently trusting in him completely to get her to safety or so exhausted that she simply had no choice in the matter. He held her around her shoulders and backstroked toward the yacht. I ran out to give him a hand.

The girl couldn't have been much more than fourteen or fifteen. Her blond hair was plastered to her scalp and half covered her face, and her skin was too pale by far. Charlie did his best to tread water as he held her up to me like she was a toddler. I'm not Charlie. He could do that without too much trouble, but I had to strain hard when I caught her thin wrists with my hands and hauled her up the ladder with me. She wrapped her arms around my neck and shivered violently. Her skin was wet and nearly as cold as ice. I made the climb back onto the deck. This was twice in one night that I'd gotten myself soaked pulling someone up to safety and it wasn't something I wanted to make a habit of. To make matters worse, she was dressed in enough wet layers of clothing to add a good thirty pounds to her weight. I was surprised she hadn't dropped like a stone under the extra layers of heavy fabrics. As I set her down on the deck to catch my breath, I couldn't help but notice that she was wearing petticoats and old-fashioned leggings under her full length formal dress.

She curled up in a nearly fetal position as I went back to the ladder to give Charlie a hand. He tossed the life preserver to me and I caught it and tucked it under my left arm before reaching down to offer him a boost. He took it gratefully and I pulled as he climbed back on board.

"Jesus Christ! That water's *cold*." Charlie shook his arms wildly, spraying salt water all over the deck and me. I was wet enough that I didn't much care.

"Let me get a couple of blankets for you and your new friend." I headed for the cabin and grabbed a few thin blankets from the supplies I kept close at hand. They could both warm up properly after they'd gotten out of the wet clothes, but the night was cold and any protection at all would do in a pinch.

When I stepped back onto the deck Charlie was looking around almost desperately.

"What's wrong?"

"Where did she go, Joe?"

"What? The girl? She's right—" I stopped myself. The girl who should have been curled up on the deck was gone. The only indication that she had ever been there was the trail of wet spots where she'd dripped as I carried her, and the larger patch of water where she'd settled after I put her down. There were no new footprints, no real signs that she'd suddenly gotten a notion to go exploring, as if she'd have even been capable.

"What the hell, Charlie?" I looked at my first mate and he looked back at me, shaking his head.

"I don't know. I have no fucking clue, Joe."

"She was right there." I jabbed my finger at the water on the deck and Charlie nodded his head in understanding.

"She was there when I climbed on deck, Joe. And then I looked where you were going, and when I looked back, she was gone."

We made a quick check of the deck and then the cabins, but I think we both already knew we wouldn't find her even before we started searching. I even checked all around the sides of the *Isabella,* just to be safe, but Charlie would have surely heard a splash if she'd gone overboard.

After a few minutes we gave up and neither of us said a word. We just looked at each other in silence and shook our heads.

We didn't want to speak about it because that would make it real. And neither of us wanted to use the words "ghost" or "haunting" right then. The air was already cold enough without adding goose bumps to the chill.

FIVE

The next morning started off with perfect weather. Just cool enough to be a relief from the worst of the summer and not so miserable that the crew from the school needed to worry about freezing to death in the water.

Charlie wanted nothing to do with it. He put on a polite smile for the people hiring out the yacht, but other than that he was cold as ice. For my part, I'd spent most of the night trying to figure out exactly what the hell had happened with the girl he pulled out of the water, and had come up with nothing at all.

Except the obvious choice I was trying to avoid. I didn't believe in ghosts. Still, there were no traces of where she would have gone, and there was no reason for a girl to be wearing the old-fashioned clothes she had on, especially in the water.

I could have told myself it was all just the booze, but Charlie made that a little harder to get away with. My first mate was not a coward, but I could see that he was shaken by what had happened. He was also staying busy enough to make it impossible for me to get him alone. I think he did it on purpose.

He offered his services to the college professor, and Ward, being a well-educated man and down one diver, took him up on it.

The kid I thought was Diana's brother stayed back at the hotel. His leg was aching to high hell, and he wasn't much up to even thinking about diving. I think she was happier with it that way. Whatever their relationship, it was obvious she felt responsible for him.

I didn't talk to too many of them that morning, aside from getting directions from Ward and his sidekick. They wanted to start the dive on the other side of the reef, as far from town as possible, and try mapping out whatever they found down below the surface.

I have to be honest here, I was a little fixated on the girl Charlie had pulled out of the water. Not to the point where I couldn't pilot a yacht, but to the point where I wasn't much good for conversation. The evidence wasn't adding up too well. Unless the girl had somehow managed to jump from a nearly fetal position and clear the railing, there should have been some sign of how she'd left the *Isabella* the night before. Every footprint that I left on the deck as I walked to get the blankets was easily seen, and the same with Charlie's tracks. So it wasn't possible that she'd just gotten up and hidden herself. Besides, I don't think she'd have been physically capable.

Belle always loved to read mystery books. I was more into reading the newspaper. My point being that the idea of actually trying to figure out what the hell was going on was never really much on my mind. The people hanging around on my yacht were the ones who were supposed to solve the strange events going on in the area. The whole thing was annoying me, the same way not remembering who sang a song on the radio can get under my skin. I kept looking out the windows as I aimed us for the far side of the reef, and I kept looking over at Jacob and Mary Parsons. The mister of the couple was talking with Ward, and whatever they were discussing had the both of them more animated than I'd seen them before. The missus was curled up in a way that only cats and women ever seem to manage comfortably, and writing notes in a ledger. I wondered if I should tell them what I'd seen.

Charlie would be opposed. Still, wasn't that the sort of thing Parsons said they'd come out here for in the first place? I looked at Mary Parsons for a while longer, enjoying the way the wind played with her hair. If she noticed me staring, it didn't seem to bother her.

Finally, I decided I'd tell Jacob. Charlie could get upset, tell me to fuck off, whatever. I couldn't bring myself not to help someone like Parsons with what I knew was a lifelong quest.

But I'd wait awhile. I didn't want a gaggle of college kids as an audience. Whatever the man decided to make of the story, I preferred he do it without anyone else hearing about it.

For a group that was spending a small fortune on renting out my yacht, they weren't exactly organized. Charlie took care of that. He very calmly set about rearranging the equipment they were taking with them and double-checking all of the gear. He wasn't the only one, mind you, but between him and Diana they got everything handled in short order.

Ten divers hit the water and sank below the surface just a few minutes after I anchored the *Isabella*. After that, it was a lot easier to pull Jacob off to the side and let him know about the encounter. He nodded a lot when I was talking to him and then he asked me a million questions regarding what I'd seen and what Charlie had witnessed. He was clinical, but I could see that he was also very excited about the notion of whatever had occurred the night before.

After he was done, I started regretting what I'd said. Not because of his reaction, but because he called his wife over to ask me the same questions all over again.

Mary Parsons was a puzzle, and I didn't much know if I felt like solving the equations that would explain her to me. For one thing, she was quieter than I'd expected. Belle always loved watching those asinine shows on the paranormal, especially around Halloween, and I'd seen the couple plenty of times. Normally, at least on the shows where they were featured, Mary did all the talking. Seeing her on my yacht, I'd never heard her say much of anything, except when she called her husband to her side.

For another thing, she was doing her absolute best not to look as pretty as she was. I'm not saying she had model features or anything, but she was good looking enough to catch most men's eyes, and as outspoken as she was on TV she was doing her very best to look and seem like a church mouse.

One thing I learned, and fast, was that she didn't stay shy when it came to the business of ghost hunting. As soon as Jacob told her I'd seen something the night before, she slipped away from her perch on the deck and came to find me, notebook in hand and tape recorder at the ready.

"So, can I ask you a few questions, Captain?"

I looked at her and wondered how I could have ever thought she was shy. There was nothing at all subdued about the way she looked at me. I don't mean sexually, if that's what you're thinking. I mean, she had a very intense gaze and I knew she was going to analyze every word I said, looking for any sign that I might be making things up just to get her attention.

"Of course. You're paying my bills." I looked over and saw Jacob pulling a cigarette out. I threw a nod and a wink Parsons' way and he tossed one over to me. I don't really smoke much anymore but I got the feeling I might need one before his wife was done with the interrogation. "I figure the least I can do is make it easier for you to get your job done."

"Thanks." She eyed the cigarette like it was one of the FBI's most wanted, but said nothing as I lit up.

"So what do you want to know?"

"Everything."

I told her what had happened the night before, careful not to embellish. When I was done she looked at me and then at her husband and for just a moment she smiled brightly, an excited, almost hyperactive grin that she shut down as soon as it showed itself. Kind of a pity, really, because she had a nice smile.

"So, you actually held this girl when you carried her on board?"

I resisted the urge to ask if I was supposed to carry her up by her hair. "Yeah. I've still got the wet clothes if you want to check them out."

"No, that's okay." She chuckled, which was good, because I sure as hell didn't want to go rummaging through my dirty laundry. "Can you describe her?"

"Looked like mid-teens, fourteen or fifteen, with dark blond hair, pale skin, might have been five-foot-four or so, tops. She was a little thing."

"You said her clothes were archaic?"

"Old-fashioned, yeah. Like they belonged at the turn of the century, maybe even a little earlier."

"You said she was cold?"

"Well, yeah, but she'd been in the water for a while before I even spotted her. I'm surprised she held on as long as she did before we got to her."

"Did she say anything? Make any noises at all?"

I had to think about that. "No." The notion made me frown; I hadn't been thinking about much of anything but pulling her from the water and how damned cold she felt. Reflecting on it, I hadn't heard her so much as breathing, but I hadn't been aware of the absence during all the chaos. "No I don't think she did." But she had to have been breathing, didn't she? I mean, I'd carried her up the damned ladder. I'd felt her moving against me, holding on to me as I scaled the side of the *Isabella*.

Mary looked at her husband and nodded. Jacob leaned back on the railing and smiled at her. I got the feeling there was something they weren't telling me.

"How long were you gone before she disappeared?"

"Maybe a minute, tops. I was in a hurry when I got the blankets." I shrugged. "Charlie was right there next to her and I don't figure he'd have looked away for more than a few seconds."

"Can you describe her face?"

"Not a chance. All I saw was hair and wet clothes."

"What do you think happened to her?" I tried to read her face, to get an idea of what sort of answer she wanted, but at that moment the light was gone and all I saw was an expressionless face that would have made most poker players sweat bullets.

"Honestly? I don't know. If I thought ghosts could touch you, I'd say maybe she was a ghost."

Mary looked away from me and crossed her arms over her chest. There was a chill in the air, but she was wearing a nice, thick sweater and the rising sun was finally getting around to warming the world around us.

"Oh, some of them can touch you, Captain Joe. Some of them can do more than just touch."

Part of me wanted to ask her what she meant. I gagged that part quickly. Not because I was afraid of offending either of the people I was dealing with, but because I was pretty sure I didn't want to know what else a ghost could do.

"I thought ghosts were supposed to be floating white sheets or little spots of light on film." I was trying to lighten the moment, but it didn't work.

Jacob looked my way and pitched his cigarette butt over the side of the yacht. That sad sack face of his scolded me with an expression as his wife seemed to almost collapse in on herself. Then he went over to his wife and put an arm around her. They still looked mismatched, like he should have been her uncle maybe, but not her husband.

I stayed where I was and watched them walk away, feeling like I should apologize and having absolutely no idea why.

When in doubt, fish. The few people still on the *Isabella* were busy doing their own things, and I decided to see if there was anything worth catching in the cove.

I don't sport fish. I eat what I catch, as long as it looks edible. I spent the better part of the afternoon reeling in a bluefish and grinning ear to ear. Even the Parsonses came over to cheer me on. The damned thing wasn't going to win me a world record, but by the time it was all said and done I was sore and the fish was dead. It looked like I'd be cooking dinner for the crew and our passengers that night. Fish steaks all around, and maybe a case of beer to wash them down. What the hell; it cut back on my expenses on the included meals and no one would have to worry about the food being fresh.

The people around me were academics. They'd gone to colleges and universities, the whole nine yards. While not one of them had acted deliberately condescending, a few of them still had a slight air of superiority. That changed a bit when I cleaned the fish right there on the deck. I've been fishing for my entire life, and I can say without hesitation that I can scale, gut and clean a fish in less time than damn near anyone.

I didn't even think about it, I just grabbed the knives and went to work, tossing the leftovers into a bucket to be dumped after the divers came back up. Why tempt any sharks into the area?

When I was done, Ward and Parsons were looking at me like I'd just scored the winning touchdown. It was nice having them looking at me with a little awe, because, honestly, I kept looking at them the same way.

Ward was skinny and meek, but he still had something about him that made his students pay attention when he spoke. Parsons was a sad looking man with a very sharp mind who had managed what should have been impossible and gotten himself a very lucrative career by chasing after ghosts.

Me? I owned a few boats and just made ends meet. Weird how that works, I guess: I'm sitting there, feeling inadequate without even realizing it, and just like that, a stupid thing like gutting dinner makes me feel better. I guess it doesn't matter what you're good at, as long as you're good at something.

Not long after I'd finished cleaning the deck—well, to be truthful, having Tom Summers swab it down, that's what I was paying him for—the divers were coming back up. They were learning very quickly why I was dubious about doing a dive in October. Most of them were shivering so hard their teeth were clicking like castanets.

Tommy took care of setting them up with hot coffee and cocoa as well as towels. I have a total of four showers on the *Isabella*. They got to use three of them. The last one is in the captain's quarters, and I'm not all that good about sharing with people I barely know.

None of them came out of the water looking too blue

for their own health, but they might have if it were any colder out there. Charlie came out of the shower looking refreshed. His skin was warm enough that he steamed as he walked out onto the deck, still toweling his hair dry.

"Everything go all right?" I asked the question as casually as I could, but he noticed that I was worried.

"Yeah. Why wouldn't it?"

"No reason. I just like to make sure."

"You afraid I might have seen another ghost? Or maybe a sea monster?" His voice was teasing, and he had crow's-feet around his eyes, even if there was no sign of a smile anywhere else.

"Did you?"

"Nah."

"Listen, I had a talk with the Parsonses about what happened last night."

"Figured you would."

"Well, just so you know in case they approach you about it."

"What did you tell them?"

"The truth. I spotted the girl, you rescued the girl, and she disappeared."

"They say they were gonna talk to me?" He tossed the towel into the hamper that Tommy would be handling later.

"No, but I figure it's what they do, right?"

"So if they do, I'll tell them the truth." He shrugged and turned away. It's a gut thing, I know, but I could tell he was still pissed at me. Not because of me telling the Parsonses, but because he was honor-bound to stay on the *Isabella*.

I'd given him an out and he hadn't taken it. I refused to feel guilty. Well, mostly I refused. There was still a little guilt.

We went back out on the deck together, and sure enough, Mary Parsons looked ready to tackle Charlie, and not for the usual reasons that women wanted to. She asked him aside and he went, suddenly all smiles and charm.

If I thought I was safe, I was mistaken. Jacob caught my arm and pulled me aside.

"Listen, Joe, is there any way we can stay on board tonight?"

"Of course you can. Hell, you're paying for the trip, right?"

"Well, yeah, but I didn't know if that meant nighttime accommodations."

"Well, they probably aren't the most comfortable, but I've got a few extra cabins I had set aside, just in case."

He nodded, his sad face looking as close to happy as I'd seen. "They'll do, as long as there's a bed."

"Why the change from the hotel, Jacob?"

"Mary and I want to be here tonight and maybe a few more nights depending on what happens."

"What happens?"

He nodded his head. "Yeah. We want to see if you have a repeat performance with the girl from last night."

"Be my guest."

"We'll have a little equipment along."

"Long as it doesn't sink the yacht, we're in good shape."

After that, it was time for a late lunch and I cooked for a change of pace. The fish was damned fine and while we ate, the professor regaled his students with tales of my fishing prowess that left me ready to blush. Some of them listened, but most of them were ready to call it a day after doing their best to accurately map out the reef.

I cooked. Tommy got to clean up again. He didn't seem to mind too much, except for the part about not hanging around with the college girls. Before we raised anchor and headed for the docks, I went for the slop bucket I'd used to gut our dinner. The bucket was still there, but was knocked on its side.

There was nothing left inside it but a little fish blood. It wasn't unsettling so much as it was weird. No one on my crew would have been careless enough to dump the bucket and not put it away. I wouldn't have hired them if they were the sort to do that. A bluefish is a damned big animal, and I'd cleaned and scaled one and left the nasty bits in that damned bucket. If what I took out of the thing weighed less than fifteen pounds, I'd sell the *Isabella* to the first bidder. There hadn't been any waves, and I knew the wind hadn't caught the bucket and knocked it over. Besides, the deck was clean.

It was possible that one of the passengers had done it, but I didn't think so. I don't think any one of them would have considered it, seriously.

But the bucket was empty and the evidence was right in front of my eyes. So was a sign of the culprit.

There was a thick trail of seawater that spilled over the side not far from where the bucket lay. I wouldn't have given it much thought, would have probably just taken for granted that it was a spill from earlier, but first, I saw Tommy take care of swabbing the deck and second, the divers had come up on the other side of the yacht.

In the end I decided to let it go. I rinsed the bucket and stowed it where it belonged and barely even gave it another thought.

Remember what I said earlier about Belle liking mysteries? I would have never made a detective in one of her novels.

SIX

Charlie wasn't thrilled about the idea of having a couple of parapsychologists hanging around on the *Isabella*. He didn't have much say in the matter. Way I looked at it was that they were paying the bills and that meant they could stay on board if they wanted to. He'd just have to deal with it.

I called Belle after we docked. I'd only been gone for a day and was already missing the hell out of her. One of the things I have always loved about my chosen profession is that I seldom had to stay out overnight and I had never had to commute across the country in order to get any business done. I know people who spend half of their time on airplanes and in hotels. They make a pissload more money than me, but they're never home. My idea of wanderlust involves going out in the morning and being home by dinnertime. I mean, what's the point of working yourself half to death for extra money if you never have the time to enjoy it?

We didn't talk for too long. Belle had her reading group to attend to, and it was her turn to host. That part made me glad I was out on the ocean instead of at home. Most of the women in her group seem to find more excitement in a book than they do in the real world. That would be okay with me, if the books they chose weren't normally whatever crap Oprah suggested to housewives all around the world.

After the phone call, I set up the Parsonses in a room near mine. It was nice enough as cabins go, but small. I figured they'd be asleep in no time, but I was wrong.

I found them up on the deck, sipping coffee and watching the waters out toward the reef. They were engaged in quiet conversation and I left them be, perfectly content to sit a ways off and enjoy the chilly night air. It was cold enough that I wore a sweater, and the air was the sort of dry that only seems to come around when it's autumn and the leaves are changing. Golden Cove was behind us, and the few lights that burned in the town were just enough to illuminate the waves with a golden counterpoint to the silver of the moon. It was nice and peaceful, just the way I like it.

I must have spent a good half hour out there, just sitting and thinking about as little as possible before the fog started coming in. You expect fog on the ocean, especially when the weather changes drastically. But there's fog and then there's the pea soup that came spilling over the entire cove, roiling in with a gentle breeze that shouldn't have been able to move the thick layer of mist that fast.

If I'd been driving a car, I'd have pulled off to the side of the road and left my hazards going. There are times when the fog along the shoreline can seem like a living thing, and this was one of those times. In a matter of seconds the reef was lost. Off to the north, about half a mile or so away, I could see the Cove Point Lighthouse, a long spire that sat in the middle of nowhere and worked to keep anyone from running into the things they weren't supposed to hit. The light was automated, and only came into play when the visibility was bad. From this distance all I could really make out was the flash of white that marked where it was whenever the rotating beams cut through the darkness. The fog was so heavy that it stole everything but the illumination. There was nothing out there to see otherwise, just like with the moon far above.

The temperature dropped a good fifteen degrees when the fog crossed over the yacht and onto the shore. I let the heavy mist wash over me and stayed where I was, ignoring the increased chill as best I could.

Mary Parsons moved closer to me and settled into the chair next to mine.

"Does the fog always come in this fast?"

I shook my head. "Now and then, but this is one of the worst I've seen."

She looked out at the water and I studied her for a few seconds. I was struck again by the notion that she went out of her way to look unattractive. I guess it takes all types, but I was still a little puzzled by it.

"Your first mate doesn't like us much, I think."

"Honestly? I think you scare him a little. Charlie's a bit superstitious."

She sighed and shook her head. "He should join the club."

"Probably would, depending on the dues."

"Do you think you saw a ghost last night, Joe?"

I thought about it, but in the end I didn't really have an answer. "Maybe. I think it's a possibility."

She sat silently for a few minutes, comfortable with where she was sitting, which was kind of nice. There aren't too many women I've met who were at ease with a relatively unknown man.

"What made up your mind about it?"

"My mind isn't made up, if you want to know the truth. There could always be a different explanation, but I think the most likely thing is that I saw a ghost."

"Does it bother you?"

"Not much besides getting wet for nothing."

I looked at her, trying to read whatever she was thinking from the expression on her face as the fog thickened even more. Mary became a silhouette, every detail of her body and face hidden by the heavy condensation. Even from only a few feet away the visibility was almost gone.

"You aren't scared of ghosts?" She seemed a little surprised by the notion.

"Well, I've only seen the one, and I'm still not completely sure she was a ghost."

She nodded.

"I think maybe you're a little worried about it though. Am I right?"

She nodded again and I could hear her swallowing before she answered. "I've seen a few things."

"Then why are you still doing this?"

"You mean the parapsychology thing?"

"Yeah. If you know that ghosts are real, haven't you already proven everything you need to prove?"

"We know there are other planets, but we still keep going out there and looking for more proof, don't we?" She turned in her seat and looked at me, her elbows resting on her knees. "We keep looking deeper and deeper into the oceans, too."

"Good point. But if a deep-sea diver gets bitten by enough sharks, he stops diving."

"What makes you think I've been bitten?"

I wasn't sure I wanted to answer that. It's the sort of question that can be a double-edged sword: answer it truthfully and you risk pissing off a client. Answer with a lie, or a half-truth, and you look insufferably stupid or weak.

"You want the politically correct answer? Or do you want it straight up?"

"I prefer straight up."

"You look haunted." It wasn't meant as a joke, but it could have been taken as one. Mary Parsons didn't take it that way.

"Do you run away from everything that ever bothered you?"

"No. But I don't always invite it to bother me again, either." And did I sound defensive myself? Probably. We all have our secrets, and I had more than my fair share.

"I take more precautions than I used to, Captain Joe, but I can't turn my back on my life's work because of a few strange occurrences." She spoke slowly and carefully, choosing each word as precisely as a surgeon chooses the implements of his trade.

"Call me Joe, okay?"

"I'll work on it." She smiled an apology that wasn't necessary.

"I think I should read a few of your books sometime."

"If I had any spares with me, I'd give them to you."

"Maybe I'll check out the bookstore tomorrow."

The lights from the distant lighthouse were working about as well as a neon sign for distracting me. Every few seconds the night turned white and then vanished again.

Mary cleared her throat. "So, Joe, when was the last time you saw a wooden ship?"

"What? You mean like a full-size ship? Not a yacht?"

"Exactly."

"I saw Old Ironsides once, when I was a kid."

She pointed out into the fog, and I followed her index finger. At first I saw nothing but more of the swirling mists, and then as the beam from the lighthouse came around again, I saw the shadowy shape of a ship, complete with three masts and furled sails. The angle was wrong to even guess the size, but she could have eaten the *Isabella* for a light snack.

As soon as I saw her, she was gone again, lost in the heavy fog and darkness.

"Jesus, Mary and Joseph. How long has that been there?"

"About three minutes."

"Where did she come from?"

"She just showed up. She hasn't moved at all."

"That's not possible. A ship that size doesn't exactly sneak in without someone seeing it."

"Joe, look at where she is in the water..." Mary's voice was very soft.

I had to think about it, because the water couldn't even be seen from where we were. Somehow the ship had gotten past the reef and never even been seen coming in. Believe me; I would have known if that had started on the docks.

The light came around again and once again the galleon cast a long shadow through the darkness. It hadn't moved at all; she was right about that.

"Are you taking any of your scientific readings on this?" I wanted to ask an intelligent question, maybe mention the Electro Magnetic Frequency readers I'd seen used on a couple of specials, or ask if they were doing anything with electronic voice phenomena, like in that movie with Michael Keaton, but the words wouldn't come out. I was too busy being stunned.

"Oh, yes. That's what Jacob is doing." She nodded and stared at the silhouette out in the distance.

We watched in silence for several minutes, while the fog grew even thicker. *Flash*: and the ship was there, followed immediately by darkness. *Flash*: and it was still there, with no changes. *Flash*: and there were figures on the ship that had not been there before, all of them seeming to face the direction of Golden Cove.

Flash: and they were gone. The ship and all of the

people who had suddenly been there looking in our direction.

"What the hell?" I stood up and walked to the edge of the deck, staring hard as if I could will it back by looking and wishing. Nothing happened.

"Ghosts keep their own schedules, Capt—" She caught herself. "Joe." Her voice was soft and almost forlorn behind me.

"You think they were ghosts?"

"Do you think they weren't?"

She had a good point there. Unless the ship had just managed the fastest sinking ever, or been rocket-propelled out of the cove, there weren't many other options. I knew what I'd seen, and I knew it wasn't a trick of the fog. There was nothing out there to cast the sort of shadow I had just been looking at, and surely nothing to imitate the shapes of people on the ship's deck.

"How many ships did Jacob say sank here?"

"From what we've been able to gather, at least seven. Probably more."

"I thought he said more than that."

"Seven that have been fully confirmed. There's a lot of background to go over in most cases." She walked over to where I was leaning out over the railing and joined me. "I think Jacob was right. I think there're a lot of ghosts in this area."

"It's never had a very good reputation. My grandfather used to say it was the one place he knew of that he never wanted to dock his boat."

"And yet you're here anyway."

"I made a deal. I probably would have charged a little more if I knew where we were going to be, but I made a deal and I like to stick to those."

"I'm glad you did. And thanks, again, for letting us stay on the *Isabella*."

"Not a problem. Just don't invite any dead sailors on board for a party."

Mary looked at me for a long moment and then cracked up, laughing as if that was the funniest thing she'd ever heard.

Before I could do more than smile in response, something hit the side of the *Isabella* hard enough to rock her slightly in the water. Let me make this clear, there is nothing light about a sixty-foot yacht. Waves don't even move the *Isabella* much unless they're big enough to break over the sides. The *Isabella* is a damned fine ship and a heavy one, too. So feeling her move was enough to make me worry about structural damage.

I calculated where the sound had come from and moved over there as quickly as I could, half expecting to see a hole in her side. Instead, I just saw very turbulent waves. The problem with that was that the waves shouldn't have been there. There was nothing to make them happen and the rest of the cove was almost placid as far as my eyes could see.

I leaned over to look and something came out of the water at high speed, lifting a good ten feet into the air. Had it been right next to the *Isabella,* I could have touched it.

Instead, all I saw was a dark shape, one that looked almost human, but not quite. The arms were too long, the head was wrong, and the faint light I saw reflected off the eyes seemed to bounce back at me from too wide a surface.

The thing twisted in the air with all the skill of an Olympic diver and dove back into the waters, barely even making a splash. I saw the body cut through the waves and then the feet and legs kick as they drove the entire form deeper below the surface.

The feet looked almost like a diver's oversized floppy fins, but not quite. Most of the diving equipment I've seen doesn't come with wickedly sharp-looking claws at the end of each toe.

Mary came up behind me and put one hand on my shoulder. "What was it? Did you get a good look?"

I shook my head, utterly speechless for a moment.

"I have no idea, and I don't think I want to know."

A few minutes later the fog started to lift and Mary Parsons went off to see her husband and find out if he'd gotten anything useful.

I stayed where I was instead, wondering about what I'd seen and whether or not my mind was going soft in my head.

How do you sleep after that?

Not well.

After the Parsonses had retired, I went to my cabin and got myself undressed and flopped on the bed, exhausted. My mind decided to start replaying everything I'd seen again and again.

The damnedest thing is it's easy to fool yourself if you want to. I caught myself trying to talk my way out of what I'd seen out there, both the ship and whatever it was that dove down into the waters. I hadn't really seen a ship, exactly, just the shadows of one. And the shadows of her crew. Perhaps atmospheric conditions were just right and what I'd actually seen was some sort of distorted reflection of my own vessel, or even another yacht somewhere out of normal visual range. The fog could have done it. This wasn't a light fog, but a heavy blanket over the whole damned area. And if I was having a little more trouble convincing myself that the thing I saw going underwater was a log, or even a guy in scuba gear, well, I just tried all that much harder.

It was midnight before I finally got back out of bed, got dressed, and headed for the bar in the main cabin. When in doubt, there's always anesthesia. I poured myself three fingers of brandy and nursed it down slowly for a couple of minutes in the nearly complete darkness. The fog was back and thick enough to blind me to the world outside.

I walked out onto the deck and shivered in the cold. All I could see was murky darkness followed by the occasional blast of light from the lighthouse. The night was so silent I could hear my own breathing and the faint sound of water lapping at the sides of the dock and the *Isabella*.

And then I heard a sound that was completely foreign to me, a deep thrumming noise that came from where I knew the marshes were, just to the north of the cove. It sounded almost like someone had recorded thunder and then slowed down the noise, stretching it out and distorting it completely. It wasn't nearly as loud as it sounds, and I think some of it might have actually been below the human hearing range.

The sound was answered several times from different areas.

I felt an additional chill run through me as I listened.

What I didn't hear, however, left me nervous. There were no sounds coming from the shore after that unusual racket. Nothing, when I knew there should have been a lot of noise. Have you ever been to a place where the local dogs don't bark when something unusual happens? Except when I was in the Navy and so far offshore that hearing them was physically impossible, I've never run across that dilemma. Dogs bark; it's what they do. It struck me at that moment that I hadn't heard a dog bark in the last two days. Not even once. Granted, I was on a boat the entire time, but even so, I should have heard a few barks, or even a yip, especially when you consider I was docking in the harbor every night.

Nothing. Not a damned thing.

I went back inside and killed off my brandy.

This time around, sleep came quickly.

SEVEN

I learned something important the next morning. I learned that science really can be a religion. The weather was crappy, with high winds, dark clouds and choppy waters. Anyone with half a brain would have called it a done deal and stayed off the waters. My employers failed to heed my advice and because they were paying for the privilege, we went out to the same spot as the day before.

I don't think the temperature broke forty degrees, but Ward insisted on having his team dive and Charlie, being a man of strong ethics, went along with them into waters guaranteed to make joints ache.

Me? I sat in the main cabin and brewed up coffee by the gallon while the divers went into the water and then deep below the surface. They'd need something warm when they came back up. I've been in that sort of cold before; there's nothing but pain involved when you come out of it.

I used to dive, a long time ago. It was a passion of mine for a few years in the Navy and afterward. People change and sometimes experiences change them. I got over my love of diving around the same time I almost bled to

death in the ocean. I got myself caught in a bad turn of
events, starting with a vicious sting from a man-o'-war.
Being hit by a jellyfish is bad news, the sting leaves ugly
red marks and even though it's seldom fatal, the pain from
the sting is enough to leave you in poor shape for a day
or so. The Portuguese man-o'-war is a nasty little surprise
that can do a lot worse to you. It's not one jellyfish, but a
colony of them all bottled into a lethal package. I managed
to run into one while diving, and got the life half stung out
of me.

That would have been bad enough, but I was stupid that
day and diving alone. I remember seeing the rocks, but not
being able to stop myself from hitting them hard. I spent
about half an hour getting knocked around and beaten by
the waves. I probably would have died there, but someone
on the shore must have seen me. Any way you look at it,
I got lucky. The Coast Guard pulled me out of the water
before I could bleed to death, but it was a close thing. I
spent two weeks in a hospital room recovering from the
lacerations and the blood loss, plus complications from
infection.

Funny thing about the accident: it took all the fun out of
diving for me. Ever since then I've thought about diving a
lot, and then decided against it. Maybe I have an overdevel-
oped sense of self-preservation.

We got out to the reef a little after nine in the morning. By ten, all of the divers were in the water and going
down again. For a change of pace, Ward relaxed a little and
stopped pacing like an expectant father.

Just because I was a little bored and not ready to go
fishing yet, I asked him why he wasn't going along on the
dive.

He smiled at me, a little embarrassed to be caught in the
act of not boldly facing any possible threats, and shrugged
his narrow shoulders. "I'm not much good at it, I'm afraid.

I'll be going down there later, but felt it best to wait until they've mapped out a part of the caves before I tried."

I looked at him for a few seconds and read between the lines. "Hate the water that much?"

"Absolutely terrified of it."

"And yet here you are, ready to go swimming through underwater caves."

"There are some things a man can let others do, and some things he has to take care of himself. I want to see those caves, and my desire for knowledge—along with a good stiff drink when we get back up—will outweigh the fear." He shrugged again and looked down at his feet. "At least that's the plan."

"Sounds like a good one to me."

"I've seen you looking. Granted it's not a part of what you were hired for, but I'm rather surprised you haven't decided to go along."

"Well, I'm not a spring chicken these days, but also, I don't dive anymore."

I guess it was my tone, but he didn't ask the reasons.

I didn't volunteer, either.

"If you change your mind, Captain, you have but to ask. I think we could find a spare mask and tank."

"Thanks. You never know. I might take you up on that."

Instead of leaving him to worry and pace, I showed the man how to bait lobster traps. We talked a bit more about not much of anything. I found out he was married and divorced. He found out I was married. Other than the job at hand, we also discovered we had damned near nothing in common.

That didn't mean we couldn't get along. The two of us sat in silence and manned the traps for a few hours. It was nice.

I didn't ask him if he and Diana were an item. It wasn't any of my business. Honestly, I don't think there was anything between them. I think there was a mutual attraction, but I also don't think he was the type to try sleeping with his students. Okay, let's be honest here: I couldn't imagine him sleeping with anyone. He wasn't a bad looking guy, but I sort of got the impression he was prissy. The idea of dirt touching him was enough to make him want to shower, and the idea of exchanging bodily fluids? I could just see him spending a week in a decontamination chamber.

That might be mean, but that was just the impression I got from him.

Close to four in the afternoon, they were done for the day. That was a good thing, because they'd used up all the oxygen tanks by then, having come up a couple of times to get refills.

Charlie was finally getting over his attitude, and that was an even better thing. He walked over to me as he was toweling off and shivering violently. Mostly, I think, because I was the one handing out coffee and chicken soup in big mugs.

"Cold enough for you?"

Charlie looked at me as he took the hot coffee and downed half of it in one gulp. I figure there were probably a few layers of his throat that weren't burned to sin after that, but only a few. "You don't know from cold, Joe. My balls didn't shrink, they disappeared."

I chuckled and handed him a mug of soup and a spoon. He was the last in line for the stuff and I had the heater going in the main cabin. He was still shivering but it was a little less violently. The thing about being in water like that is your body adapts to a certain extent. It feels a lot worse when you come out and your blood starts flowing again. Charlie was proof of that. He was practically doing a jitterbug; he wasn't trying to. A couple of the kids who'd been down there were still shaking so hard they were having trouble carrying their mugs without covering themselves in coffee or soup. I don't think they minded much when the hot liquid spilled over them.

I'd thought long and hard about telling Charlie what I'd seen along with Mary Parsons. In the long run, I decided to keep my mouth shut unless he asked about it.

Instead I brought up the dive.

"Did you see anything interesting down there?"

"Oh, yeah." He nodded hard and fast.

"Seriously?"

"Very seriously." He settled down and I sat across from him on a couple of the chairs. "Those caves, Joe, they're unbelievable. We've mapped a big part of them with the sonar, and I swear, I think they could go on forever." He sounded as stunned as I guess he should have. I was trying to picture the caves and having trouble. "There's this little tunnel—I guess you'd call it—and it goes on for a damned long time, but once you're past that, it opens up and it's huge."

"What the hell causes something like that?"

"Doc Ward says it's probably gas bubbles from when the reef formed in the first place." He frowned. "I dunno. Parts of it seemed almost too smooth, does that make sense?"

"Too smooth?"

"Yeah, like they were polished." He sipped at his soup, and then broke down and used his spoon like a human being.

"Yeah. I think that's called erosion."

"Underwater?"

"Ever hear of a current? See, now and then water moves along the same course for a long, long time and as the years go by, the water's constant motion makes the stone break away a little at a time. You can even find pebbles that are almost as smooth as glass." Was I being sarcastic? Yes, I was. Did Charlie catch it? If the middle finger he waved at me was any indication, then yes.

"You'd have to see it, Joe." He got an innocent look on his face. "Oh, I forgot. You don't dive anymore."

Charlie was one of the people who knew about my little diving accident. Normally he'd have the good taste not to mention it, but in his defense, I probably had it coming. Of course, being as we were friends, a little ribbing was to be expected.

Charlie went to get into real clothes and I went off to pilot us back to Golden Cove. I had a few books I wanted to look into, and I needed to get things in order. Meanwhile, I had my other crew members and the good professor pull in the lobster traps. We got enough of the damned things to make dinner an easy choice for everyone.

Before dinner, however, all of the divers that weren't staying on the yacht went back to their rooms to get properly dressed in heavier clothes. I took that time to go into town for the first time.

Golden Cove was just as nice to look at up close as it was at a distance. The difference was you could see that most of what was there was still new. It was like what I suspected walking onto a Hollywood movie set would be like: everything was real, but it didn't really feel like it was.

The only bookstore I found in town was a place called Eats and Reads. It was exactly what I would have expected to find in a touristy little bookstore. There were a dozen books with pictures of Golden Cove, complete with one about how the town was rebuilt from the remains of Innsmouth. That one was mostly filled with pictures and a few notes about the different buildings and what they had been in the past. I bought the damned thing, but mostly because the photography was damned nice.

I had an attendant from the moment I walked into the shop. There was a girl there who was dressed in jeans and a T-shirt, both of which were topped by an apron with a name tag that told me her name was Kathy. I think that if she'd actually been doped to the gills with Valium, she might have been less interested and maybe even less dazed.

Despite her sloth-like tendencies, the girl managed to find me three books written by the Parsonses. I spent a little over a hundred dollars buying those books and a magazine about yachting. Belle would have been proud of me; that was more than I normally spent on books in a year and she always thought I should read more.

The sun was setting by the time I started back toward the *Isabella*. The glare off the water dazzled my eyes and left me feeling disoriented. I thought back to the fuzzy pictures Jacob had shown me on the first day, and tried to imagine what it would have been like to walk toward the shore when those dark shapes came up from the water and attacked. Did anyone even know what was coming for them before it was too late? I didn't like to think about it. The more I considered the devastation and considered the vague gray forms, the more I wanted to head for home and screw the fat check I'd already deposited in my checking account.

It didn't help that I couldn't get the thing I'd seen the night before out of my mind. Only a quick glimpse and I was convinced that there was something going on at Golden Cove, and not necessarily something that would make me sleep better at night.

The absolute worst part of my little trip into town was the certainty that I was being watched. Paranoid, right? Who the hell cares about a boat captain taking a walk? The most frustrating part of the situation was that there were plenty of people around, walking on the streets and minding their own business, and I wanted to look at each one of them to see if I caught them giving me a hard stare.

By the time I got back to the *Isabella,* the team from Ward's expedition had returned and Tommy had started the water for boiling up the lobsters. He'd also managed to work up a decent macaroni salad and a few extras.

Diana had brought her little brother back with her and the kid looked like crap. His skin was pasty and his eyes were surrounded by dark bags. I saw that the wound he'd gotten on his leg had been treated, and when I asked about it, Diana told me he was on antibiotics. I told her she needed to check with the doctor again, because whatever he was taking, it didn't seem like enough to handle the job.

It's possible she would have listened to me a little better if Charlie hadn't come along just then and distracted her.

So instead of talking with the head of the diving team, I spoke to her brother. "How you doing, Jan?"

"Doctor says I got blood poisoning from the bite." He looked at me and then looked back at the deck as if moving his head was too much of an effort to sustain.

"Ouch. They put you on antibiotics?"

"Yeah. But they aren't doing any good as far as I can tell."

"Well, sometimes they take a while to work." What else could I say? That I thought he was right? The kid wasn't looking good and he seemed to feel even worse than he looked. "You have any appetite? Fresh lobster for dinner."

He nodded and smiled. "I wouldn't miss it. I love lobster."

"I love seafood. I don't even care what kind it is." I looked at his leg, and even through the jeans he was wearing, I could see the thick layer of bandages and gauze over the wound site.

"Seven stitches." He pointed with his right hand and I nodded.

"When did you see the doctor?"

"We went to the emergency clinic right after we got off

the boat." He pointed in the direction that I assumed was the emergency clinic. "Gotta say, that was the ugliest doctor I've ever seen."

"That bad?"

"Three miles of roadkill ugly. If his eyes were bugging out any more, I think they would have just fallen straight out of his face."

"So when can you dive again?"

"Not for a week or so, at least. I have to let the wounds heal up completely and even when that's done I have to beg Diana."

"She's your sister?"

"Yeah." He looked away from the ground long enough to spot her where she was standing with Charlie and another couple that looked like they should still be in high school. Seemed like every year the kids that went to college looked younger. I'm guessing it was just my age showing. I don't remember ever being that young. I'm not bothered by that so much as I'm amused by it. Just a different world after a certain point, if you get my meaning.

"So what has your sister said about the expedition? Is it going well?"

"She's excited. Said they didn't get this far the last time before everything went wrong."

"Did she ever tell you what happened the last time?" I was making conversation. I figured Jan would get bored to tears being stuck on the yacht with no one to talk to, and all of the college kids looked like they planned on tossing back a few drinks and having a party. Diana was busy making time with Charlie and that left her little brother to tend to himself.

What I didn't expect was the answer I got from the kid. He looked away from me and shook his head. "I'm not allowed to tell anyone about that." His voice was defensive and a little angry, like I'd asked him to tell me all about his sister's sexual encounters instead of a previous dive.

I held up my hands to show my willingness to just let it go. "Don't mean to cause problems, Jan. I was just making conversation."

He looked down at his feet again and I stood up to leave him in peace. I'd tried to be nice, but I learned a long time ago that not every person wants to have a conversation.

"It's just...she doesn't talk about it. Whatever happened, I mean." His voice was very soft, almost a sigh.

"Don't sweat it. Some things are private, I can respect that."

"No, I mean, you should know, but I can't tell you out here, where everyone can hear us."

I was intrigued, but decided not to push it. "You tell me when you feel comfortable, if it's important. No rush." I gave the kid another smile and then moved off to help Tommy with the dinner preparations.

It was over an hour later, after damned near every lobster we'd pulled from the water had been cooked, shelled, and drowned in butter and devoured, that Jan pulled me aside to have that little chat.

I was feeling particularly pleased with myself, having killed off two of the finest lobsters I'd ever consumed, when Jan moved over to where I was sitting and sat down facing me. His knees were almost close enough to brush my own and he leaned in so that no one could possibly hear him without him wanting them to.

"No one knows what killed the other diving team. Everyone says they got lost inside the caves down there. There were no bodies, see? None. No one ever found them and people tried, believe me. They had the Coast Guard down in those caves and everything."

"According to Charlie, those caves are mighty deep, Jan."

The kid shook his head, once again looking at the deck between his feet. "That's just it. My whole family came here when everyone disappeared. We were worried sick about Diana, but she was the only survivor of that last dive. I was with her in the clinic when some men in uniforms came and asked her questions. She told them about the mapping project and all of that stuff, and she said the bodies could be anywhere, because the caves go on just about forever."

He looked around the room making sure that no one at all was listening in and then spoke again, softly. "The guys from the Coast Guard? They told her she had to be wrong, because they'd looked over the entire cave down there and they said it only went in around twenty feet before it closed off."

"Excuse me?" I had to be hearing him wrong. "Jan, your sister and half a dozen other people were in those caves all day long. It doesn't take that long to map out a twenty-foot cave." The kid had to have misheard the conversation.

"I know that." He raised his voice a little when he started and lowered it again when he realized how loud he was. "I know that. And so does Diana. But the guys that went in looking for the rest of the divers, they do this sort of thing all the time, right? So I don't think they would have missed the sort of caves Diana was talking about."

"Jan, caves don't disappear or grow smaller."

"No, but maybe they can be hidden."

"How?"

"I don't know." He sighed and shook his head. When he moved his legs around to get more comfortable, I saw him wince as he bumped his wounded calf against the edge of his seat.

"So maybe there's more than one cave." I shrugged, at a loss for what else to say.

"No." He shook his head. "I was down there. There's

only one cave in the reef, only one cave entrance. What I saw was a lot bigger than what the rescue team saw. You know what I think?"

"Tell me."

"I think something down there doesn't want to be seen and whatever it is, it has a way of hiding the size of the cave."

"You think there's a fish down there that can hide the cave? What? A smart sand shark with good camouflage netting?" I shook my head and stared at the kid. He was thinking way too hard about this.

"I don't know what I think." He finally looked at me again and this time he looked at me hard, like he wanted to know if he could trust me. "But I know one thing for sure, and that's that it wasn't a shark that pulled me down the other day."

"No? What was it then?"

"I don't know. But unless it had one tooth on the bottom of its mouth and four on the top, it wasn't a shark." He looked at me again and his eyes narrowed just a bit. He pulled up his baggy jeans' pant leg and quickly unwrapped the bandage covering his wounds. They were red and angry and obviously infected. "Looks like a handprint, doesn't it?"

"You'd know better than me, Jan. You were there when it happened. I just tried to treat it."

I left him alone after that, unsettled because he was right. I could see the red marks where his skin was cut and festering and I could see the dark bruises where his leg had been held by what looked a lot like a hand. Only, the person leaving a print like that would have to be enormous or at least have paws the size of a polar bear's. Yeah, he was young and he was even a little skinny, but the hand that held his leg and pulled him down—if it was a hand and not my mind playing tricks—would have to be very powerful to leave those marks and at least a few inches wider and longer than my own.

I didn't want to think about whatever might be underwater and capable of using that much force.

EIGHT

Have I mentioned how much I hate nightmares? Dreams are easy; they may not make sense when you wake up, but at least when they're done you know it was a dream. Nightmares don't seem to play by the same rules.

Maybe I had a bit too much to drink. Normally I limit myself to a shot or two. I broke that little rule and had a total of five drinks before I hit the sack.

Belle always says that rich foods can give you strange dreams, so maybe it was the lobster, or something in the macaroni salad. Whatever the case, I got myself one hell of a nightmare for my troubles.

In my dream I was underwater, diving, breathing recycled air and looking at the underworld through a mask. The damnedest thing was I knew I shouldn't be going down into the waters; even in the dream I knew I didn't dive anymore.

The water was murky and dark, but I could make out the details of the rocky surface on my right and I knew that I was at the Devil's Reef, searching for the cave that was supposed to be there. I didn't see anyone else at first, but I knew that there were other people diving with me. In the dream I knew as sure as I was diving against my own better judgment that Charlie was there, to my left, coming closer. All I had to do was look over my shoulder and I'd see him and a few others, too. Dream logic, I guess. He was supposed to be there, and I accepted that. Charlie was down there, and so was Diana and her brother Jan.

The entrance to the cave was a black pit far enough down that I felt the pressure in my ears and temples. Deep enough down that no one would ever see the damned thing unless they were actively looking for it. The edges were rough and almost looked like they'd been expanded by someone using a pickax.

You remember going to the movies when you were a kid and taking in the cheesy horror flicks? There was almost always a scene where I wanted to scream at one of the characters up on the big screen and tell them not to be stupid. It was obvious in a lot of cases that whatever they were about to do was going to get them killed.

That was how I felt about what I was doing in that nightmare. I knew that going into the cave would be disastrous, but I couldn't make my dream-self stop. Instead I just watched on, my stomach tight with tension and my heartbeat pounding the hell out of my rib cage as I slipped into the dark opening and slid through the water in search of something I couldn't even see.

There was light coming from behind me, and I turned to see the other divers as they approached. All of them had lights, but for some insane reason, my dream-self was too stupid to bring one. So I made do, swimming in the lead and using the light provided by smarter divers to see my way around.

The cave wasn't very wide, or very deep for that matter. But it led to another tunnel, a darker spot in the darkness that I knew would be much larger. I swam toward it, consciously terrified of how abysmally stupid my dreaming self continued to be.

I went down into the deeper darkness of the narrow tunnel, swimming with the casual grace of a longtime diver, just like I knew I would in the waking world, if I were foolish enough to dive again. My dream-self went with all the confidence of a professional and the dreaming me who observed everything tried to cry out warnings that fell on deaf ears and left me wondering exactly when I'd grown terminally stupid. And behind me the others followed suit, their lights hinting at what lay ahead, showing me just enough to make me want to scream as the forms came toward me from the darkness. They were not human, but there were hints of the human shape to them. They had legs and arms and heads. Their skin was dark, but not quite as dark as the rocks of the reef, and their eyes lit up with an internal luminescence.

One of the things grinned as it turned to face me, a flash of sharp teeth bared as the thick lips pulled away from each other. It could hardly be called a smile, the expression that revealed itself on that shadowy face, because it turned downward at the edges.

Powerful legs propelled the thing toward me with the speed of a torpedo. The lights of the other divers lit just enough of the thing to let me see the hands that came toward me, hands with long, thick claws and heavy webbing between the fingers: hands made to catch the water and claws made to rip through flesh with the greatest of ease.

I woke up gasping for breath and soaked in a heavy sweat. The heaters were working on the *Isabella* but I still felt chilled. In the darkness of my cabin, I let out a moan of disgust and fear, and shivered. The only sounds I heard were the waves tapping along the stern of the yacht.

And then I heard that drawn out noise again, the same

as the night before, a deep bass thrumming noise that made my bones hum and my ears tingle.

Despite my chill, I wanted to know what was out there. I climbed out of bed and staggered to the window, looking out at the waters and the distant reef.

Something moved in the water, several somethings, actually. Dark shapes that rose and dipped with the waves, but broke through the waters and moved away from land toward the Devil's Reef. I watched them, unable to make out more than vague black shapes in the water. I didn't move to investigate this time, but instead did my best to make out the forms for what they were.

They were gone from sight in only a few minutes— gone, but not forgotten.

Morning brought a new series of challenges, but happily they weren't mine to deal with. The college kids and the older passengers for the daylong dive were just boarding the *Isabella* when a police car pulled up on the docks with lights flashing and a siren that died away as it stopped.

I stood on the bow of the yacht and watched as two uniformed men approached the group and brought them to a quick halt. The cops were just possibly the most brutal looking individuals I'd ever seen, with broad shoulders, thick necks and all the swagger of the terminally cocky.

Charlie slipped up next to me and offered a mug of coffee. The day was cold and overcast, so I took the offered drink and sipped it as quickly as the heat would allow.

"Any idea what's going on down there, Charlie?"

"Diana said the cops here like to give them shit from time to time. It happened on the last expedition, too." He didn't seem overly worried about it and neither did the professor or his students.

Sure enough, as we watched, it was Diana who answered

the questions from the local police, and she answered them
with a heated expression on her face. The police officers
looked absolutely unperturbed by her attitude. They merely
stood there with their thick arms crossed and looked at her,
blinking slowly and shaking their heads.

"Think I should go down there and see what's happening?" Charlie sounded a little anxious and I knew why. He
was starting to fall for Diana. I'd known him long enough
to recognize the symptoms when it came to Charlie and
infatuation. I won't call it love, because I honestly don't
know that Charlie was ever capable of feeling love. If so,
he'd always hidden it well.

"No. They'll tell us when it's all said and done. Why get
yourself noticed by the local cops?" I could tell he wanted
to say more, do more, but he understood what I was saying
to him. We were the hired hands, and whatever the problems were that the college team and the Parsonses were
suffering, they made no difference to whether or not we got
paid. It wasn't my place to interfere and it wasn't his place,
either. He didn't have to like it, but he had to deal with it.

Sometimes I wondered why Charlie even put up
with me.

The discussions down on the dock took a while, and
probably would have gone on for an hour or more, but Jacob
Parsons stepped forward and pulled a sheaf of papers out of
his jacket pocket, handing them over to the policeman who
was doing most of the questioning. After a quick examination of the documents, the cop nodded his head curtly and
then handed them back. A minute after that, Parsons, his
wife and the whole group of divers came on board.

Diana looked pissed and none of the others seemed like
they were in the mood to party. I was thinking the day was
off to a bad start, and I have to tell you, I wasn't wrong.

The weather started poorly and got worse from there.
The winds were picking up and the clouds that were dark-

ening the day grew heavier. By the time we'd reached our destination the sky was spitting fitfully and the water was choppy enough to make the *Isabella* rock back and forth even after I anchored her. Still, Charlie and everyone else got into their suits and climbed into their gear.

I thought about my dream of the night before and had to restrain myself from turning the yacht around and heading back toward the docks. I was here to make a buck and maybe catch a few fish, not to investigate whatever was under the water. I'd told myself at the beginning of the job that whatever they did out there wasn't my concern and I intended to keep it that way.

Jacob Parsons watched them as they went into the water and paced a little, worriedly. He headed my way and pulled out his cigarettes. He didn't bother asking but just tossed one to me instead. I figured the man was going to destroy all my efforts to quit smoking and was grateful for him.

"You look worried." He spoke the exact words I was going to say to him and threw me for a loop in the process.

"Not my job to be worried, Jacob. I'm just here to play tour guide."

He looked at me with almost no expression and then nodded his head. "Yeah, I can understand that. But you still look worried."

He was perceptive, and that annoyed me just a little. "I didn't sleep much last night." I couldn't think of anything else to say. We stood in silence for a few minutes and then just to kill the time, I asked, "What was all that about on the docks?"

"I get the feeling the locals aren't really thrilled to have us around." Jacob pointed his chin at the Devil's Reef. "Seems like us doing dives over here is bugging the hell out of them. Unfortunately for them, I have all the paperwork and I have copies of everything, to boot."

"Sounds like you were expecting trouble."

"Try working as a parapsychologist sometime. You'd be amazed how many people don't like hearing there might be something unnatural going on where they are."

"What? Like you're to blame for whatever you might find?"

"Oh, yeah. Lots of that. It's like they think the property values will drop and their neighborhoods will turn into a ghetto overnight."

"And does it? Drop the values, I mean?"

"Not hardly." He chuckled. "I had one guy call me and thank me. Not only did he get validation from us on his place being haunted, but he also had an offer from a couple who wanted to buy the house and paid him almost twice what the market value of the place was."

"Nothing like free advertising, I guess."

"Exactly. And for all the people who scoff at ghost stories, there are a lot of folks who want to experience a haunting firsthand."

"Well, that's just fried."

"What?" He smiled and put out his cigarette. "Never wanted to know about life after death?"

"I'm still working on the life part. I'm not really in a hurry to check out the death thing."

"Now, see, normally when I ask someone that question, they start spouting religious doctrines." He chuckled and shoved his hands into his coat pockets.

"Never much cared for church philosophies." I shrugged. "I figure I'll skip the middleman." I looked back over at the town in the distance and felt a shiver. "You think the locals can cause you a lot of trouble?"

"I figure they'll want to, especially if they decide they have something to hide."

"Like what?"

"Like their own little Bermuda Triangle, if the stories are true."

"How are you going to find out if there's any truth to them?"

"Research, research, research. There are always things you can learn with research."

"Thanks, but I still prefer fishing."

Jacob winked at me and settled himself a little closer to the wall of the cabin. "Well, I would, but there's that whole water thing that slows me down."

"Now, see, my grandfather always said the only way to beat a fear is to face it." I looked at him and watched his face carefully. I was teasing, but doing my best not to let it show. Who the hell was I to talk about facing your fears when I was watching other people take a dive into the caves that I was growing more and more fascinated by? I mean, seriously, I was scared of getting stuck underwater and he was just plain scared of the water.

Jacob looked at me for several seconds, his face back in that poker expression that made me know he wouldn't be a good man to underestimate. "That's on the agenda already, remember, Joe? I'm diving once the whole thing has been mapped."

I nodded and kept my mouth shut after that. He had the balls to face his fear. Me? I was perfectly fine watching from the sidelines. At least that's what I kept trying to tell myself.

Belle called me a little after noon. She was packing her things and getting the car ready for driving up to see me. I have to say, the notion of spending some quality time doing nothing with her had a lot of appeal. Sounds strange to some people I suspect, but seeing as my wife is also my best friend, the idea was leaving a grin on my face.

So the day was finally starting to look a little better; I got the boys to do a once-over of the cabin and the yacht to make it as presentable as possible for Belle's arrival. They worked a lot faster when the college kids weren't back from diving and this was no exception. I took care of the captain's cabin myself and even changed the sheets, which, as Charlie would tell you, is not one of my favorite things to do.

After a half hour of frenzied cleaning, it was back to business as usual and I went to the far side of the yacht and started fishing. I got lucky and the drizzle had stopped. Judging by the recent track record, I was beginning to think Golden Cove was one of the best kept secrets in New England when it came to sweet fishing spots.

Mary Parsons came out and sat near me, taking a breather from the research, I suppose. It wasn't unusual for her or Jacob to keep me company while relaxing.

She did that cat curl thing as she sat down and put her chin on her knees while watching my line bob in the water. I handed her the fishing pole and she took it as I put bait on another one. Unlike her husband, Mary seemed okay with the whole idea of fishing.

"Davey says your wife is coming out to stay a few days?" Her tone was conversational, but I looked her way just the same.

"Yeah. I guess she wants to see me."

"Good." She nodded her head, satisfied, and then got a small smile on her face when the line started pulling. "Charlie says she's something special. I want to meet Mrs. Joe."

I set down my newly baited pole and reached over to help her when the line on her pole shifted hard in the water. She had a fish and by the way it was moving, she had a big one. Mary let out a sound like a teenaged girl at her first boy band concert and sat up straighter in her chair as the fish on the other end started putting up a proper fight. The 400-pound test line drew tight and then took off, heading farther out to sea, and I resisted the urge to take the pole away from her, instead just giving encouragement and advice. I figured if she got too tired I could help, but otherwise whatever she had was all hers.

My father always took the pole away from me when I was a kid and I always let him, but I never liked it. How could it be my catch when he was the one that reeled it in? If you see my point. I always did my best not to do that to other people.

I think we must have spent almost an hour working on that fish. I know that Jacob came out to watch and so did Davey and Tom. It wasn't anything special to watch me fish, but this wasn't me. This was Mary Parsons and she was having a blast. I could see the strain in her shoulders and neck, and I could see the sweat on her brow, but she was determined that the fish on that line was going to join us on the yacht for dinner.

Whatever she had on the line was getting tired and desperate and I wound up helping her, but only long enough to let her slip into the harness that Davey got for her. With a harness in place, she'd have a chance to brace herself properly and not risk losing the pole, but just as important, I could literally anchor her to the yacht. Once she was strapped in, I did just that, too, because I don't figure she weighed much more than a hundred and ten and I didn't really want to go in after her if the fish she was fighting with got bitchy.

Good thing we were prepared. After almost another full hour she finally managed to reel the thing in—with my help and even Jacob's—and it outweighed her. She'd managed to hook a blue fin tuna and it took everyone on board to pull the thing onto the yacht. If it was less than seven feet long from snout to tail, I'd have been surprised.

I had a lot of fun taking pictures of Mary and Jacob next to her catch. Jacob was smiling and looking a little seasick at the same time and Mary was grinning ear to ear and looking like she was all of twelve next to that monster. We took the photos, and then Tommy and I gutted and cleaned the tuna. Jacob made a point of being elsewhere for that part, but Mary watched on, fascinated by the entire process.

Once again, we used buckets to hold the guts. I don't worry too much about shark attacks along the coast of New England, but only a fool would have dumped all of that chum into the water while there were divers nearby.

Tom cleaned the deck with Davey's help and we took the catch into the refrigerator to wait for dinnertime. Or maybe just to hold for another day. I'd planned on steaks for the dinner that night because after a while, most people don't want to look at a fish anymore.

It was while they were cleaning up and Mary and Jacob were chuckling about her conquest of the seas that the diving team came back up. Charlie was first, and then two boys I'd barely spoken to, along with Diana and Professor Ward, who was already shivering violently.

Charlie practically hauled people out of his way as they climbed, barely even taking the time to toss his oxygen tank aside. No one was talking and every face was tense. I know the signs of trouble when I see them, and I moved over as quickly as I could, calling to Davey and Tom at the same time.

The last two divers were still in the water when Charlie scurried down the ladder and pulled the burden the two were carrying up and onto his back. The one he was carrying wasn't moving at all, except when his head rolled to the side.

"What happened?"

Charlie ignored my question and started peeling away the equipment that covered the kid's face and body. The teenager looked deathly pale, his lips almost blue. I squatted and checked his pulse. It was there, but very weak.

As the dry suit was peeled away, the red marks were revealed. Long strands of deep scarlet ran over his torso and along the side of his neck.

"What the hell?"

I looked at the red, raised welts and felt my skin crawl. I'd seen the same sort of marks before, back when I ran into the man-o'-war years ago. I knew them all too well, only the marks on the boy were worse. They were thicker, and there were fine lines of blood in the center of each mark.

Charlie looked at me, and shook his head. "It wasn't a jellyfish and it wasn't a man-o'-war, either, Joe."

I nodded my head. I'd seen jellyfish stings plenty of times, but never one that showed up where fabric was protecting the skin. Whatever had stung him had gone through the heavy layers of his suit like it wasn't even there. "What attacked him?"

"Joe, it was a man that did that. A man, and he was under the water, in the caves."

I heard the voices of several of the students murmuring agreement and that creeping flesh feeling hit me again.

"That's impossible."

"Hey!" Diana's voice was loud and cut away the confusion I was feeling. "Worry about that shit later! Right now Corey needs to get medical help!"

I nodded my head. "Charlie, get us turned around and back to the cove. Call for an ambulance. Diana, tell Tommy to get you as much vinegar as he has." Vinegar, for the record, stops the venom from jellyfish stings. I was hoping it would work on whatever the hell had hit the kid.

They both moved, not bothering to question me, and I was grateful but chagrined. This kid, Corey, needed medical assistance and all I could do was think about an oversized jellyfish that almost killed me once.

We turned back toward Golden Cove and I did what I could for his wounds, all the while listening to the voices of the people around me. They were background noise, mostly. But now and then I heard a phrase that caught my attention. Little things, like "no dry suit" and "he had claws."

They were talking about whatever it was that had attacked the kid, and they were completely serious. I looked down at my patient and did what I could with the supplies I had on board.

And I worried. I worried a lot. Mostly about what I had signed on for and what Belle would think when she got into town.

And about Corey, of course, who was dying in front of me, a little at a time.

NINE

There's a damned big difference between trying to treat someone with an ambulance full of supplies and trying to treat them with a few bandages and some apple cider vinegar. I looked down at Corey and hated that there wasn't more I could do for him while the yacht cruised back toward the docks. He'd been on the *Isabella* for several days and I don't think I'd spoken four words to him in that time. Believe me, I was feeling like shit about that; the kid was barely old enough to shave and instead of worrying about whether or not he could get a date for the weekend he was lying on the deck of my boat and turning paler by the second. Despite the cold, most of the kids from the school were hanging around and watching while I checked their friend's pulse and respiration as best I could without any decent equipment.

The ambulance was waiting when we got to the docks and the attendants were first rate, checking his vitals and actually listening when I told them about his rapidly declining health. They managed to stabilize him and then took off with Corey and Professor Ward. It was out of my hands, and all I could do was hope it turned out all right. The weather was looking even worse by the time the ambulance took off and after the stress of the day it was decided that the expedition was done for now. That was just as well, because I was seriously considering calling it off myself.

The divers were still showering and drying off in shifts when the rain started in earnest, a heavy downfall that turned the air silvery gray and made enough of a racket to convince me to stay inside the main cabin. I watched the rain from inside, and saw the drops of water pelt the ocean hard enough to subdue the waves.

I tried not to think about the claims that something was in the caves, something that looked a little like a human being and had put that massive a hurt on the college kid being treated at the local hospital.

Charlie came over and stood near me after pouring himself a serious glass of scotch. I waited for him to talk. He'd get around to it in his own way and I knew the scotch was as much to make that easier for him as it was to make him numb.

"It wasn't a man, Joe. But it looked like one."

"Then what was it, Charlie?" I looked at his reflection in the glass. His ghostly double looked back with knitted eyebrows and a scowl on his face.

"I don't know." He shrugged. "All I know is it came out from the lower part of the cave and it moved like a bullet." He paused to consider his words and I finally turned to face him. "Joe, the damned thing had eyes as big as my fist and they were glowing."

"So maybe it was a weird dry suit. Maybe it was someone with a custom-made job who was trying to freak you out."

"No bubbles, Joe. The mouth opened and closed and not a single bubble came out when the thing was breathing."

"He could have been wearing a re-breather. Hell, Charlie, it could have been somebody from town trying to make sure nobody stays around whatever is down there. Seems like they'd prefer that to having a good tourist business."

"Yeah, that sounds like a plot from a Scooby Doo cartoon. We aren't looking for Ahab's hidden treasures here."

"A man in a full face mask with a weird getup isn't as far-fetched as a fish-eyed monster, sport."

Charlie shook his head. "I don't think so. I think it was some kind of fish man." It would have been easy to laugh it off and push thoughts of what he was saying away, but it was Charlie I was dealing with. Charlie was superstitious, sure, but he was also not prone to exaggerating.

"Okay, so where did it come from?"

"Joe, believe me, you'd have to see those caves to believe them. They go straight down, and a lot farther than I thought was possible." He shook his head. "Ward says the reef is pretty much the end of the continental landmass. It's possible those caves go all the way to the bottom and end up in the deep ocean. Of course, no one can prove that, because no one can get down low enough to test it out."

"Yeah? Well that doesn't explain how no one has ever seen one of these fish men. This isn't an area that's exactly unmapped, Charlie." He sighed and got a look on his face that said he was ready for a long, drawn out argument. I held my hands up in surrender. "I'm not saying you're wrong, or you didn't see what you think you saw, Charlie. I'm just trying to understand how anything like that could exist."

"That's what Ward's been trying to figure out, too."

"I thought he was trying to map the caves."

"He is. But that's only part of it. Seems he's heard rumors of some kind of mermaid population or something that lives on the outer edges of the reef."

I shook my head. Not out of disbelief, but out of disgust. Perfectly educated professors who look for Atlantis off the coast of New Hampshire aren't overly bright in my book. Suddenly I wasn't so shocked to find out that the university didn't feel like footing the bill for the expedition taking place in their own backyard.

"Yeah, and in ancient times, they sang sailors onto rocks and made them sink their ships."

Charlie got that just-smelled-something-nasty look on his face. "Yeah, I know. 'Charlie's falling for another ghost story.'"

"Look, Charlie, I'm not saying anything like that. I'm saying be careful about it, okay? You saw something in a dark cave. It could have been a diver. Maybe it was something else, but it could have been a diver. There's not a lot of light down there, right?"

That's another thing about Charlie. He normally had to concede when logic was pushed in his face. He didn't have to like it, but he wasn't a complete idiot.

"Yeah, okay, but that doesn't explain what happened to Corey."

"We don't know what happened to Corey. All we know is he was hurt. Just because it looks like a jellyfish stung him doesn't make it the right answer."

"It wasn't a jellyfish, Joe."

"Did you actually see the thing that attacked him? Could you get a decent picture with a sketch artist?"

"I don't know. Maybe."

"Not a great answer there, Charlie. Not the sort that convinces most people."

"I'd think you'd take my word on it, Joe. I've never lied to you about that sort of thing." He was getting upset, and his face was starting to get a red color that wasn't exactly healthy.

"You don't have to convince me. You say it was a fish man, I'll at least accept that it looked like one in the dark cave where your flashlight was showing you the way. But the professor and all of his students and you need to have more than just eyewitness accounts if you want to prove something like that to everyone out there. A picture would be good, or a video."

Charlie waved his hand in the air, dismissing everything I said, like he was swatting at an annoying bug, and then he turned and walked away. I didn't try to follow him. Charlie was a big boy and if he wanted to believe there were fish men wandering around under the water that was his decision to make. I had seen a pair of legs go under the other night and they'd looked about as normal as a wild boar at a high society gathering, but that didn't mean I was willing to accept that they belonged to an extra from the *Creature from the Black Lagoon.* Show me a shaggy man with fangs under a full moon and I'm not going to decide I saw a werewolf, either. Does that make me stubborn? Maybe, but I can live with that.

We got the news almost three hours later that Corey was expected to make a full recovery. Ward came and told us all about it himself. After that, he went off the docks and headed for the hotel where he was staying. He had plans of sleeping on dry land.

Not long after the professor left, the students took off as well, including Diana. Charlie went with her and chose to stay in a hotel room, too. That left me and the boys for dinner that night because, though they planned to stay on the *Isabella,* the Parsonses were also going into town to discuss matters with Ward.

I went with steaks, and as I was getting ready to cook them, Belle showed up at the docks, dressed in a pair of jeans and one of my flannel shirts. The old flannel looked like a tent on her, but she'd managed to tuck it in well enough that it accented her figure. How the hell do women do that? I wish I knew the secret.

By the time she reached the yacht her clothes were soaked from the continuing downpour. I gave my wife a hug and spun her around me on the deck of the yacht I'd named in her honor, not giving the least bit of a damn about the cold and rain that soaked me. I don't think it'd be possible to write down how much she means to me. I won't even try. Let's just leave it at I was very glad to see her, and almost overwhelmed by the way the stress left my body when she showed up. I hadn't realized how much the trip was affecting me until I saw her.

I let Tom take care of the steaks after that, and went out to the parking lot to get her overnight bag and her small suitcase. We took a quick shower together and then got into fresh clothes not long after that.

We ate, we talked, we slept. What else happened that night is no one's business but mine and Belle's.

It was a little over an hour before dawn when I woke up. The air was even colder than before, but the rain had stopped. I'm not normally a light sleeper, but I'd heard something that was loud enough to wake me up. I heard it again a moment later: a very soft knock at the cabin door. Instead of getting royally pissed off, I slipped on a pair of sweats and answered the knock before it could wake Belle. I figured if I had a reason to get bitchy, I could do it after I'd left the room.

It was Davey. He looked a little nervous about waking me, which according to my wife is always wise. I stepped out of the cabin and ushered him down a dozen feet or so before asking him what was up.

"Sorry to wake you, Joe, but I keep hearing shit outside, and with all the talk of fish men, I'm not checking it by myself."

"Where the hell is Tom?"

"I dunno." He looked around nervously. "He isn't in his room."

I stifled the desire to curse up a blue streak and nodded my head instead. With everything that had been going on, I didn't really want Davey trying to find out anything on his own. He was a good kid, but he was also not exactly designed for dealing with any serious threats. Like I said before, he looked like a freshman in high school.

We grabbed up a couple of makeshift clubs; mine was an old-fashioned harpoon from back in the whaling days and Davey took a cast-iron skillet from the mess. Either one would do the job of bashing in the skull of anyone that had no business being on the *Isabella*.

We were thorough, too. We looked in every single room on the yacht, except for the Parsonses' room, which was locked up. There was no one to be seen, no one hiding in any corners or lurking in any shadows.

There was also no sign of Tom. Either he was in my cabin with Belle, which I knew he wasn't, or he was in with Jacob and Mary, also unlikely, or he was gone from the yacht.

Here's the thing: Tom was a big boy. I was worried about him, but I also acknowledged that he could have decided to go for a late-night walk, or even to find a hooker. Davey was worried and so was I, but we both agreed that we should wait at least until the next night before we decided to report him missing.

Yeah, Belle didn't agree. That pretty much resolved the matter.

So instead of heading off immediately for the reef, my wife and I found our way to the Golden Cove Police Department and filled out a missing persons report. The detective who came to speak to us was one of the square-shouldered goons from the previous day. Up close he was just as unattractive. Not surprisingly, he said they couldn't act on it for twenty-four hours because Tom was an adult. Still, I have to admit I felt better for making the report early.

"We should tell his parents." Belle said the words as calmly as if she had just suggested that we perhaps have spaghetti and meatballs for dinner.

My response wasn't quite as calm. "Oh, hell no!"

"What?" She didn't sound defensive. I was hoping for defensive because there would have been less of an argument then. "They have a right to know that their son is missing."

"And that's just fine, but he isn't missing yet. He's missing after twenty-four hours and I'm not ratting out a college kid to his parents until the allotted time has passed."

"Are you serious?"

"Of course I'm serious!" I couldn't believe she would even ask.

"So if Laurie or Mike didn't come home from a date you wouldn't worry for a full day?" She shook her head. "No, screw that. If one of our children vanished without telling anyone where they were going, you wouldn't want to know?"

Leave it to a mother to know how to make a father feel guilty. We have two wonderful kids and both of them are in college. Mike I trust to handle himself. Laurie I trust to try, but let's be honest here, I'm a guy and I'm a dad. I know how some men think and I have always worried about my baby girl's safety. She could be surrounded by a hundred armed eunuchs who were being paid top dollar to protect her, and I would still worry. It's what dads do, I guess. Belle knew how I felt; I knew she thought the double standard was wrong. It was something we had always agreed to disagree about.

I didn't think she was going to accept my usual chauvinistic ways this time around.

"Belle, that's different and you know it." Okay, I confess. The argument already sounded weaker than I wanted.

"Why is it different, Joe?" She crossed her arms over her chest and shook her head. "Because he's not your son?"

"Yeah. That's a big part of it, Belle. He's my employee and he's a kid. He's also a kid who might be sleeping with one of the girls from the dive for all I know."

"Fine." I felt the temperature drop in the car as surely as if I'd turned on the air conditioner. "So if he's not there when your divers show up, we should call his parents."

"If he's not there when the divers show up, *you* can call his parents." That was the best she was going to get from me and she knew it and accepted it.

Tom hadn't shown up by the time the divers were ready to go. Davey had tried his cell phone several times before discovering that it was halfway under the bed in Tom's cabin.

Belle kept her word and called the Summerses', playing phone tag until she could get his mother on the line. Meanwhile, I watched the divers getting ready. They had new equipment this time, and not exactly the sort I was expecting to see. In addition to the usual tanks, lights and sonar devices, they had two of the *Isabella*'s harpoon guns, complete with harpoons, and Charlie had also confiscated one of the smaller nets.

I looked at him like he'd lost his mind.

He looked back at me like I could go fuck myself.

"Going fishing, Charlie?"

"I figure if something shows up again, we can defend ourselves. If not, they don't weigh that much."

"What are you going to do with whatever you catch?"

"If it's a fish, I'll cook us a nice dinner. If it's a man, I'll turn him over to the authorities."

"And if it's a fish man?"

"Well, then we have a nice addition to the doc's research, don't we?"

I could have told him to leave the stuff behind, but what was the point? He wanted to go fishing for mermaids; I wasn't really that worried about stopping him. Still the idea made me a little nervous.

Off in the background, I heard Belle talking into the phone, trying to placate the woman she had no doubt sent into a frenzy. I know she hated being the one to make the call, but part of me was still sure she was overreacting. It was hardly the first time I'd had a college kid on my team who didn't show up for a shift, and I didn't think it would be the last time, either.

Charlie and Diana paced impatiently as I started the yacht and piloted us out to the reef. The black stone shelf seemed bigger today, but that was probably just because the tide was going out.

As I pulled the yacht into the same spot as the day before, Charlie walked back over to me, his face set and almost unreadable.

"You gonna wish me luck, Joe?"

I looked at him for several seconds, unable to answer him. I wanted to wish him luck, but I didn't really know what he was looking for. Finally, I nodded and offered him my hand. "Good luck, Charlie. Be careful."

He smiled when I made the peace offering. Sometimes he was too sensitive for his own good.

I watched them go down the ladder on the side of the *Isabella* and felt nervous. The day was nicer than the day before, but I was still getting the feeling that things were going to go wrong. When they were gone, I went into my cabin to get away from everyone for a while. Belle was still on the phone, but I didn't want to hear it anymore.

I wanted to relax and I knew that wasn't going to happen.

So I waited, just like everyone else.

And I worried that I'd never see Charlie again.

TEN

I guess it's safe to say that I drifted off to sleep for a while, still in my thick pea coat. I woke up covered in a light sweat, with my arm shoved under my body at an awkward and uncomfortable angle. I had a few seconds where I wasn't really sure where I was, or at least when. I knew I was on the *Isabella,* but I couldn't grasp why that was so important. Then I heard Jacob Parsons laughing and remembered.

A quick look at my watch told me I'd been out for almost three hours. The tanks the divers were using weren't good for that long, so either they'd come back up and gone down again—the tanks were only good for a little over an hour and after that they'd need to come up and spend a little time recovering—or they'd never returned. I decided to hold off on any panic attacks until I knew one way or the other.

A quick look told me that Belle had met up with the Parsonses and was having a good time. She had a look on her face that seemed reserved for rare occasions, like Christmas. I left them in peace: right now, near as I could tell, Belle and I were not really on the best terms and I figured she'd have a lot more fun if she was chatting with celebrities rather than remembering to be pissed at me.

Besides, I wanted to see what was up with Davey. I wanted to know if Tom had come back and what was going on with the divers. I had to look for him outside in the cold and I swear, I think I felt the perspiration on my body freeze solid the second I walked out there.

He was cleaning up the decks, mopping away the excess water from where the divers had been a little while earlier, when I found him. There were several empty tanks to be put away, and I helped stow them in the right area, careful to mark them.

"So, anyone hear anything from Tom yet?" I paused in my efforts and looked at Davey. He shook his head, focused on finishing his mopping or on not looking at me; I couldn't decide which.

"You worried about him, Davey? Or does he pull this sort of thing at home, too?"

"He wouldn't have left without his cell phone."

"You sure about that?"

Davey nodded and finally got around to looking at me. His eyes looked bleary and red. "Yeah, I'm sure. Stupid thing is practically fused to his hip, Joe."

That worried me a bit more than I wanted to be worried, and I decided that maybe my refusal to actually call Tom's parents was a sad case of me being a jackass. Yeah, he and Davey were both old enough to vote, but in a lot of ways they really were just kids. Hell, if he'd been seventeen instead of nineteen, I'd have been legally responsible for his safekeeping on the yacht and here I was arguing semantics with Belle over the situation because I was afraid of violating Tom's personal space. It was one thing to make him gut a hundred fish for a group of tourists and another to check in on him when he was sleeping on the *Isabella*. Not my wisest move, maybe, so I nodded my head as I finished putting the spent tanks into the hold.

"Did he say anything at all about going for a walk or something?"

"No. He said he was tired." Davey shrugged. "He was gonna call Theresa and then he was going to sleep."

Theresa was his girlfriend back in Bowden's Point. She was still in high school and graduating in the spring. After that they were planning on going off to college together. Tom was the one who'd been extra happy about getting the late gig, because it was more money he could sock away for college when the time came.

Theresa Lattimore was more important to Tom than a little shameless flirting with the college girls. That was what I'd managed to forget along the way. Tom was about as quick to flash her picture at someone as a gunslinger in Deadwood was to draw his iron and fire six bullets into someone trying to make a name.

I felt my stomach tighten up and forced a breath out from my lungs. This was looking about as bad as it could without a body popping up. It was looking even worse to me, because I'd been an ass and never realized how stupid I was being.

I mumbled something under my breath in Davey's direction and gave him a wave to let him know I was heading off. I wasn't ready to talk with Belle and admit that I was being stupid, not just yet. I wanted to think things through first, to double-check all of my facts and make sure I wasn't missing anything.

I did what I've almost always done to help myself relax: I stared at the sea and reminded myself that my problems, no matter how immense they might seem, are little more than a speck of dust in comparison to the enormity of the ocean that surrounded me.

The breeze was coming in from the ocean but now and

then it shifted a bit and I caught a whiff of the marshes to the north of town. They smelled stagnant and foul, as if some-one had been dropping the remains of fish there for months and letting them rot. I looked in that direction and saw the seagulls swooping and diving down to feast on whatever might be over there. The birds were so much a part of my life that sometimes I failed to notice them. The gulls up here are great gray monsters, big enough to scare the life out of someone when they get an attitude. I'd seen them dive out of the air and snatch everything from hamburgers to pizza out of careless people's hands, and while a lot of people thought they were nuisances, I'd always liked them.

Damnedest thing: not a one of the seagulls had ever come near the yacht. Not while we were docked in Golden Cove and not when we were out at the reef. It was like the lack of dogs, something I should have noticed from the beginning, but had overlooked. I'd left over ten pounds of raw fish innards in a bucket on the back end of the yacht and not a single gull had come over to take a few sample bites. Damned unsettling is what it was. My skin tried to shimmy across my body and I felt the gooseflesh pimple over my arms and neck.

I stared out at the ocean until the divers came back up, lost in my thoughts and an increasing sense of discomfort.

Belle came up behind me as I was staring into the waters and slipped her arms around my waist. She rested her head against the back of my shoulders and I closed my eyes, savoring her presence.

"I'm a dumb ass, Belle. I'm sorry."

"I was just going to say the same thing to you."

"What? That I'm a dumb ass?"

"No. That I am."

"No one gets to talk about my wife that way, not even

my wife. Watch yourself." I turned to face her as I spoke and pulled her into my arms. There has never been another person who understood me as well as she does, or who has had a better sense of timing. Not in my world, at least. We held each other for a few minutes and I lost myself in her. Belle is my favorite way to get lost.

"What did Tom's mom have to say?"

"She's worried, but she knows you'll look out for him." Ouch. That hurt, too.

"Davey's worried and that makes me worried."

"Well, hopefully he just got drunk and picked up a hooker."

"I don't think so. I wish it was that easy, but I don't think it will be."

"Neither do I." Belle barely knew Tom except as the kid who worked on the yacht whenever he could. She had maybe met him five times in her life, but she was like that. She made worrying about other people an art form. I didn't let myself worry about too many people. I had Belle and the kids and Charlie. That was about enough.

And now I had Tom.

On the brighter side, Belle and I were back on speaking terms, and that meant more than you know to me. The idea of her being upset was normally enough to give me a headache. The idea of her being angry with me was enough to make the world seem bleak. The world didn't seem to need much help in that department right then. Tom was missing and the divers were down in frigid waters carrying enough weapons to almost guarantee someone getting hurt if anyone made a misidentification. I knew Charlie wouldn't get stupid, even if he panicked about bugaboos under the water. Charlie had a level head, and always looked before he acted. It's one of the reasons I hired him and one of the reasons I kept him on.

Still, I worried.

I was fretting away at high speeds when I heard the splashing noises and then heard Charlie calling out to me.

"Joe! Get over here, damn it!"

Something in the water with him let out a deep bleating honk and I let go of Belle and ran for the portside ladder where I heard Charlie's voice. I got there just in time to watch Charlie go under, his face locked into a gasp of surprise or pain; I couldn't tell which. His arms were wrapped around something that was fighting back, something that thrashed and bucked against the net wrapped around it.

"Jesus Christ on a bike! What the hell did you catch?" I stepped onto the ladder, hanging on tightly with my left arm as Charlie came back up and rammed whatever he was fighting with against the side of the *Isabella*. It let out another deep croaking noise and then sat still, pressed by his weight into the side of my yacht.

By the time I was low enough to offer a hand, Charlie had help. Diana was there, one of the harpoon guns held in her hand, the point of the business end pressed against the thing they were struggling with. Whatever it was, it seemed to know that the weapon was deadly and it stopped throwing itself around.

I reached down and caught a portion of the netting. I felt the rough sandpapery skin of the thing they held and pulled the net tightly toward me. Charlie lifted from below and both of us were grunting with effort as I started back up the ladder and Charlie climbed after his prize, both hands holding on to the net where whatever it was gasped out breaths and shivered.

In the water below Charlie I saw the rest of the diving team as they bobbed up to the surface and started swimming toward the yacht. I think most of them would have been babbling but they all still had their regulators in place.

As soon as it was out of the water completely, Charlie's

catch started throwing itself around violently from side to side. I hauled on it faster as my right arm was sent all over the place. The damned thing was strong and it was pissed off.

I had a moment where I was pretty sure I was going to come off the ladder and hit the water below and I probably would have, but Jacob Parsons was there and he grabbed my shoulder and my belt and started hauling me back. It made it much easier for me to keep a hold on Charlie's prize. With Jacob's help I was back on the deck in short order and hauling the wiggling package of net and fish onto the yacht proper.

I let it go around the same time the thing inside the net tried to bite me with a mouthful of some nasty-looking teeth. I heard the sound of the teeth snapping together and felt the vibrations from it near my hand. I couldn't help but wonder what would have been left of my fingers if I hadn't seen the motion.

Charlie climbed to the top of the ladder, panting and dripping seawater. His face was red from exertion, but he was smiling about the nastiest smile I'd ever seen on him.

"I got that sonuvabitch! Yes!" He kicked off his flippers and was halfway out of his buoyancy control device before the next person came up the ladder. And they came quickly, eager to see what they had caught.

The thing in the net wasn't nearly as happy about being there, and it showed its dissatisfaction by trying to head back for the water. Diana put a stop to that when she pressed the sharpened tip of the harpoon gun against the flesh near the mouth of the thing. It stopped struggling and instead laid back, panting and gasping for a good breath. The heavy nylon cords that made up the netting around it were strained, pushed against the grayish flesh, but not cutting into the thing, despite all the struggling. Most people would have at least had some serious friction burns by then, but whatever Charlie had brought back with him was apparently made of sterner stuff.

It was tangled very thoroughly into the netting, and I could see what looked at first like a fin protruding from the webbing. I looked more carefully and realized it was a foot, complete with individual toes.

The thing croaked again, a loud, rattling noise that shouldn't have been possible from a human throat. That, more than the teeth that almost removed my fingers, made me realize it wasn't just a guy in a costume.

Professor Ward walked closer, peeling off his mask and regulator as he got to where he could get a clear view of the thing. He had a dozen different expressions trying to make themselves known on his face and none of them were very pretty.

I realized right around that moment that I didn't know Ward. Not at all, actually. He was quiet when he was around me and I had just taken that to mean I wasn't important in the scheme of things. He was a professor on a mission and I was someone who was working for him, nothing more and nothing less.

But the thing that Charlie and the others had caught? Well, that was a very different story. He looked at the writhing package on the ground with the same sort of obsession that a religious fanatic would display when encountering the Holy Grail.

"This is a great moment." He spoke with that sort of reverence, too.

"No, it's a fish." I couldn't resist giving my personal editorial on the situation.

"A fish?" Ward looked at me like I'd just taken a piss on the altar of his preference. "It's not a fish, you moron! It's a Deep One!"

I got in his face. I don't normally do that sort of thing. I usually just shrug and grin when someone gets stupid with me, but today I was missing one of my crew and I didn't feel very charitable to the idea of being called a moron by some stuffed shirt with delusions of Nobel Prizes for Pomposity.

"Who are you calling a moron, you little shit?" I don't think he could have backpedaled faster if I'd pulled a knife and set it against his crotch.

Charlie stopped things from getting worse. Several people actually came forward to help, but some of them would have had to step over the thing between us and them and Charlie was just a fraction faster.

"Calm down, Joe. He didn't mean it, did you, Professor Ward?" Charlie had that purr going in his voice. It was the same tone he used to sweet-talk the ladies and the same tone I'd heard a few times when he realized things were about to get ugly.

Here's the thing: it's normally me talking Charlie down and I couldn't for the life of me figure out exactly why I was getting so completely pissed off about what was basically a social screwup. Believe me when I say the opinions of people like Ward meant very little to me, because I knew his kind. He was only comfortable when he was nose deep in a book. He probably hadn't meant to open his mouth at all, and I know he didn't intend to insult me. I've ignored much worse insults without batting an eye, because it's my job to ignore rude comments. You don't get to stay in business for long, especially when you run fishing trips for a living, if you don't develop a thick hide.

But, damn, I wanted to knock his teeth down his throat right then and maybe break a few of his ribs in addition.

I stepped back and made myself calm down. It wouldn't do me any good to get into a fight with a man half my size. As my grandfather used to say, five minutes of satisfaction isn't worth six months in the local slammer. Belle would never forgive me, and I didn't want to come out of this looking like the bad guy. So I closed my eyes, thought about the chunk of money sitting in my savings account, and nodded my head.

"I'm terribly sorry, Captain Joe..." I looked at Ward and he looked appropriately apologetic.

"No problem. I guess we're all a little edgy today." I put out my hand and smiled a closed mouth little smile. It was the best I could do. Charlie nodded his head, glad that everything was calmer.

And the thing in the net lunged, and snapped its teeth together on the edge of my shoe. I know it wanted more, but all it got was the tip of my loafer. I felt its cold breath and felt the spray of moisture from its mouth as it spat out the leather and tried again. All of us backed off a little as it struggled and let out a roar that shook the bones in my legs.

Ward looked around like a deer in hunting season and stepped back even more as it shook and growled and clawed at the netting. Three thick claws, each as long as the last two knuckles of my fingers, ripped through the nylon rope and cut at the air.

Several people made loud screaming noises. I could barely hear them over my own. Despite everything, I was still convinced it was just a strange-looking fish up until that moment. I've never in my life seen a fish with an opposable thumb, and the thing in the net had at least one, judging by the hand scratching at the deck.

"Charlie, what the hell did you bring onto my boat?" I was barely even aware of speaking.

Charlie stepped forward and then thought better of doing anything. His feet, minus the flippers, had only a thin layer of canvas for protection. Davey wasn't worried about that. Davey was a fisherman first and a sailor second. He brought down his steel-toed boot and slammed it against the claw on the deck. The thing let out another roar and started struggling, but I took the harpoon gun away from Diana and clubbed it a few times in the head with the butt of the thing. It stopped fighting as much and Charlie looked at me like I'd lost my mind.

"What? It stopped, didn't it?"

"We want it alive, Joe."

I looked at Charlie for a few seconds and tried to read what was going on in his head. Finally, I shrugged. "So bind the damn thing up properly. And you better figure out where you want to keep it, because there isn't a fish tank on this rig."

I looked back at the thing. It was still there, still breathing and unconscious and still mostly wrapped around itself inside the netting.

I didn't like it and I didn't want it on my boat, but unless it gave me a reason, I'd tolerate it being there. Besides, it was only for a few hours, right? We'd be back at Golden Cove in a little while and all would be well.

Damn shame how things never work out the way we want them to, isn't it?

The thing had to go somewhere, and it would need water to survive. Luckily for the people who wanted it intact, there were three showers available for their use. That might sound cruel, but it was all I could think of. Also, I noticed that it was breathing outside of the water, so I had to guess it was an amphibian of some kind. Either that or it was taking its own sweet time with the whole suffocating thing.

So it went into a shower and stayed wrapped up inside its netting. I watched the whole operation because—I have to be blunt here—I didn't like the idea of the fucked-up thing on my yacht. Three separate ropes tied the beast in place as far from the glass door of the shower as possible, anchoring it to the showerhead and to the two handles for adjusting water flow.

I looked it over carefully in the stark light of the bathroom and finally got a decent idea of what it looked like. In a word: ugly. The hide was a mottled, dark gray with lighter patches and an almost white belly. Even through the coarse netting, I could see the face well enough: it had wide, round eyes that were eclipsed by a prominent brow, a pair of thin slits for a nose, and a mouth that drew downward the same way as a barracuda's. The shape of the head was all wrong, longer than a human head should have been and set almost improperly on a powerfully wide neck that sloped into equally brutal-looking shoulders. There were gills on either side of that neck, running from directly below the mouth down to the bottom of the skull. You look at enough fish and you get familiar with the shapes that gills can take. These reminded me most of a shark's: streamlined and almost invisible if you weren't looking for them.

The legs and arms of the thing were disproportionate to the body. They were longer than I would have expected from a human shape, and all of them ended in a collection of lethal weapons. The claws I'd seen earlier were attached to hands and feet that were also too long, with a heavy webbing of skin between each digit that I was sure worked like a diver's flippers, only with a lot more efficiency.

Somewhere along the way, nature had played as poorly with this thing as it did with the platypus. It was functional, and about as ugly as a hidden sin left to fester. I couldn't decide if it wanted to be a man, a fish or a toad. It seemed to have features from all three, and none of them matched together well. There were spines along the back of the thing, running from the top of the skull and down to the small of the back. They varied in length and thickness and had a symmetry about them that seemed perfectly in line with any number of fish. Have you ever seen the spines on a catfish? They're thick and sharp and flexible. If you don't know better, you'll mistake them for decoration, but I know from experience that the damned things are capable of cutting through skin and muscle like it's not even there. I had the tip from one of those barbs stuck in one of my fingers for a few weeks once; no matter how often I cleaned the wound it refused to stay healthy. I had infection after infection until it was finally removed. When the doctors were able to figure out that part of it was still inside my skin, it took almost two hours to extract it.

Thinking about the spines on the back of the thing in that shower was enough to make my testicles want to shrivel up and hide. Did I mention the stink of the thing? I guess maybe to its own kind it was all right but there was an odor around it that made salt marshes smell like roses. It was like a blend of rotting fish and mildewed seaweed. I didn't think it was any sort of pollutant in the water, either, because the rest of the area around us didn't reek that way and the divers came out smelling like the ocean, not like something that died in it.

I examined it from as many angles as I could to take in the full impact of what I was looking at. While I was doing that, the good professor was taking pictures.

Diana was watching it, too, but the expression on her face was as dark and ugly as I had ever seen. I don't think she could have looked more disgusted or homicidal if she'd been offered a million dollars to put on the best mean face she could.

I left the bathroom with the full understanding that at least one person would be watching over the freak of nature at all times. Frankly, the idea of that thing getting loose inside of the yacht sat about as well as the notion of force-feeding my right arm to a rabid bear.

"Money talks and bullshit walks," ever hear that one?

That's the reason my common sense was in check, just for the record. I was being paid to let these people use my yacht and if that meant they caught something other than the usual fish, what could I do?

I left the bathroom and stepped outside to get away from the stench of the thing. Jacob was waiting, and handed me a cigarette. I nodded my thanks and then used his lighter to fire it up.

"What the hell is that thing, Jacob?"

"Bad news."

"Yeah? How you figure that?"

"Okay, maybe we should go into a little more detail about what exactly was supposed to have happened here."

I looked over at Jacob and he was looking back, his face even more mournful than usual. I nodded and we moved to the back of the yacht and settled down on one of the benches there, partially sheltered from the worst of the wind that was cutting across the deck.

I waited for a few minutes, both of us smoking our cancer sticks, before I grew impatient. For his part, Jacob stared out at the water and the black mass of the Devil's Reef. "So, you were going to say something about what used to be here?"

"Well, remember, I'm a parapsychologist, so I tend to listen for the weird and wild, right?" I nodded, and he continued. "My interest in this place, me and Mary's, is all of the stories of shipwrecks. You were out the other night when we spotted the ghost ship or whatever it was, so you know we've already had some success."

I nodded again. "I don't know what it was, but it was impressive to see."

"Okay, so Martin Ward isn't interested in ghosts at all. He and I have had several debates and he thinks ghosts are nothing but figments of overactive imaginations. He's interested in anthropology with maybe a side order of xeno-biology thrown in for fun."

"Want to explain that last part?"

"Xeno-biology is the study of strange life-forms. Someone says that Bigfoot is running around and it's the xeno-biologists that check out the possibilities and come up with all sorts of conjectures. They're also the ones who've been looking out for giant squids for centuries.

"Anyhow, we aren't here for the same reasons, but the reasons we're here are the same."

"Want to pass that by me again?"

"I'm here for the ghosts. He's here for rumors about an underwater city."

"Okay. So he thinks Atlantis is under Golden Cove?" I was very good at not laughing about that. Really, I was.

Parsons smiled tolerantly. I guess he was used to that sort of smart-ass comment.

"No, Joe. He's looking for evidence of a city created by creatures just like the one in your bathroom."

"Are you serious?" I tried to wrap my brain around the idea of a place the size of Manhattan populated by those things. It wasn't a pretty notion.

"Oh, yes. Completely."

"And you footed the bill for his research?"

"Not quite. I added his research bill onto mine. I've known Martin for a lot of years, Joe. He's actually a very sharp man when you get to know him."

"Really? Because I have to tell you, Jacob, pissing me off earlier and calling me names? That wasn't very smart."

"I know it and so does he." He waved a hand and shrugged his shoulders by way of apologizing for Ward's earlier behavior. "The thing is, he's never been able to get any backing on the idea, because the sources for all of his research are either dead or missing."

"I'd think that happens a lot with anthropologists."

"You'd be right, too, but the physical evidence for what he's been looking for is very scarce and most of the notes he could find regarding this underwater civilization are second- and thirdhand reports from people who came into Innsmouth for whatever reason and left in a hurry. The closest thing to any physical evidence is a crown that sits in a museum in Newburyport. All anyone can say about the crown is that it's old, made of gold, and has some finny-looking pictograms on it."

"So you decided to be a Good Samaritan and cover his bills."

"No, I have exclusive rights for publishing the scientific findings that he comes across in exchange for a very sub-stantial amount of my money covering his expenses." He shook his head. "I look for ghosts, Joe, but I'm not soft in the head. If there's any truth to what he's after, it's the sort of news that will at the very least knock the scientific com-munity on its collective ass."

"You think so?"

"Think about that thing in there. I'm not saying it's human or a missing link, but the ramifications of an intelli-gent, aquatic, humanoid life-form wandering around in the sea for millions of years will cause all of the biologists on the planet to reassess the creation of man."

I did think about it, and I couldn't help but grin a little at the idea. Every Bible thumper who screamed that evolution was a scam and that God had created the world in seven days would have a cow if this thing was legitimately one of a larger collection of creatures. Every Darwinist on the planet would have screaming orgasms at the idea of some-thing that could be linked to the idea that man evolved from fish in the sea and they now had proof.

Finally, I nodded. "So he's off the hook for calling me an idiot earlier. Tell me more."

"Here's the thing. From what little Martin could find, these Deep Ones, as he calls them, aren't just around here. They're all over the planet and deep, deep down in the waters. Someone named Obed Marsh—and I've researched the hell out of him, Joe, believe me—brought these creatures into this area in the latter part of the seventeenth century. He allegedly made the townsfolk mate with them."

"Okay, that's got to be a crock of shit."

Jacob did that patient smile of his again. On some people I would have called it patronizing, but not on him. I don't think there's a patronizing bone in his body.

"Here's the next part of the scenario that gets weird, Joe. There are documented cases of a very localized genetic disorder called 'The Innsmouth Look.' This particular malfunction of the human body normally started in puberty and continued on for years, slowly altering the way a person looked. It started with swelling of the joints in a lot of cases, and progressed to bulging eyes, a distinctive swelling of the lips, compounded by a gradual alteration to the entire skeletal structure. There were a lot of reported cases in Innsmouth back in the day, but only a few were ever documented and only one or two were ever actually photographed, mostly by a few biologists at the Miskatonic University biology department."

"You ever see any of the pictures?"

"Oh, yes. It caused a very noticeable change in the shape of the body and skull. Most of the people who suffered from it apparently lost their hair at a young age and I mean all of their hair, not some of it."

"And this is documented?"

"Oh, yes. I've seen pictures of several cases, and in one case there was a family that moved from the area to Boston. One of the children was perfectly normal, and the other started showing signs of the Innsmouth Look at around the age of twelve. She was a plain-looking girl to begin with, Joe, not exactly what I'd call a looker, but the doctors were very careful to document the changes. They took blood samples; they measured her arms, her features, everything."

"How bad did it get?"

"In ten years' time before the girl left the area, they saw physical changes that shouldn't have been possible. The girl complained of headaches, and it was easy to understand why. Her bones changed. There are certain diseases, neurofibromatosis and Proteus Syndrome, as examples, that can cause rapid changes in bone structure but those are always random. It might make one portion of the face bulge and distort but leave the other alone. Joseph Merrick, the Elephant Man, is an example."

He paused to light another cigarette off the butt of the one in his hand and gave me another. I figured I was going to have to buy him a carton before it was all said and done.

"Joe, the thing here is that all of the changes that happened might have looked incredibly strange, but they were balanced; both of her eyes and the sockets around them distorted in equal measure. They also shifted in her skull, like a flounder's do when it gets older."

"Jesus." I shook my head and felt my skin crawl. "No wonder she bitched about headaches."

"Exactly. The photos I saw showed the changes every year, and they were getting progressively more intrusive as time went on. The girl's entire body was changing along the same lines and the last time she came in for pictures she'd developed a rather extreme skin rash that the doctors discovered was a side effect of her skin not getting enough moisture. They gave her a lotion and within days it started clearing up."

"So you think that somehow the thing in there and the girl are related?"

"No. I don't think any such thing. I just think it's interesting to note that the ways in which her body changed looked a little like what that thing looks like."

"So these Deep Ones could mate with humans?" The thought sickened me.

"Maybe. Or maybe it's that they always start off as human and change. There's a lot of talk in the circles that believe in this sort of thing, that they're an offshoot of Homo sapiens that never left the water, or that adapted to stay in the water. I don't know. It's not my area of expertise."

"So what makes him think there's a city of these things down there?"

"Because according to a couple accounts, the FBI attack that effectively killed Innsmouth was done to try to destroy the city and all evidence of its existence before word of these things could get out."

I was still thinking about the possible ramifications of a government cover-up on that scale when the screams started.

ELEVEN

Well, it didn't take long to figure out where the commotion was coming from. Diana's voice carried through the yacht like an air-raid siren. I went back to the bathroom that had been commandeered for holding the fish man in time to see three students pulling her back from the shower stall, straining to keep her away from the thing inside the net. Her face was furious, and her body was all coiled muscles and flailing limbs.

One of the guys holding on to her was telling her to calm down and so far she was ignoring him completely.

"You get that sick fucking thing away from me, you hear?" Diana's voice was hoarse and shrill.

"What the hell is going on here?" I made sure my voice was as loud as hers and walked into the already crowded room. In the shower, the creature was still wrapped in its netting, but it looked like a few more of the cables that made up the net had been damaged somewhere along the way. The only good news was that it had managed to tangle itself up even more in the efforts to get free. It let out a panicked croak that was loud enough to rattle my ears and

I spared it a disgusted look as I walked over to where Diana was still kicking and trying to get free from her captors.

Another kid I barely knew, I think his name was Roger, this one was decidedly more athletic, and had a deep tan, shook his head. "Sorry, Captain, but that thing licked Diana and she got a little upset."

"Put her down." It wasn't a request, and they listened very quickly. I may not be as big as Charlie, but I can be downright bossy when I have to. I looked at Diana and she looked back, her face still furious. She did not, however, try to get past me to get to the fish man in the corner. "Why the hell did you get close enough to that thing to let it lick you?"

"I was five feet away from it!" She moved her hand up to wipe at the side of her face, where I could still see a faint trail of slime. "The sick fucker has a tongue as long as a fishing pole!" She shuddered with revulsion and I couldn't say that I blamed her much for it. I could smell the thing's odor in the air; it was permeating the room.

"Just go and get yourself washed off. God only knows where that thing has been." She looked at me like I'd just sent her to her room for misbehaving and she wasn't thrilled with it. I resisted the temptation to tell her to swim her ass back to town if she didn't like it.

She tried to stare me down and failed. I was about done with the insanity on my boat, and I was definitely sick of getting attitude from my passengers.

Mostly, I was going to be very, very glad when we got the thing in the shower stall off my boat. Jacob could talk all he wanted about the thing in there being a part of scientific history, but for me it was just an oversized, smelly nightmare.

I went out of the bathroom after Diana vacated the area and up to the main cabin. It was time to head for shore. At least that was the plan. As I moved toward the captain's

deck and got ready to start the *Isabella* on the way for the
cove, Jacob and Martin Ward were waiting for me.

Jacob looked at me like he wanted to be almost anywhere else. "Joe, I know you'd like to head for the docks,
but is there any way we can convince you to wait until after
the sun has set?"

I looked from him to Ward and then out at the water
lapping along the edge of the reef. From a weather perspective, it wasn't a problem. From a there's-a-freaky-thing-on-
my-yacht perspective, there were definite issues.

"I'm not really comfortable with the idea, Jacob."

Ward spoke up, his lean face pulling a lemon sucker
expression on me. "Why is that, Captain?"

I guess I was supposed to be intimidated by the frosty
voice, but it didn't work. Jacob shot him a withering look
and then waited for me to answer.

"Because according to what Jacob told me, that thing
you caught is only one of many. Is that right?"

"Well, yes, that's a possibility, but not really likely."

"Yeah?" I looked at him nice and hard, to make sure
he was paying attention. I didn't want to repeat myself
with him. "So suppose there are more of them. How do
you think they'd feel about having one of their own taken
away?"

"Every indication that I've run across about these creatures says that they're emotionally detached."

"Really?"

"Yes, of course."

"Read up on them a lot, have you Professor?"

"What are you getting at, Captain?"

"If you're wrong, if there's more than one of them hanging around, I don't think it would be very wise to be sitting
on the water if they decide to come up and see what happened to their buddy."

"I have certain methods of stopping that from happening." He was trying to sound confident, but I wasn't falling for it.

"I have a great method myself. It's called not having a fish monster hanging around on my yacht."

Jacob came forward and put a hand on my shoulder. "Please, Joe. It's a situation we can't do too much about. You saw the way the local police acted when we were ready to leave yesterday morning. It can only get worse if they catch us with a find like this."

"Why, Jacob? What's so horrible about finding a new fish?"

"Because it's not new, Joe. Not to them. Did you look at the police officers we have around here? Did you notice anything unusual about them?"

"You mean aside from the fact that they're incompetent? No." But I thought about them as I answered and wondered a little about whether or not what I said was true. The one I dealt with was a big bruiser, and he sort of gave me a weird feeling. More of a sense that he wasn't someone I wanted to trust, than a feeling I should actually be scared of the man.

"Did you look at the features on his face? The rough patches of skin? The receding hairline? Joe, for all we know he could be a descendant of the original townsfolk."

"And for all we know he could have dry skin and a family history of baldness." I shook my head. "What happened to being an impartial scientific observer, Jacob?"

He looked at me like I'd just slapped him in the face and looked away, a little ashamed, I think.

"Let's get this straight, gentlemen. I don't know what, exactly, that thing is, but if there are more of them out there and they might want to come back to help it, I consider that a serious threat. My wife is on this boat and so is yours, Jacob. I don't care if the thing in there is the secret to every evolutionary question ever posed. My first priority is for the safety of the people on this vessel."

"The Deep One is bound and harmless, Captain..."

"The 'Deep One' just licked your sidekick's face from two yards away. Damned thing has a six-foot tongue and claws like knives. What else can it do that you haven't told me? What else should I know before I decide to head straight back to the docks, Professor?"

"Did you ever think there might be more danger from the police in Golden Cove than there is from the Deep Ones in the sea?" Ward was staring hard now, his face reddening. He wasn't used to being challenged and it didn't sit well with him.

"Of course the easiest way for me to take care of the whole thing is to throw it back into the water." I shrugged and stared at him some more while he made his own fish faces.

"You wouldn't dare!" He pushed past Jacob, his hands clenched into fists at his sides, and leaned in close enough that I could see the pores on his nose.

"You want to test me? Keep getting in my face and we'll see how long it takes." I admit it. He was starting to piss me off again. I didn't know why that was, but something about him creeped me out the same way as the cops in the town did. Frankly, I'd have already had the *Isabella* turned around and docked if it weren't for Jacob.

Just to make my point as clear as possible, I leaned toward him this time. He backed off.

Jacob shook his head and looked at me, his face resigned to accept whatever I decided.

I nodded my head, unwilling to speak just then. Then I went to my room. I didn't want to deal with either of them anymore, and much as it was against my better judgment, I left the damned yacht where it was.

I think Jacob said something by way of thanking me, but I brushed it aside.

My mood was definitely getting worse, and I didn't like

that very much. I have never liked being the heavy in any situation.

I found Belle talking with Mary Parsons. I didn't bother them. They were having too much fun getting to know each other. Belle has always been good at meeting people. It's one of her many gifts. From what I could tell, they were talking about the fish man. I can't say as that surprised me very much.

Davey came up to me and stood nearby, moving from one foot to the other like a kid who had to pee and felt he needed to ask permission. That was Davey when it came to anything he thought was awkward. He hated having to share bad news.

"What's up, Davey?"

He spoke in a very small voice. "Joe, do you think that thing might have done something to Tom?"

I've heard of people reacting like they'd been slapped when they heard a comment, and I always thought that was a little dramatic license. I learned right then that it was a real reaction. I'd completely forgotten about Tom in the last little while. Oh, I knew he was missing and all of that, but it was just background information. It never once dawned on me that he might have been hurt by the thing in the shower or another one just like it.

Davey looked at me like I was supposed to give him all the answers. I wished I could right then.

"I don't know, Davey. But I think maybe we ought to look into it."

Without another word, I headed back for the shower where our fishy friend was spending his time. Davey followed me; I could hear his footsteps after he hesitated for a few seconds.

Roger was still in the bathroom, looking at the fish man

as it looked back at him with narrowed eyes. Both of them
turned their heads sharply as I walked into the room.

I didn't bother with Roger, ignoring my own advice to
get to know the kids spending time on the *Isabella* a little
better. Instead, I walked closer to the thing wrapped up in
netting and stared hard into its unblinking eyes. Not really
unblinking, by the way. It had translucent lids that were
covering the actual eyeballs. I saw them flutter up and
down a few times, but mostly they stayed over the delicate
tissue, probably to keep the eyes wet enough.

"Can you talk?" I asked the question as casually as I
could, and in response, the thing turned its head a little,
like it was listening for something that made sense.

"It's a fish man. How could it talk?" That was Roger. I
went on ignoring him.

"Pay attention to me." I moved closer and the thing
opened its mouth, baring teeth that I had no doubt could
take off half my face if given a chance. I held up one hand
and continued. "Let's pretend you can understand me for a
minute. If your tongue comes out and touches me, I'll cut it
out of your mouth. You understand?"

The thing turned its head a little more and then closed
its mouth very abruptly. Nothing like a threat of physical deformity to get most intelligent creatures to behave;
with that simple gesture it convinced me that it understood
everything I was saying.

"Good. We understand each other. Can you speak
English?"

The thing looked at me and blinked its eyes, but otherwise did nothing.

"I have a crewman missing from my yacht. His name is
Tom. He disappeared last night. If I don't find him, and I
decide that you had anything to do with his vanishing, I'm
going to kill you." I walked even closer as I spoke and once

again it opened its mouth. I saw the tip of its pale tongue lick across its thick lips and I reached for the gutting knife I kept on my belt.

Roger started to say something, but Davey shushed him.

I moved closer still, knowing all too well that I was risking getting myself cut into ribbons if it got out of the netting. "I've been fishing these waters for a lot of years, you smelly bastard. I can clean a tuna inside of three minutes. Want to test me, you'll let that tongue of yours move out a few more inches. I don't much care for you and I don't care if you're alive or dead. But I want to know about my shipmate. You understand me?"

Roger left the room, calling for Professor Ward. In front of me, the fish man closed its mouth again.

"I don't much care what language you speak. You can nod your head if you have to. Did you do anything to Tom?"

And damn me if the thing didn't shake its head from side to side in a very human gesture that said no.

Then it looked at me and stared hard and I learned a thing or two that I wasn't expecting to learn. First and foremost, I discovered that some forms of communication have nothing to do with speech.

They say the brain doesn't have any nerves, that it can't actually feel anything. But I'm here to say that they just might be wrong. Maybe I imagined what I felt and maybe it really happened, but the wide dark pupils of the fish man's eyes seemed to flare even wider and I felt something like a cold pressure inside my head, deep beneath the skull. An instant later I saw an image form, one that superimposed itself over what my eyes were seeing. I heard and felt and smelled things that I shouldn't have, and all the time it was happening, I still saw the thing in front of me as it looked into my eyes.

I saw the Isabella *from a new perspective, from a distance away, as if I were in the water. It was dark outside and the waters were cool and soothing. I felt my webbed hands and feet kicking at the sea around me, keeping me afloat, and I felt the fluids breathed out of my gills and opened my mouth to fill my almost dormant lungs with fresh air.*

I almost staggered back, almost lost the contact I was experiencing, but made myself stay where I was. I could see the fish man, could tell that he hadn't moved at all, even as I watched Tom moving along the side of the *Isabella,* staring out at the waters and in the direction of the Devil's Reef.

Faintly, off in the far distance, I heard a girl crying for help, heard her splashing in the water. I turned my head and saw her, a frail, desperate form that splashed in the sea and struggled to swim toward the shore beyond where I treaded the surface of the water.

And I saw Tom, poor, stupid Tom, grab one of the life preservers and dive off the side with the reckless skill that seems to be granted to the young.

How can I explain this properly? I knew it was Tom I was seeing. I knew him as well as I ever had, but at the same time, the memories, or images that I received looked at him differently, as if he were an alien creature. I saw him as ugly, deformed and pale and weak, even as he dove into the water. I watched this imaginary Tom as he cut across the waves, seeking to reach the girl in the water, the same girl I'd seen my first night in the cove as she swam toward the *Isabella.*

The images disappeared in an instant, and I shook them off, even as the fish man in front of me pushed itself against the tile of the shower stall and let out a bleating protest.

Professor Ward was standing next to me, putting something in his pocket. I didn't have time to think about that, but instead could only focus on what I'd almost learned. Somehow the thing in front of me had reached into my mind and spoken to me without ever saying a thing. Telepathy? Sure, I'd heard of it, but like ghosts and fish men, I'd assumed it was all a crock of delusions.

Ward pulled a piece of paper from his pocket and I saw a long list of gibberish words, phrases of some kind that had been spelled out in block letters, but that made no sense. Ward opened his mouth and then started making noises that strained his vocal cords. It sounded like he was trying to belch out the Russian alphabet or something.

When he was done making odd faces and odder sounds, the fish man looked at him and bobbed its head enthusiastically. It let out a series of barks and grunts that sounded a good bit like what Ward had just tried to recite.

Ward held up a tape recorder, one of the little ones you sometimes see people using to make notes to themselves, and recorded everything that came out of the fish man's throat.

They had a few interchanges, with Ward speaking and then recording what was said. When it was over with, the professor turned off his recorder and nodded his head.

"What did you just do?" I wanted to shake him, wanted to rattle his smug expression clean off his face for ruining the communication I'd been having with the fish man.

"I saved your life, I suspect."

"What do you mean?"

Ward looked at me, and instead of being smug, he looked troubled. "I don't know what was happening between you and the Deep One, but you looked like you were about to pass out."

"I think he was talking to me. With his head. You know, telepathy."

Ward looked at me and nodded, not seeming to doubt a word I was saying. "I've heard of them doing that. Be careful if it tries again, Captain. I can't say for sure it was trying to hurt you, but there are always risks when dealing with new life-forms."

"What are you talking about?"

Instead of trying to explain it to me, he pointed away from the fish man toward the sink along the far wall. I looked where he was pointing and then looked again, almost certain that I had to be dreaming.

My reflection in the mirror looked back at me with wide eyes. Eyes that were suffering from several burst blood vessels, apparently. The whites of my eyes were crimson, and I could see streaks of red running down my face from my tear ducts. My skin was pale and wet, and now that I could see the wound, I could feel that I had chewed half-way through my lower lip.

"If young Roger and then Davey hadn't come to get me, Captain, you might well be dead by now." Ward sounded smug enough, but didn't look it. He looked shaken.

"What the hell did it do?"

"I know it sounds strange coming from me, of all people, Captain, but believe me. There are some things we aren't meant to know. I recorded what it said and I asked it a few questions in what I'm hoping is its language. Try not to look it in the eyes again. Deep Ones are supposedly very cunning."

I left the room before I could do something very stupid, like ram my knife through the creature's brain pan. My hands were shaking and my head was beginning to ache.

Much as I hated to admit it, the professor was probably right. He'd probably just saved my life. Unfortunately, he'd also left me wondering exactly what the hell had happened to poor Tom.

TWELVE

The tension stayed thick on the yacht. There were a lot of people who were under a lot of stress and most of them were just stewing in their own thoughts. I felt like, if I wanted to, I could have just stopped and listened and heard everything they were thinking. It was a soft noise inside my head, but I thought I could make it louder. I was afraid to try. Maybe it was a side effect of whatever that thing had done to me or maybe it was my imagination, I can't really say. Eventually, I calmed myself down. The catch was to look at this the same way I would any other job. The bosses paid the bills and they were right. So the fish had legs. Not their fault. Professor Ward went looking for some under-water pottery and came back with an actual fish man. It wasn't expected, and that meant he had to make arrangements. I could make myself see their point when he wasn't in my face. I could accept it if I had to.

It was only a few hours until the sun set, but damn, those hours seemed to crawl. Instead of going stir-crazy I found Charlie to keep me occupied. He was still grinning the same sort of smile normally reserved for fishermen who caught a big fish and hunters who bagged a ten-point buck.

There was work to be done on the *Isabella* and he was already doing it. I decided to help him. In this case, the work was mostly cleaning up after the divers and getting everything ready for tomorrow when they went out again.

"You gonna get a picture with your fish over there, Charlie?"

He shrugged his shoulders and winked. "Can you imagine that thing stuffed and mounted over a fireplace?"

"Well, it'd be an interesting conversation starter. Or stopper, but I get the idea Diana wouldn't be thrilled."

"Yeah, I heard about that." He looked away for a second and his face got stormy. "She's got issues around here."

"How so?"

Charlie stopped working, looked around to make sure no one was listening in on us, and then stepped closer. From a lot of people, I would have thought that was extra drama. Not from Charlie. He was deadly serious when he came closer to me.

"Remember, she was here before and the expedition went sour. She hasn't said it, but I think those things in the water killed off the crew she was with."

"Jesus. How did she get away?"

"She didn't dive that day. She wasn't feeling up to it. They went in cold season last time, too, and she got herself a bug."

"So how does she know what happened?"

"She doesn't for sure, but she said some of the divers said they felt like they were being watched under the water."

"You think it's all that smart, her coming out here again?"

Charlie shrugged. "She's a big girl, Joe. You know what it's like. She decided she had to do this again to prove something to herself."

He might have said more, but right around then, we heard Diana's voice calling out to someone else. She sounded like she was coming closer. A few seconds later she wound up where we were, smiling at Charlie as she came up.

"Beat me to it. I was just going to start setting everything up." She nodded to me and gave Charlie a hug around his waist.

Diana was a muscular girl, but next to Charlie she looked like skin and bones. He leaned down and kissed her on the forehead. "We were just finishing up."

"Yeah. Charlie was telling me how he's gonna get his catch of the day mounted over his fireplace." I swear to you the words just came out of my mouth. I had been thinking them, sure, but I didn't expect to say them.

Diana looked my way and smiled. I was glad. I didn't want to start any troubles for her and we were already on thin ice after the great licking incident earlier. The smile fell away from her features when she got a look at my eyes. They were still bloodshot as all hell and felt like someone had been at them with sandpaper.

"Jesus. What happened to your eyes?"

"Nothing to worry about." It was my turn to shrug and even feel a little embarrassed as she came closer and looked at my eyes.

"I saw the same thing on Terry Wallace with the last expedition." She spoke softly, all the while looking at me with the sort of intensity you normally only get from a lover. I think I actually blushed.

"Who's Terry Wallace?"

"He was a diver. A kid in the same grade as me. He was good." She looked away and shook her head. "I'd get that looked at."

"How's your little brother?" I asked the question just to get her off the subject of my eyes. Charlie was watching the both of us and I think maybe wondering about why she was staring so hard himself.

"Jan? He's doing a little better. The infection is stubborn. Corey's doing better too. I just got off the phone with him at the hospital. They want to keep him a few more days for observation, but his folks are coming up tonight to see to him."

"What about your folks? They worried about Jan?"

"They said it's up to me to watch him. They're off in Europe on a trip. As long as he doesn't lose his leg, they're okay with it." I was amazed by that. My parents would have been by my side in five minutes, regardless of any physical laws they had to break to get there, and you can bet money I'd have been by Belle or the kids just as fast. That's just the way it's supposed to be done, if you get my point. Still, it wasn't for me to judge.

Diana must have read something in my face, because she got a sheepish look on hers. "I know. But they've been planning this for three years and I swore to them I'd take good care of him."

"Don't mind Joe. He's just a stick in the mud." Charlie was joking, trying to lighten the mood. I chuckled along with him.

Diana didn't. She looked at him and then at me, and then shook her head. "No. He's just old-fashioned. I admire that."

"Not old-fashioned." Charlie slapped me on the shoulder. "Just old."

"You keep it up, Charlie. I'll have you stuffed and mounted for my fireplace."

"That thing." Diana shook her head and looked in the direction of the shower, as if she could see through the hull and study the fish man from where she was. "That thing should be fed to the sharks, not put on display."

"Can't learn as much from a pile of shark shit." Charlie was still joking around. I don't know if he didn't see how serious she was, or if he didn't care. Sometimes it's hard to say with him.

She wheeled around on him fast, pointing a finger at his chest like a knife. "Don't you tell me about learning from them, Charlie. I already know all about that!"

"Diana, what?" Charlie stepped back from her finger and looked at her like she'd lost her mind. I kept my tongue and watched what happened next instead of interfering.

"You haven't had one of those things touch you, Charlie. You don't know shit about them!"

Diana stormed off after that, shaking her head and muttering. Charlie looked at me and I used my head to say he better go after her. He nodded and went.

And I finished cleaning up, feeling a cold dread start in my stomach.

Why would Diana know anything about having one of those things touch her? It might have been the tongue thing earlier, but I doubted it.

She knew more than she was saying about the fish man. I knew that for certain right at that moment. I also suspected something else. I suspected she hadn't been sick the day the last group of divers had their accident.

I think she'd been there with them. I thought about that a lot while I stowed the last of the equipment. Half an hour later, the sun was setting and it was time to head for shore. I didn't even notice at first. I was still lost in Diana's reactions and wondering what secrets she was keeping. And why.

I watched the sunset with Belle. It was a nice day for it, and the buildings in Golden Cove looked as pretty as any I'd ever seen as the sun's last rays faded behind them.

Davey had the engines all nicely warmed up and Charlie raised the anchor; it was time to get away from the water for a few hours. There were a few nice restaurants in the cove, at least according to Charlie, and I intended to find one for Belle and me to enjoy.

I was going to have a good time, and I was going to relax. That was all there was to it. The fish man was leaving my yacht and he wasn't going to be my concern anymore. He would belong to the scientists, and I would be perfectly happy to never see or think of him again.

I told Charlie to get us back to the docks and he nodded. He wasn't smiling much right then. I didn't know what happened between him and Diana, and was doing my best not to be nosey. I know he wasn't looking happy and I know she'd spent most of the last few hours sitting at the back of the yacht, drinking coffee like it was going out of style.

Several people tried to approach her and she politely, but firmly, told them to leave her alone. I barely knew her, so I didn't even try. If she wanted or needed to talk to someone there were plenty of readily available sources.

Can you guess who got her to talk? If you said Belle, you guessed correctly. I don't know how it happened—I have a suspicion it might have been Charlie's handiwork—but whatever the case, by the time we were heading back for the port, my wife and Diana were thick as thieves and discussing whatever it was that had the girl so stressed out.

We'd made it most of the way back to the cove and were doing fine when the thing inside the bathroom started letting out enough noise to wake a volcano. I was just about to step inside anyway when the sound started. The deep thrumming noise caught my attention (and everyone else's) around the same time that the lighthouse in the distance cast its beam in our direction. I mentioned a noise I'd heard off in the marshes a few nights earlier. Well, this was the exact same noise, only bigger. I also said the thing in there had made noises loud enough to make my ears ache, and that was still true but I swear to you, I felt the sound in my bones when it let loose with the latest surprise.

I didn't stop to think about what might have caused the noise. I didn't have to think about it. Nothing human could have made that sort of racket. Not in my experience, anyway. I headed for the shower immediately. I guess I wasn't alone in my thinking because several other people got there before me.

The fish man let out another noise, and it echoed around the small room and the people inside it. I moved in, covering my ears with my hands, and looked at the thing where it stood. It was still wrapped up, but the chest was distorted. Instead of the wrinkled flesh I'd seen before, the skin was drawn tight and the chest had expanded to almost three times the size it should have been. All I could think of was a bullfrog in mating season, calling out for potential lovers with its odd noises.

Think about that. Forget the part about lovers. It was calling for more of its own kind. I suppose I was a little overzealous, but all I could imagine was a hundred more of the damned things climbing onto the *Isabella* and trying to free their fellow frog man. I pushed past a couple of the kids who were looking at the thing and maybe trying to remember their own names past the noise, and I pulled my scaling knife for the second time that day.

This time I used the blade. No, I didn't aim to kill it. Instead, I aimed to keep it quieter. One swift stroke of the blade was all it took to cut open that bloated air bladder on the thing's neck. The explosion of air felt like cold steam and smelled as rancid as anything I've encountered in my entire life, but the end result was exactly what I expected. The thing reared back and let out a shriek as the air bag exploded, and then it started thrashing around, determined to get free or get away from me. I backed away as fast as

I could; the violence and the noise making me feel very claustrophobic in the small bathroom.

Professor Ward and Jacob Parsons came into the room right around the same time, and Ward took one look at the thing where it was thrashing in the corner of the shower, took one look at me, and then took a swing.

I wasn't ready for it by any stretch of the imagination and his fist caught me perfectly on the side of my jaw. The knife went one way and I stumbled right into the shower stall, slipping on the slick tiles and landing on my ass not two feet away from the screaming fish man.

I was hurt and pissed.

The Deep One was feeling the same way, only the object of all its anger was yours truly.

Everyone was talking at once. Parsons was screaming for Ward to back off. I was screaming at the sea monster looming over me to do the exact same thing. Ward was hollering about me being an unthinking animal, and the fish man was screaming for my blood.

I knew it was strong, had guessed it was fairly dangerous in a close-up fight, but never once expected it to shred the net that had been holding it at bay. Both of the clawed hands hooked into the netting and it let out a roar that sprayed me with warm blood and cold spit as it tore through the nylon bindings.

I pushed away from the thing, my feet sliding across the damp tiles, and sought my knife. It was somewhere beyond the small army of legs in my way.

One of those legs came up and kicked me across the side of my face. I recognized the loafer attached to the offending foot. It belonged to the professor.

Much as I'd love to tell you the exciting story of how I got up, fought off the monster, and kicked Ward's ass all the way to the west coast, that just didn't happen.

Instead, I fell back to the ground and felt my skull knock

against the tiles again. I wanted to get up, I really did. But my body refused to listen to any of my desperate pleas.

Ward was aiming for me again, when Jacob grabbed his shoulder and spun him around. From my perspective they looked like giants. Ward cocked back his arm, and I thought for sure he would hit Jacob, but at the last second he seemed to come out of it.

Both of them looked at me and then past me as the scaly bastard behind me finished ripping free from its net. I heard it moving forward and knew I was a dead man. Hell, I could see its shadow suddenly covering my body, and closed my eyes, praying as hard as I ever have for a few more minutes of life. Long enough to let me tell Belle how much I loved her and maybe just long enough to rip out Ward's throat with my own teeth.

"MOVE!" I heard Charlie before I saw him knocking Ward and Jacob aside. He came on like a freight train and launched himself over me, his feet barely missing my prone form as he rammed into the thing that was about to kill me.

Charlie must have hit it a fearsome blow. All I can say for sure is that his shadow replaced the fish man's and I didn't end up dead right then and there. Instead, I heard the monster let out another croak of protest and then heard the sound of meat hitting meat again and again.

That was about the time my mind decided it had had enough.

Macho man that I am, I passed out.

THIRTEEN

Little something I've learned as time has gone on: sometimes reality can mess with your dreams. I had a nice thing going on, me and Belle on the beach, sunning in the summer heat, somewhere in the Caribbean, I think. Maybe it was supposed to be Hawaii. Either way, it was warm and sunny and the water was as clear as blue glass. There were a few people around us, but not too many. Just like the sort of place where I've often dreamed of us retiring.

When the clouds came in, I barely even noticed. But Belle got a nervous look on her face and started fidgeting. Before I could even ask her what was wrong, the sky darkened and the rain fell; torrential, bitterly cold drops that hit like ice pellets. So in the dream as we both got up to run, the rain got worse and the ocean bubbled, the pristine water turning slate gray and green as the waves grew to tsunami-sized walls of water.

And then the frogs fell, hundreds, thousands of black frogs with red eyes and fangs in their mouths. Everywhere they touched me, biting deeply into my skin and Belle's, and I heard Belle calling my name as the damned things hopped and flopped and chewed on flesh.

I tried to turn to Belle, tried to protect her, but the pain was too much. And then to make matters worse, something rose out of the water, a bloated thing, almost too big to fully see, but just as vile as the frogs. It let out a noise, a wet, throaty roar, and...

I woke up covered in sweat, disoriented as hell. Some things are obvious to a person with proper sea legs, like when you're on solid land instead of on the water. That was my first hint that I wasn't on my yacht anymore. The second was the smell of antiseptic.

I was in a hospital room. One thing you can always count on in a tourist town is that they'll have a facility for taking care of injuries.

It was three hours later than it should have been by my reckoning. The doctors had already done most of the workup on me by then. I didn't have a cracked skull, but I did have a minor concussion. Also, I had two stitches in my head from where I'd cracked my noggin on the shower stall tiles.

I found all of that out after I opened my eyes and saw Belle, Jacob and Charlie all sitting around the cot the hospital had chosen for me. Belle had my hand in hers. If I hadn't already been head over heels for her, I would have fallen in love right then.

Charlie was looking just fine, except for a few bandages on his right arm. And by a few, I mean it looked like he was working as a hand model for *The Mummy*. He also had a bruise doing ugly things to the left side of his face and a grin that said he was happy to see me alive.

Jacob wasn't looking as thrilled, but then again, he almost never managed so much as a smile. It just didn't seem like he was designed for them. Also, I bet Jacob was maybe just a tiny bit worried about the fact that I was going to sue the bejesus out of his buddy, Professor Ward.

I felt along the new stitches on my head while all three of them chatted away and asked me how I felt. My head hurt where the stitches pulled my skin back together, and my jaw was throbbing dully to its own beat. All I could think about was how much I wanted to tie a certain college teacher to an anchor and drag his sorry ass across the ocean floor for a few hours.

When the pleasantries were done, Jacob got straight to the point.

"Joe, I'm so sorry for what Martin did."

I nodded my head. "Don't feel too bad. I'm sure the local police will treat him just fine."

"So, you're pressing charges?" Jacob was looking a little crestfallen.

"I'm either going to press charges and have him put in a jail cell for a few days, or I'm going to beat the ever-loving shit out of him. Right now I don't know which one sounds better to me. Hell, maybe I'll press charges and then beat him black and blue."

"He thought you were going to kill his fish man."

"No, I just didn't want it calling a whole bunch of friends in to save it. I'm silly like that. I don't want to get eaten by fish people."

"We figured that out later, Joe."

"After he sucker punched me?"

"Well, yes."

Jacob looked all apologetic and I did my best to look unforgiving. But the thing here is I wasn't mad at him. I was mad at the college boy who decided to do me in for playing with his fish.

"So did he get his fish man off my boat?"

"Yes. All went well."

"Good. From now on he's not allowed on the yacht."

"What?" Jacob and Charlie both looked like I'd stolen their favorite toy. Jacob I could understand, but Charlie made me a little worried.

"Your expedition goes on just fine, Jacob. But Professor Ward is no longer allowed on the *Isabella*." I looked him dead in the eyes and he looked back without flinching. Again, not a man I'd ever play poker with.

"How can he do his research if he can't get out to the reef, Joe?"

"He should have thought about that before he hit me."

"Joe, we all make mistakes..." I held up my hand to cut off Charlie. This wasn't his decision to make and it wasn't his fight.

"I can see where you're coming from, Captain, but don't you think you're overreacting?"

"No, I don't." And don't think I missed the cold in his voice or the sudden reversion to my title instead of my name. I was a little hurt by it, too, because I liked Jacob. "I might be overreacting if he hit me once, Jacob. But he kicked me when I was down, while you were trying to restrain him. I don't think he's playing with a full deck of cards. So here's the thing: Diana is welcome on the yacht and so are all of his people. But Professor Ward is not welcome. He can stay back on land and study his precious fish man. He can even get on the yacht when we are docked, but he is not welcome on my yacht when we're away from land and I can't call the police to subdue him."

"He's offered to pay your medical bills."

"Last I checked you were footing his bills for this little expedition, Jacob. I'm insured and I can certainly send the deductible to you. But his generosity with your money isn't winning him any points right now. Maybe I'll change my mind after I have a little time to calm down, but I don't much take to people trying to kill me."

Was I acting like a spoiled brat? I didn't think so. The

educated man of science had gone over the edge as far as I
was concerned. I don't like to fight; I never have, but I don't
back down from them either. The man was dangerously
obsessed with his work as far as I was concerned. He'd
come close to killing me for preventing imminent danger,
and small as he was, Jacob had been hard-pressed to stop
him from doing it.

Charlie was itching to have it out with me. So I decided
to let him. I was feeling a little scrappy, even with a headache trying to crack my skull open.

"Belle, honey, why don't you ask Jacob here to get you a
cup of coffee? I get the idea Charlie would like to discuss a
few things with me."

Belle smiled at Jacob and then nodded her head. She
knew I wasn't dismissing her. I'd never dismiss her from any
serious discussions, but she also knew Charlie well enough
to know that things were going to get ugly very fast and that
she would probably want to jump into the middle of things.

I know that sounds odd, but Charlie and I have had a
long understanding about how we settle matters. Mostly I
say how high he should jump and he does it, even if he
disagrees. When he feels the need to argue it out, we've
always done it in private. It's only fair to my way of thinking, because Charlie can be a bit old-fashioned, and by
that I mean he can clam up if there's a lady present. Some
things don't get said that maybe should if we're around
mixed company.

Belle gave me a kiss on the mouth and I held on to the
feeling. It helped keep me calm while she and Jacob left
the room. We waited a few moments and Charlie settled in
for a proper argument.

"You think I'm being an asshole?" I decided to get right
to the point.

Charlie shrugged. "Yeah, Joe, I do. I know why you're
being an asshole, but I think you should reconsider."

"Man hits me with a sucker punch he doesn't exactly get onto my Christmas card list, Charlie."

"Okay, so maybe he's a little obsessed."

"Yeah, so were the terrorists who flew planes into the World Trade Center, and the Pentagon."

"Don't be an idiot." He scoffed at the idea. "He's not a terrorist."

"You don't have to be a religious man to be a fanatic about something, Charlie."

"Look, you're the one who signed us on for this gig in the first place."

"And you're the one who joined the diving team and hooked up with Diana. And more power to you, but that doesn't mean I feel like having a fruitcake on the yacht who likes hitting people when they aren't looking."

"Just kick his sorry ass and be done with it, Joe. Jesus."

"Okay, fine. I'll let him back on the yacht, Charlie. But the next time he does anything, I'm holding you account-able. You okay with that decision? Because it's all up to you, big boy." He started to look happy about getting his way until that last part. Then he got thoughtful and nodded his head.

"Okay, Joe. You have a deal."

"Fine. Go tell Jacob his pet professor can come out and play."

"Want me to get Belle for you?" He stood up and shrugged on his pea coat.

"Yeah. And have her get the doctor. I'm getting out of here."

"Sure you shouldn't stay for observation?"

"Hell will freeze over before I will spend a night in observation because a geek kicked my ass."

Charlie got a shit-eating grin on his face and chuckled. "A geek kicked your ass, Joe."

"And I'm gonna kick yours if you don't get out of my

face, you prick." We were both grinning by then. Now and then you have to let your friends have their way or nothing runs smoothly.

I was out of the emergency room and clinic just before midnight. We stayed in a hotel room that night at Belle's insistence. Who am I to argue? We got a nice room at a decent price, and in the morning I found out that Jacob had footed the bill. I wasn't going to stop him. I felt like getting a little pampered after having Ward kick me in the head.

Belle, God love her, made me take a hot bath and then gave me a massage across my back and shoulders. We ate steaks and room service meals that cost as much as I normally spend in a week on food, and then we talked and caught up.

"Mary Parsons is something else," Belle said, looking at me with a little mischief in her eyes. I think she knew I found the other woman attractive. Happily, she also knew I'd never consider doing anything about it.

"Yeah, she's a sharp one. What did you two talk about all afternoon?"

"Mostly about all the stories of the town that used to be here and about her ghost hunting."

"You get the impression she's seen her fair share of ghosts?"

"Oh yeah." She nodded vigorously and then cut another piece of well-done steak for herself. Me, I've always preferred my steaks rare, but Belle can't stand the idea. "She's definitely seen a few things. She told me about an asylum in New Jersey she checked out once. Said the place was about the worst she's ever been in."

"Well, it's an asylum. Not just ghosts, but crazy ghosts."

"Exactly what she said."

"What else did you talk about?"

"Girl stuff."

"Yeah? You comparing notes on me and Jacob? 'Cause I gotta say, he's winning in the financial stability department." What can I say? It always bothered me that I could never give Belle all the fine things I thought she deserved. I tried not to let it show, but now and then I brought it up just to see if it bothered her as much as it did me. If it did, she never even gave a hint.

"She didn't say how much he's worth, but yeah. I think so." Belle chuckled. I loved her laugh almost as much as her smile.

"She tell you about the ghost ship we saw?"

"Yes, and I'm staying a few more days 'cause I want to see it."

"I only saw it the once, but you never can tell." We sat in silence for a few minutes and ate our dinner. It was a damned fine meal and I didn't want to see it go to waste. We had crème brûlée for dessert—pure poison for the system, but worth the health risks.

"Anyone hear anything about Tom yet? Did he show up?"

Belle looked at me and shook her head. "No, and I'm starting to really get worried."

"Me, too. So in the morning, we'll drop by the police station and make sure they get their sorry asses in gear."

"It's just not like him, Joe. Tom is responsible."

"Belle, there isn't much we can do about it. He's a big boy and I agree he should be back by now, but there's just so much we can do. I'd call him but his phone is still on the boat. I'd look for him but where do I look in a town like this?"

"I'm not blaming you, honey. I'm just worried." She put her hands over mine and made sure I knew she wasn't just saying the words.

"I gotta say, this day has sucked."

"Well, but the dinner was good."

"The company was better." I stood up from the table and put the remains on the tray to slide outside the door. Belle followed after me and put up the DO NOT DISTURB sign.

Sometimes she makes my world just about perfect.

The next day started nice and early, just the way I knew it would. My head was only throbbing a little as we went down to the police station and made sure they'd follow up on Tom's disappearance. The cop I dealt with looked at me a little funny, and I couldn't blame him. The lump on the side of my face wasn't looking all that pretty.

He didn't ask who hit me and I didn't volunteer anything. We got along just fine that way.

The morning sun came up and lit the entire area with high wattage warmth. For about ten minutes. After that the clouds moved in and brought back the cold with a vengeance. By the time we were on the *Isabella*, I was ready to settle in for a nice cup of coffee and to put on my winter coat. I got to the coat before Ward found me.

He walked up looking sheepish, and I ignored him completely. It's a gift I learned from my grandfather, who always advised against starting the day with a shit-kicking.

"Captain?"

"You don't exist for me, Professor Ward. Keep it that way."

"I'm sorry?" He sounded as confused as he looked, so I decided to clarify it.

"If you existed right now, Professor Ward, I would have to lose my temper. So for right now, you don't exist. Don't make me remember you."

"I'm not sure if I follow."

I put down my coffee as carefully as I could and looked

at him. He hadn't listened. I really wished he had. So did Charlie, who was watching the whole exchange.

Being a smart first mate, he didn't interfere.

The stitches in the side of my head were pulsing with my heartbeat, which was racing a bit as the adrenaline worked its way into my system. I reached out and grabbed Professor Martin Ward by his jacket collar and hauled him up into my face. He let out a little squeak that did me a world of good and then grunted when I slammed him against the wall. Both of his hands reached for mine, to break my grip, I'm sure, and I shook him as hard as I could to make sure he knew not to do anything else that was stupid.

"You hit me when I wasn't looking and you kicked me in the face you pissant little fuck." I saw the spittle coming from my mouth land on his face and even that made me angrier. I also saw Charlie thinking about doing something, but he stopped himself. "The only reason you aren't in jail right now is because I like Jacob Parsons and he thinks you're an okay guy. The only reason I'm not feeding you your own goddamned spleen is because Charlie asked me to play nicely with you."

He let out another groan and started stammering something in my face. I shook him again until he shut up.

"I don't like people who take cheap shots and I really don't like it when they take them at me. So listen very carefully and we'll get along just fine. You don't talk to me until I speak to you. You don't look at me and you don't dare touch me, or I swear to you, I'll break every finger on both of your hands. And if you decide to get bitchy about that, I'll pry your teeth out of your mouth and make you swallow them. I don't like you and I don't want to deal with you anymore. You're on my Shit List, Ward. It's not a good place to be and it's worse if you're using my boat. Stay away from me."

I let him go and went back to my coffee. He stayed

against the wall making faces like his pet fish man, big eyes, gaping mouth and all. When he'd calmed down, he moved away from me as carefully as he could.

That made me feel much better about him being on the *Isabella*. It made me feel like I could trust him to behave for a few hours. Charlie poured himself a cup of coffee and leaned against the edge of the seat across from me and never said a word. Ten minutes later we were on our way back out to the reef and another day of fishing. I'd feel a lot better when Ward and his cronies were in the water.

And because I'm a nice guy, I decided I wouldn't leave them out there.

In hindsight, maybe I should have. It would have saved a lot of problems later.

FOURTEEN

The weather got worse, with winds coming from the northeast and threatening clouds turning the early morning the color of evening darkness. By the time we'd reached the Devil's Reef, the clouds seemed to have lowered themselves right over the water and then they let loose with a constant drizzle, the sort that creeps past all of your clothes and soaks you to the bone.

There were fewer divers than usual, and Jacob—who had taken my shaking his friend in stride and was just happy to have things back to normal, apparently—explained that three of the students were staying in the warehouse that had been rented for the next two months. They and two people I'd never met were going to be studying the Deep One in greater detail, starting with getting the damned thing sedated and then taking measurements of every part of its body. Diana was on the yacht and diving, but she sent her brother along to watch the fish-faced bastard get measured, weighed and tested. He was supposed to film the entire procedure. Apparently Ward wanted to be there, but he couldn't pull himself away from his aquatic caves long enough to do it.

Yippee.

The team went down, and I got busy making lunch for when they came back up. Tommy being gone was not only a personal sour point, but also a guarantee that I was going to stay busy. With Charlie on the dive team and Davey taking care of the engine and generator on the *Isabella,* I had my hands full.

Luckily, I had two perfectly willing sidekicks to help me. I guess it's a testament to my cooking that both Belle and Mary decided to come to my rescue long before I'd managed to get properly started. I'd planned on making the steaks I never got to the night before, but Mary volunteered her tuna to the cause and I wound up cutting the steaks off the cleaned, monster-sized fish before they took over and kicked me out of the galley.

Jacob was waiting for me. I found him in the main cabin, with notes scattered all over the place again. This time he waved me over and showed me the papers.

Mostly what he had was the sort of stuff that means nothing at all to me. Charts and long lists of statistics that had been written out over the last few days. I didn't bother with trying to read measurements from sonar printouts or studying the alterations in the temperature underwater. I knew it was a big cave and I knew the waters were damned cold. That was enough for me.

Not for him. He'd been busy drawing detailed schematics of the cave's layout. For the first time I got to see just how big a deal the caves were. The first part of the place, the antechamber is what he called it, was about thirty feet across and twenty feet deep. He'd made a mark that clearly showed where the tunnel leading to the rest of the cave was, and explained that it went sideways into the reef for almost a hundred yards before it dropped down into deeper waters. That was really all that the divers had managed to discover so far. He also showed me some of the pictures Ward and his students had taken of the walls in the cave. There were some fairly simplistic carvings in the rock, most of them thick and crude and a little disturbing to look at. They seemed like pictograms of creatures that lived underwater, but they didn't hold to shapes that quite made sense.

And it wasn't the shapes so much as the effort to carve them that surprised me. It looked like someone had scraped them at least a quarter inch into the stone, and unlike most of the walls in the cave that were covered with algae and slime, the carvings were clean. That might have been the divers themselves, but really, how would they have noticed the damned things in the first place if they hadn't been cleared away?

"How old would you say those were?"

"What? The carvings?" Jacob looked at me and frowned in thought. "Hard to say, but they don't look very old, do they?" He had mercy on me and gave me a smoke. I nodded my thanks and lit up.

"They look like they could have been done a few weeks ago."

"For all we know, they were."

I shook my head. "If that was done in the last couple of weeks, Ward's fish man is an industrious little shit."

Jacob looked at me and nodded. "Or he wasn't alone."

"Yeah, that's a comforting thought."

"You're the one who brought it up first, you know." His voice was half teasing but his expression was completely serious.

"Well, if we get overrun by toad men, I did my part."

We sat in silence for a while and just smoked, looking at the pictures they'd managed to bring back so far. Aside from the carvings, they were nothing all that spectacular.

"What do you think, Jacob? Do you think there's more than one of them?"

"Honestly? Yes. I do. I think there has to be, because I

can't imagine just one of those things living by itself in the water."

"So how come they were never discovered?"

"I shouldn't have to explain that to you, Joe. We've barely even touched on the things in the water. There're too many obstacles to slow us down."

I nodded at that and thought about it for a while. The human body is an amazing machine, but it was never meant for diving deep into the ocean and even the best equipment only allows us to go so far into the depths.

"You think they're intelligent?"

"At least smart enough to write on the walls."

I thought about that as I finished my cigarette. I thought about it some more before I spoke. "What would you do if someone came into your house and took Mary by force?"

"After I was finished having a panic attack I'd call the police."

"What if you knew where they had taken her?"

Jacob looked at me and shrugged. "I suppose I'd come after them with as much help as I could get." He shook his head and sighed. "I know what you're getting at, Joe. I do. But you're applying human emotions to these things."

I shook my head. "Not human emotions, just emotions. Bears protect their young and wolves look out for their own."

"Sharks don't care about their schools and frogs could not care less if someone grabs their neighbor."

He had me there. "I hope you're right on this one, Jacob. I wouldn't want to be your professor if I'm right."

"There are no certainties in this sort of business. But I'll tell you something, Joe. I was very glad to see what you did when that thing started calling out."

"Why's that?"

"Because if it was calling for help and nothing had a chance to respond, then maybe, even if those things act more like bears than they do sharks, there's nothing to worry about. If they could have tracked the one we caught, they probably would have by now."

"Well, here's hoping you're right about that, too." I saluted him with my empty coffee cup and then went to fill it. The coffeepot gave me a great view of the choppy waves between the reef and the town off in the distance.

Outside the cabin the winds were picking up and the storm was blowing harder. Fat raindrops fell from the sky and killed themselves on the deck, leaving everything wet and slippery as all hell. If it got too much worse, I'd call the day finished when the divers came up for replacement tanks and surface time.

I thought I saw something in the water, a gray movement that vanished as soon as I noticed it. I looked at the water a lot more intently after that, and while I couldn't be sure with the size of the waves, I might have seen something.

"Okay, Jacob. Call me paranoid, but I think there's something out in the water."

He stood up and moved my way, never hesitating. I made room for him at the window and we both spent some time looking for any signs of life out in the water, but to no avail.

After a few minutes, we gave up. Or rather, Jacob did. I chose to go outside and risk the nasty weather for a better look. I've never been one to give up easily if I think I saw something. I was almost sure that I had seen a shape moving along the tops of the waves.

I got myself dressed in a slicker and a hat, feeling ridiculously like one of those little wooden sailors you could find in damn near any port town, and walked out onto the deck, careful to keep my footing on the slick surface.

Maybe I was being paranoid, I don't really know, but I kept seeing that fish man in my mind's eye and it wouldn't leave me alone. There were four people other than me on the *Isabella,* and I didn't want to take any chances with their health.

The sea was churning up a lot of waves and several that were larger than usual were bouncing around the edges of the reef and rocking the yacht a little. A smaller vessel might have been in trouble, but so far there weren't any waves big enough to make me sweat. I stared out at the water, looking nowhere in particular and trying to catch that motion in the water again. The thing about watching the waves is once you're actually looking at them, they seem to hide whatever secrets they have. You only get lucky enough to catch the oddities from the corner of the eye. Or at least it seems to work that way for me.

I was so busy looking at nothing that I almost missed the gray thing the next time it showed up. It bobbed in the water for a second and then ducked down behind a wave that swelled and grew, like a man drawing in a deep breath. This one was going to hit the *Isabella* hard, I could tell by the way it seemed to hesitate for a moment even as it grew larger. It wasn't going to be big enough to wash everything off the deck, but it was probably going to cover me with water up to my knees.

I realized that just in time to know it was too late to get away. I backed up as fast as I could, but some things can't be escaped very easily.

The water hit the side of the *Isabella* and rose up in a swell, spilling over the railing and sloshing forward with enough force to shove me into the wall and knock me off my feet at the same time. I tasted salt water and felt the cold ocean wave soak my clothes and chill my flesh. I also got a mouthful of the stuff that tried to force its way into my lungs. While I managed to cough it out, it was the sort of thing that took all of my energy. So I barely had any fight left as I grabbed for anything I could use as purchase, because as the water pulled back away from the *Isabella,* it tried to take me with it.

I think I would have wound up in the ocean, but lucky me, I managed to hit one of the railing posts and it slid up the inside of my leg and landed firmly in my crotch. Ever been kicked in the testicles? This was worse. I wasn't capable of moving after that. Instead, I spent a couple of minutes making sure everything was where it was supposed to be and then I carefully pulled myself away from the edge of the yacht and crawled up against the cabin wall.

"Joe." The voice was soft and cold, like the sound of the waves slapping against the reef, and I turned to the source without thinking, without wondering who I knew that sounded like that.

And when I saw him, I screamed. Was there ever any doubt in my mind that Tom was dead? Maybe, but it was removed the second I saw him hanging on the railing, his face turned toward mine. He was still wearing his jacket, the battered old thing he always wore when it was cold. It was waterlogged and hung from his body heavily. He was barefoot, and aside from his coat the only thing he sported by way of clothes was a pair of dark gray sweats I knew he slept in when he had to work on the yacht.

Tommy pulled himself up higher on the railing; his face sagged a bit, but he managed the feat. He made me think of a bloated spider hanging in a web and I think I tried to scream, but all that came out was a whimper. Everything about him was unsettling. He was dead; I had no reason to believe otherwise. I could see the places on his body that had been nibbled at by fish, and I could smell him as the wind shifted a bit.

"Tommy?" I barely recognized my own voice. Knowing full well that he was dead, that he was dead and climbing up the side of my yacht, I still moved toward him instinctively. Some part of my brain decided that dead or not he had to get away from the railing and I listened to that part. My hands caught hold of his jacket and I started pulling him toward me.

His flesh peeled back under the fabric. I felt it happen and I let him go, staggering back with a scream trying to get past my clenched teeth. Tommy fell forward and landed with a wet sound on the deck. He stayed there for a few seconds, a lifeless, broken form, and then Tommy looked at me again, his eyes staring not at me, but through me.

"Joe. Listen. They're going to come for you and everyone on the boat. Be smart. Take Belle and get out of here."

I heard the words, but I shouldn't have been able to. He opened his mouth to talk and the water poured out in a nearly steady stream.

"Tommy, what happened to you?" I was shaking my head back and forth, and my mind felt frozen in molasses. I knew I was in shock, but knowing something doesn't mean you can override it.

"That doesn't matter, Joe. Listen to me. They like their secrecy. They haven't forgotten what happened the last time people found out about them, and they will stop anyone from finding out what they're doing. You have to leave here. You have to go away and stay away before they come." He spoke with urgency and I listened, finding it easier now that he wasn't talking through the water coming from his mouth.

"Tommy, please!" I was starting to think right again, but it was hard to get past the dead man talking to me. My mind accepted the fish man just fine, but seeing a kid I'd worked with since he was sixteen crawl out of his watery grave was pushing too damned far.

Tommy stood all the way up and staggered back against the railing as another wave hit the *Isabella*. He was walking, but he didn't seem to have a lot of strength in his limbs and coordination was a pipe dream.

"Shut the fuck up, Joe. Listen to me. Get out of Golden Cove and don't come back. Stay away from this place. It's gone bad and it won't get any better. They are unforgiving, Joe. They..."

The wave that hit this time was big enough to send me back against the wall and knock me down, but when it hit Tommy it threw him down and dragged him back into the ocean with it. Whatever he was trying to tell me, was lost with the water.

I moved back to the railing, still stuck with a mind that didn't want to work right. I think I went over there to try to rescue him. I think I planned on getting him back on board and somehow making him all better. All I know for sure is that I went over there and I reached for his flailing arm as it moved with the bucking waves.

He pulled his hand away before I could touch it. Tommy looked at me with dead eyes and I think he even shook his head, but that could have been caused by the water he was sinking under.

I think I would have gone after him. I know it was in my mind to dive in and grab him and haul him back to safety; I know it was, because I was climbing over the railing when I saw them.

They came from below, dark shapes, with large, almost luminous eyes. I could barely see them save as silhouettes at first, but they came closer at the sort of speed I thought was reserved for torpedoes.

The waters off the starboard side seethed and the waves fell apart from inside as the things rose up and grabbed Tommy. He didn't struggle, but went with them, covered by their webbed, clawed hands and then overwhelmed by their bodies.

Three of the things rose out of the water and looked at me. Not a one of them was quite the same as the other. Each had certain similarities to Ward's pet fish man, the same rows of teeth, the same basic shape, but the faces were as different from one another as human faces could be and one of them, I swear to you, one of them had tentacles growing from the area under its eyes.

They were only there for a second, maybe two, but I studied them the entire time and I know they studied me in return.

A moment later they dropped down into the water and sank like stones.

Jacob and Belle found me a few minutes later. I was still clutching the rail and looking down into the water, trying in vain to find some sign of Tommy. He was gone and so were the fish men.

"Joe, Honey?"

"Tommy was here. He said we have to leave."

"Tommy? He was here?" Her voice went from softly worried to desperate and urgent.

"He's gone now, Belle. They took him."

"Who took him?"

The Deep Ones. They took him with them! I wanted to be coherent, to make everything clear as fast as I could so we could be out of here, but my mouth said what it wanted, still held by the shock. "The fish men. I guess he was talking too much. Dead people shouldn't talk. It's a little disgusting."

"Joe? What are you talking about?" Belle had a hand on my shoulder and was trying to urge me away from the edge of the boat.

Jacob lightly brushed her aside, turned me to face him, and slapped me across the face. Not hard enough to hurt me much, but definitely with enough force to get my attention. Just to make sure he had it, he did it again.

"Joe! Come on, man, make sense!"

I shook him off of me and actually took in a deep breath for what seemed like the first time since I got hit by the water.

"We heard you screaming, Joe. What happened?"

I looked from Jacob to Belle and then back again and shook my head. "We have to get the hell out of the water. We have to get to shore."

"Joe, you said something about Tommy." Belle was tugging at my wet sleeve.

"Tommy's dead. I saw him in the water." I was moving now, heading for the cabin. I wanted us out of there immediately.

Jacob spoke softly, but clearly. "Joe, we can't leave yet. The divers haven't come up."

That one stopped me cold. I was afraid. No, I was terrified, but I couldn't leave the divers out there. The waves were too rough and the tide was rising. They'd never be able to stay afloat and they'd get torn all to hell if they tried staying on the reef. The waves were almost cresting the damned thing now, and the top of it would be underwater and covered with enough water to knock them down again and again in a very short time.

"Goddamn it!" I didn't want to be on the water anymore. Not in Golden Cove, not anywhere near it. I thought of the things I'd seen take Tommy away and of the cold eyes that looked at me, and studied me like a bug, and I wanted to be far, far away.

"How much longer until they're supposed to come up, Jacob?"

"Any time now, maybe fifteen or twenty minutes."

I shrugged off my coat and headed down to Davey's territory, where he was probably working on the engines and fine-tuning everything. He was obsessive about his engines and that was one of the things I loved about him.

Belle watched me go and left it alone because she knows me. She knew as well as anyone could that I'd be back up when I was done telling Davey what I had to say. Jacob followed after me instead.

"Davey!"

"Yeah, Joe?"

"Warm us up and get everything ready. The second the divers are back, we're out of here."

"You got it."

Jacob followed too closely behind me and I almost knocked him over when I turned around. We both apologized and I pushed past him. I had a ton of nervous energy going nowhere fast and I was feeling jittery.

"Joe, what did you see?"

"I saw Tommy out there. He came on board and he told me that there are more of those things and they were going to come for their little friend. We have to get the divers up and we have to get the hell out of here. And if you're very smart, you'll get Ward to let go of his fish and call it done."

"But you were just saying that Tommy's dead . . ."

"That's right, Jacob, I did." I turned and faced him and he didn't even flinch when I stared hard at him. He was dead. It wasn't makeup and it wasn't my imagination. I sniffed my hands and shoved them at his face so he could get a good whiff of what was left on me from touching Tommy. "He's dead. And he was talking to me. Looks like you got your ghosts, too."

If he was happy about what I'd just told him, he did a great job of hiding it. He also didn't so much as flinch when my hands were in his face.

"Joe. Calm down. You're not going to do yourself or anyone else any good if you're panicking."

"I'm not panicking!"

"Yes, you are. You had a scare. It's a natural response. Now calm down and take a few more deep breaths. Calm. Down."

I don't normally like being told what to do, but I also know when what I'm being told makes sense. I drew in a few good lungfuls, in through the nose, and out through the mouth. I nodded to let him know I was calming down.

"Joe, I believe you. I believe you did see Tommy. But you have to tell me what he said, word for word, or we might be in trouble here."

"He said we have to leave. He said they're going to come for us." I told him everything I could remember, and I made sure he knew I was serious when it came to them taking his body back down. Jacob got a little nervous, but he kept his cool.

"So, we'll talk to Martin when he comes back and see about releasing his special guest. He may not like it, but he'll listen."

I could feel the tension crawl out of me when I heard those words, like someone had lifted a weight off my chest.

"I hope you're right."

I was about to say something else when I heard Belle scream. The sound was distant, but after twenty-four years of marriage, I knew damned near every sound my wife could make. Jacob was fast on my heels when I reached the deck, scanning everywhere and looking for her. Instead of my wife, I saw Mary Parsons, staring at the waters and shaking her head, a look of pure horror on her face.

"Mary? Where is Belle?" The words came from Jacob and mirrored what I was thinking. I was looking at the water, where Mary stared.

"Jacob?" Her voice was so small, so very faint, and I could hear it with crystal clarity, as if the wind and the waves and everything else in the entire universe had faded away. "Jacob? They took her. One of those things took her. I saw it."

I couldn't feel my own legs. I couldn't catch a breath. All I could think about was Belle in the water, dragged down as fast as Tommy's corpse had been taken.

FIFTEEN

There was plenty of equipment on board waiting and ready to replace the spent tanks the divers were using. I didn't bother waiting myself. Instead, I stripped down to my underwear and climbed into a dry suit as fast as I could.

I worked quickly, because I didn't want to give myself time to think. If I let myself dwell on anything, I thought I might just go crazy. I was about to do something I'd sworn off of a long time ago, something that scared me, but not as much as the idea of losing Belle. I couldn't afford to lose time to anything but the need to find Belle. Somewhere under the water, my wife was waiting, dead or alive, and I needed to find her more than I needed anything else in the universe. If I took time to think about the fact that she might already be dead from drowning or the extreme cold, I might have let myself panic and I couldn't afford that. So instead I focused on getting into the equipment and grabbing whatever I could find to use as a weapon. Jacob was along with me, and looking like he wanted to help. I didn't think there was anything he could do, but the gesture helped me focus. I didn't ask if he knew anything about diving. I just went about taking care of what I could.

I don't know if I broke any records, but I tried. I grabbed a harpoon gun and three extra spears. I made sure I had my knife in easy reach and tested the blade for razor sharpness. And then, forcing the dread out of my system and practically breathing in rage to take its place, I went for my first dive in years.

The water was cold. It tore at me and drained the heat away from my exposed hands and face in a matter of seconds. I didn't let myself stop and think about that. I just went down as quickly as I could, weighted down with the gun in one hand and a waterproof flashlight in the other.

I needed to find Belle before it was too late, before she drowned in the ocean or was torn apart by one of the freakish things that lived in the waters off the reef. Stupid, I know: there was no way she could be alive still. There was nothing to stop them from tearing her apart or feeding on her like sharks going after a goldfish, but I had to believe there was a chance, or I would have gone insane right then and there.

They had every advantage. Even if there was only one of them involved in stealing away Belle, that single creature was in its natural environment and didn't need to rely on a mask to see. It could use both eyes and have peripheral vision that I lost because of my mask. It didn't need to come up for air sooner or later and if it was cold-blooded like most fish, the freezing temperature would barely phase it. Whatever effects the chill had on the thing were already in effect and would do no more to slow it down.

I knew where the cave was supposed to be, and I went in that direction. I got lucky: the divers had a lead rope running down to the entrance. I don't think I'd have seen it otherwise.

I made it to the entrance without any problem and

then I pushed into the darkness of the cave with an unsettling sense of déjà vu. Damned if it didn't look just like it had in my dream. The area was dark as midnight and the flashlight beam barely seemed to cut through the murk at all.

I looked around the area as carefully as I could, but saw nothing moving despite my hopes. My mind kept trying to tell me I was being suicidal, reminding me of what happened the last time I decided to go diving alone. I didn't let myself listen, at least not enough to make me turn back.

It took me almost two minutes to find the entrance to the secondary cave. If it had been possible I'd have been screaming the entire time. Belle didn't have two minutes unless they gave her air. Even as I started down into the long passageway, I was already starting to think along the lines of revenge instead of rescue. Much as it hurt me, I didn't give my wife the best odds of being alive when I found her. Not if, because I knew I wouldn't stop looking until I found her one way or the other.

I almost cut loose with the speargun when I saw something coming my way. Like I said, the flashlight worked, but only so well, and when I saw motion my first thought was of the damned things I'd seen in this very spot in my dream. Happily, I controlled my reaction and managed not to shoot Diana in the chest.

She was followed by the rest of the team, all of them swimming carefully and two of them carrying something that looked like chains wrapped in muck. In my haste, I forgot all about them needing to come up and get new air tanks. I stayed to one side and they had to swim past me. Most of them were used to the idea of close quarters, I suppose. Only Charlie looked at me with a stupid expression on his face, because only Charlie knew I didn't dive anymore for very personal reasons. I shook my head and urged him on. I didn't have time to explain and there was no way in hell I could even if I wanted to. He nodded and kept going.

I knew he'd be back after me ten minutes after he climbed on board the *Isabella*. I didn't have time to wait. I kept going deeper into the tunnel.

What can I tell you about it? The passage was dark and cramped, and made me remember that I can be a little claustrophobic. I just couldn't spare the energy to think about my personal fears. I only had room in my head to worry about Belle's safety or killing whatever had hurt her.

There are a lot of things you forget when you haven't been diving for a while—like that the human body doesn't handle extreme pressure changes very well. I don't know how deep down I went, but it wasn't too long before I started feeling like someone was trying to crush my eardrums into my brain. I didn't let it stop me. I had to keep going.

When I saw movement coming from below me the second time, I took careful aim. The divers were all above me, maybe. It was always possible that someone held on for a few more minutes.

What came at me was not a straggler from the team. One of the fish men tore up through the passage like a guided missile, heading straight for me. The first thing I realized about it was that it was much, much bigger than the one we'd had on the *Isabella*. The second thing I registered was that it intended to tear me apart.

I fired the spear when it was within ten feet of me; the gas-powered lance met the monster head-on and ripped through its eye. The thing reeled back from me, and spun in a half circle trying, I suppose, to protect itself from the shaft that was sticking in its face. I'd hit it, yes, but other than skewering its eyeball, I'd failed. I'd been hoping to kill it and instead I'd left it wounded.

Wounded, and very, very pissed off.

I had roughly two seconds of being satisfied with

my aim before the thing turned back around and let out a roar, even as it knocked the spear away from the thick ridge above the eye where it had landed and stuck. It might not have been using its lungs, but it definitely knew how to let loose with a sound underwater. I was stunned by the sound, not because it was so loud, but because it was unexpected.

You ever see a man get mauled by an animal? I got to see it up close and personal. If it had been a little better at judging distances with only one eye, I probably would have died then and there. Instead, I got lucky and the webbed hand that raked my chest only peeled back a few layers of skin as it ripped through my suit. The pain was a series of hot needles, but they were drowned out by the sudden, numbing cold that washed over me. Dry suits keep the water away from you, and as cold as it was under the water, when the moisture hit me it leeched away my body heat like a vampire sucks at blood.

I didn't make as much noise. My screams were cut off by the regulator I was using to breathe.

I didn't think well enough to draw the knife on my belt. Instead, I used the speargun again. I shoved it toward the thing's face and pressed down the trigger, blasting a thick plume of compressed gasses into the butt-ugly fish face that was coming closer to mine.

I got blindly, stupidly lucky.

The expanding gasses caught the fish man in the ruin of its eye and blasted the rest of the torn organ free from where it belonged, leaving a cloud of red between us as the wound expanded. Instead of tearing me apart, the Deep One pulled back, letting out a high, keening sound and tried to protect the open wound on its face.

I released the speargun and let it drop on its tether. I needed the flashlight to see and I needed a weapon that did more than inconvenience the thing in front of me. My skinning knife came out fast, and I swam backward, only slow-ing down when the side of the tunnel got in my way.

The thing turned toward me a second time, bleeding heavily from the ripped open eye socket. It fixed me with its one good eye and like an idiot I looked back... and saw the images it forced into my head just as the one on the *Isabella* had done before. This wasn't a memory; it was a warning. I could still see the wounded thing in front of me, but transposed over that image was Belle, struggling in the waters, surrounded by the Deep Ones and drowning in the cold ocean as they circled her like hungry sharks. I knew as soon as I saw it that the image wasn't an event that had happened. Belle was wearing the wrong clothes: she was dressed as I most often saw her, in her favorite pair of jeans and a T-shirt she'd stolen from me right after we got married. Her hair was wrong, too, and I understood that it wanted to tell me something, wanted me to understand the implied threat of what it showed.

The image changed, and Belle transformed into a much clearer replica of the fish man that Ward and his people had taken from the *Isabella*. The size was perfect, the depth of detail much richer than the image of my wife. In the new image the captive fish man was diving into the ocean, escaping the land and swimming toward the caves hidden on the distant reef.

The image changed again, to one of Belle alive and healthy, unmarred as she climbed from the waters and swam toward the *Isabella*. The communication was crude, but effective. I could have Belle back if they could have their fish man back: a trade-off.

The one-eyed fish man turned away from me and was suddenly swimming back down into the tunnel, still mov-ing at insane speeds as it dove deeper.

My head felt like it would explode and my body felt fro-zen with an arctic chill as my dry suit filled with water.

Light spilled across my arms and body from behind and I
turned in time to see four figures swimming my way. They
were wearing diving masks. They were human.

I stared at them, barely able to move, as the world around
me started to fade out. I nodded my head as Charlie swam
close enough for me to see his face. Moments later he was
moving me, pulling on my arm and hauling me away from
the darkness in front of me.

I barely remember the trip back to the surface. I know
we paused a few times to let our bodies adjust to the difference in water pressure. You don't handle the depths with a
little respect and your blood becomes a toxic mess: nitrogen bubbles get out of control in your system and you're
stuck with nitrogen narcosis, which often causes dementia
and death. We had to go slowly to avoid a bad case of the
bends. Other than that, I only remember glimpses of the
cave walls and the sight of the other divers looking at me
every now and then, and hitting me with the high intensity
beams from their flashlights.

I didn't struggle. I couldn't. My oxygen was almost
completely depleted. Somehow, I had lost over an hour of
my time under the water. I guess the process of making me
see things took more time than I realized.

By the time I was back on my yacht I was shivering violently. Charlie and two of the college kids helped me out of
my suit and into my bed. That's all I remember of the trip
back.

That, and darkness as deep and complete as I have ever
encountered.

SIXTEEN

About an hour later I woke up to a headache that was trying its best to crack my skull. I could feel the pressure in my head beating to a different tempo than my pulse, and it hurt like hell. I was in my cabin and my clothes were dry, but my hair was damp. It took me only a second or two to remember all of the details of what had happened and that was enough to get me up and moving. My eyes burned and my balance was off when I stood up.

I didn't care. I wanted to find my wife.

Charlie was waiting for me, his face set in a grim, worried expression that didn't seem right on him.

"Joe, what the hell happened?"

"Those fish things took Belle." I put my hand on the edge of the bed and steadied myself. Seemed it wasn't just my sense of balance that was out of whack, so was the whole yacht. I understood why when the lightning flashed outside of the window and I had a chance to see how turbulent the ocean was around us. Anything smaller than the vessel we were in would have probably been thrown into the reef or just knocked over by the waves. I was lucky

enough to have a good crew and they were smart enough
to know how to keep a boat facing the waves and cutting
through them instead of letting us get thrown over by the
first big one that came along.

There comes a point in a storm where you're better off
not trying to reach land and judging by what was going
on outside, I guessed we'd reached it. The cove wasn't the
roughest waters I'd ever been in, but it was close. One mis-
calculation when you're in the wrong area and a sixty-foot
yacht becomes toothpicks. Put another way, if you're heading for the docks and a wave catches you the wrong way on
a turbulent sea, you might well ram the concrete moorings
and break apart on impact. I hated that we were stuck out
in the waters, but even worried about Belle, I knew the *Isabella* was in a bad situation.

"How long has this been going on?" I didn't really have
to explain what I was asking to Charlie. He knew me and
understood that I was asking about the storm.

"It started around the same time we got out of the water.
Hit all at once and wasn't playing any games." He shook
his head. "Joe, there was no way I was going to leave you
down there."

"Good. I didn't feel much like drowning today."

"What the hell was going on down there, Joe? You were
just staring at that thing when we found you."

"It was . . . It was talking to me." Charlie looked embarrassed, and he was doing his best to look like he believed
me, but it wasn't working out very well. "Charlie, it told me
I need to give back the fish man or Belle is dead."

"How could it, Joe?"

"I don't know, damn it!" Charlie flinched a little. I wish
I could say I felt bad about that, but my mind was on one
goal. "But I know what it said and I know that if I want
Belle back in one piece that fish thing has to be set free."

"Martin isn't going to like that." I know—deep inside

my heart—he didn't mean it to come out like it did. He was thinking aloud, something he'd done for years.

If looks could actually kill, I'd have vaporized him right then and there. "Do I look like I give a good goddamn what 'Martin' wants?"

"I didn't mean—"

"Belle is missing because you caught one of those things, Charlie. Not your fault. I'd have done the same thing I guess, but now that it's gone wrong, I need to get my wife back." I stood up and steadied myself against the rocking of the boat and the spinning pressure between my ears.

Charlie shook his head. "You're right, of course, Joe. Of course we're gonna do anything we can to get her back." He held out placating hands. "I just opened my mouth and it came out."

"Don't apologize to me, Charlie. Just get me to Ward or Ward to me so we can talk this over." Charlie nodded and then left my cabin. As soon as he did, I sat back down on the bed and waited for my legs to feel like they could hold me. I ached all over and most of the muscles in my body were protesting the abuse I'd given them.

I didn't even notice the bandages on my chest until I went to scratch at the persistent itch I'd been ignoring. I looked under my shirt and saw a layer of gauze with white medical tape. I had no idea who'd worked on me, but they'd done an excellent job based on the outside of the package.

The scratches ached, but not enough for me to examine the wound. I was still fixating on Belle.

Another wave slapped against the side of the *Isabella* and staggered me. If I'd been standing up, I'd have kissed the deck. Instead, I just fell on my side and let out a groan. I got off the bed and headed for the main deck. I couldn't sit still: there was too much going on in my head. Mind you, walking was a bit of a challenge, too, with the way the waves were knocking us around. The main cabin was filled with more people than I'd expected to see. Of course the college kids were all there because they couldn't very well go back down in this storm. It had nothing to do with the waters near the cave, those were deep enough to avoid any real impact from the waves. It had to do with getting away from the *Isabella* without getting smashed by the yacht.

Most of them were looking a little green around the edges. Seasickness, most likely. It's one thing to dive and another to deal with the constant motion of a violent sea. I walked over to the medical supplies without even thinking about it and laid out two packages of Dramamine. Several faces made grateful expressions as they reached for the stuff.

Martin Ward was in a heated conversation with Charlie and Jacob and I could guess what the source of the debate was.

"I didn't say you can't have the Deep One back. I said it was a shame to have to let it go." Ward saw me coming and his tone changed from angry to conciliatory. I could see that both Jacob and Charlie were taken aback by the sudden change in tone. Charlie glanced in my direction and I saw understanding move over his features.

Ward was scared of me. That was a good thing.

Jacob took advantage of his friend's change of demeanor and jumped on it like a predator at the first sign of weakness. "Glad to see you coming around, Martin. We can try again for one of the Deep Ones if you like, but I think the important thing to remember here is that we're dealing with sentient creatures. They can speak and reason and as we've just unfortunately learned, they can retaliate." Even as he spoke he pulled out a pack of cigarettes and tossed it to me. I was definitely going to have to buy him a carton or two.

All three men looked at me, and I knew they were waiting to see how I would respond to Ward's sudden offer of sacrifice. I knew how much his fish man meant to him. I understood the scientific significance it offered to the world at large. I knew that the doctor would be able to write his own checks when it came to future research. I nodded my thanks and headed past them and into the hold of the yacht.

There was something I had to find that would make this whole thing much easier for the doctor to swallow. I've been in business for a long time and I know just about every trick there is to catching big fish. Some of them aren't very sporting but they're not always illegal. If a rich man wants to cheat to catch a bluefish, who am I to stop him? It's his money and his vacation. I won't let anyone blatantly break the law on my yacht, but a little leeway is a plus if you ever want to have repeat business.

One of my regular clients every year was a man named Oliver Townsby. I have no idea what he does for a living and I don't care. What I cared about right then was that the oversized, middle-aged man who liked to date girls who were barely out of high school was a guarantee of two weeks' worth of work, that he tipped handsomely, and that half the time he left behind whatever gadgets he'd brought with him. I left them on the *Isabella* for two reasons: first, you never know when you might have a use for some of the gadgets; and, second, the man had a mind that was unbelievably sharp and had, from time to time, brought up the stuff he'd left behind. It was like he was testing me to see if I was honest. I was, and the end result one year was a five-hundred-dollar tip when I gave him back a fifty-dollar piece of electronic junk he swore worked to increase his fish haul.

I pushed past a few boxes worth of leftovers from fishing trips gone by and finally found what I was looking for after finishing off the first of my cigarettes. The whole thing was awkward as hell, but only because it was still in the box. I think Townsby used it once and then decided it was too much of a waste of time with all the dials and knobs.

They were still talking when I came back out and all three men looked at me as I carried out the box. Charlie chuckled and Jacob looked puzzled. Ward looked unimpressed until he read the fine print.

The wonders of modern technology never cease to amuse me. Townsby had spent a fortune on the thing in my arms and couldn't have cared less after it started to bore him. Ward looked at it like it was the Holy Grail of fishermen's tools and actually smiled for the first time in days. That didn't make me like him any more, but it stopped me from wanting to hurt him.

It was a global positioning tracker, state of the art two years ago and still a couple of thousand dollars on the market. The GPS unit wasn't what made it special. What made it something to notice was the fact that it was designed specifically for tracking larger fish in the water. Good up to fifteen atmospheres according to the box and with an effective range of two hundred miles. The transmitter was supposed to be delivered with a dart from a speargun. Just to make sure no one got it wrong they even included the gas-powered device that was half the size of the ones on the *Isabella*. I opened the case and showed Ward the specifics. He picked up on it quickly enough.

"When we get back to the docks, all you have to do is stick that thing in the back and let it go. You'll get to keep track of your frog man. I'll get my wife back in one piece."

That was as close as I could come to a peace offering. He accepted it gratefully.

Now all I had to do was wait out the storm, which by the way the *Isabella* was rocking, seemed to be getting worse.

Either that, or Davey was doing a crappy job of facing into the waves. I went to see how he was doing while Ward and Charlie discussed the best way to set the whole thing into action.

Davey wasn't on the bridge. He should have been. The door was open and the rain was spilling across the deck, sloshing back and forth with the surge of the waves. The radio was on, the sonar was going, and everything was where it should have been, except for Davey.

Like I needed any more complications. Maybe he'd gone to the head and forgotten to mention it to anyone. I didn't want to panic until I knew there was a reason to get worried. So I walked onto the bridge instead and went to see what was going on.

The sonar was completely clear and I froze as soon as I noticed that. The sonar shouldn't have been clear, you see. What it should have been was very busily pointing out that the Devil's Reef was less than three hundred feet away on the right. It should also, maybe, have been letting us know that Golden Cove was off to the left and behind us.

I checked the readings twice, made absolutely sure that there was no mistake, and then I started panicking. Who knew how long we'd been away from where we were supposed to be? I had no clue. I only knew that we were adrift, and at least a mile or so away from where we had been anchored.

Davey was missing and we were out in the middle of the ocean in one hell of a storm. And while the fish man hadn't given me a time limit for getting his friend back to him, I didn't like Belle's odds if I couldn't get her away from the underwater demons sometime in the very near future.

I couldn't change much about what was happening until after the storm finished with us. The only good thing I had going for me was that the sonar wasn't warning me about a really big rock, or maybe an oil tanker, that would break the *Isabella* into kindling. I took a look at the surrounding waters and then I got busy with a little creative steering. The waves were just as fearsome as I was afraid they'd be and it took a lot of concentration to maneuver the yacht through the worst of them.

I guess a few of the passengers must have started getting a little worried because Charlie came along and checked to see what was up. Nothing good was the answer and after a few minutes spent explaining everything, he went off to find Davey.

It wasn't looking good. I probably already said that, but it bears repeating. Time sort of played with my head for a while. I didn't have the energy to focus on anything but steering the *Isabella* through the storm. I know that Charlie told me Davey wasn't on board, but I couldn't afford to leave the ship floundering and go looking for him. I was far too busy trying to outsmart the waves that seemed to want me dead.

Did I do well? My only answer to that: I'm here now and writing this. The *Isabella* took a beating, but aside from Davey, no one was lost during that storm. We took on water, but there are pumps designed to take care of that sort of problem and they worked. We had a few pieces of furniture go sliding, but none of the big stuff and the worst that happened was one of the college kids got a bruise on his shin from a runaway chair.

So, yes, I think I did all right. No one died and the yacht didn't settle down with a new address under the sea.

On the other hand, Davey was missing. Our Davey, my Davey; the kid I'd taken on because he loved the sea and was good with machines. The sun was gone, lost behind the clouds and I was nowhere near Golden Cove as far as I could tell.

Somewhere between Golden Cove and my unknown location, I'd lost a crew member. The tough part would be finding him again.

First thing you learn when it comes to sailing or working a boat is to know where you are. I'd gotten cocky. I hadn't actually bothered to check longitude and latitude when I took us to Golden Cove. I'd eyeballed it. So it took a while to figure out where we were. We'd been washed around four miles off course. Happily, there weren't any other reefs hiding just under the water to break the *Isabella* in half.

I tried to radio the Coast Guard and got no response. It had been a bad storm and there was always the chance the transmitter had been knocked off. In the dark there wasn't a whole lot I could do about that, so we were on our own. What, because I needed more reasons for the tightness in my chest and the pain in the pit of my stomach? I was having trouble catching a decent breath, and I knew why. There's only so much you can take at one time and I was fast approaching my personal limit. The idea was to make myself look calm for everyone else.

It's easier to get dragged out to sea with an anchor in the water than you might think. Anchors only work as long as they stay stuck to the bottom of the seabed, and in the case of Golden Cove, the land drops away very abruptly. As I understand it, and I have to be honest and say I haven't really examined the notion too carefully, the Devil's Reef is right at the edge of the continental shelf. So it wasn't very hard to get lifted up by a big wave and suddenly discover that the bottom had literally dropped out from under the *Isabella*.

The end result was a long stretch of ocean where a person could have fallen from the boat and wound up damned

near anywhere. It wasn't a soothing thought. I'd lost my
wife only a few hours earlier and now Davey. Much as I
wanted to find Belle, I felt obligated to take it slowly on the
way back to the cove. Not that it did any good. I looked, and
so did everyone else on board. We searched carefully, using
the spotlights that adorned the yacht. There was nothing
to see but water. The storm was gone and the ocean was
almost as calm as glass, as if recovering from the rough
workout brought on by the earlier weather.

The water was calm. I was not. What I wanted to do was
speed like a madman and find Belle. No one else mattered
as much to me, not even poor Davey. Belle wouldn't have
agreed, and I made myself think like she would.

We may as well have been combing a beach for one particular grain of sand. The waters were still, and anything
that had been floating would have been spotted with ease,
but that changed quickly when the fog started up. Have you
ever really looked at fog? Not the low-lying stuff you see
on the road now and then, but the pea soup stuff that comes
from the ocean. It's almost alive with the way it moves.
This was like a serious pea soup. It didn't drift down from
the skies and it didn't blow in from anywhere. It just erupted
from the waters around us.

Fog does not, for the record, erupt. But this one did. It
came on heavy and grew until the spotlights were useless.
All they could illuminate was the swirling cloud of vapor
that danced around us.

Charlie walked past me with a grim expression on his
face and muttered something under his breath.

"What was that, Charlie?"

"I said 'The Parsonses are getting excited and I'm going
to my cabin.' "

I must have had a stupid look on my face, one that
showed I had no idea what he was talking about. I was wor-

ried about Belle and Davey. The Parsonses getting excited meant nothing to me.

"Joe, pay attention to me here, okay? There's a fucking ship out there. Maybe more than one." He talked to me like I was a feeble-minded toddler.

"Well, then maybe they can help with the search. What's gotten into you?"

Charlie's face was pale and he was shaking. It took me a second to notice that, but eventually I caught on.

"It's a goddamn ghost ship, Joe! There are dead people out there looking us over!" He was a wreck.

"Well that's fucking perfect, Charlie! That's just exactly what I need from you right now!" I knew there'd be no help from him. That didn't stop me from taking out a little of the pressure I was feeling. I saw the look of hurt on his face and I knew I was countering it with an expression of pure disgust.

"Go on, Charlie," I finally relented. I watched him head to his cabin. The man had wrestled a monster out of the water and grinned all the way through it. He'd taken the same monster on with his fists alone when it was ready to tear me in half. Yet the thought of a dead person looking at him from the side of a ghost ship freaked him out completely. I didn't try to understand it; I just accepted it. We all have things that scare us, right?

I left the yacht to steer itself for a few minutes and headed out to see what was happening in the fog. The ship was the same one we'd seen before, or at least it looked the same to me. I couldn't make out all that many details.

But I could see the shadows on board. I could feel them looking at the *Isabella*. And damned if I didn't look back, trying to see if there were any new crew members on board that shadowy galleon.

The college kids and everyone else forgot the search for Davey. All around me the people were looking at the

spectral vessel that waited only a few hundred feet away.
I looked as closely as I could, hating that the faces of the
people on that ship were shadows. There was a part of me,
damn it all, that wanted to see their faces, that wanted to
know that neither Belle, nor Tommy nor Davey was on that
boat full of dead people. I was just reaching for the spotlight when I saw a form dive from the clipper and drop into
the water.

Whoever it was that dropped down hit the calm seas
with a tiny splash, and then started swimming toward the
Isabella. I watched the shape heading for the yacht, wondering if this was a real person coming to visit or if this
was, like the girl we'd pulled from the water on the first
night, an apparition.

It only took a second to get to the spotlight and aim it at
the figure. Whoever it was had dark hair and was dressed
in some form of jacket. Beyond that I had no idea who I
was looking at.

Finally, after several moments of watching the stranger
swimming over, he made it to the edge of the yacht. I
looked down at him and he looked back up. I'd never seen
the man before. My heart sank a bit when I realized that.
It shouldn't have; it was a good sign maybe. But he was
just a man, dead or alive, and he couldn't answer my questions. Without asking, he climbed the ladder on the side
and made his way to the deck of the *Isabella.* I don't know
all the fancy terms that go along with older fashions. I just
know the clothes he was wearing were a few hundred years
out of date.

The man stared around with a quizzical look on his face
and his gaze cut right through me. As he looked, his face
grew angrier. He was shorter than me and I don't think he
was being rude. I don't think he saw me for whatever reason.

"Can I help you?" I honestly couldn't think of another
thing to say.

He walked past me as if I weren't there, and I watched the water falling from his body drip across the deck.

I reached out to touch the water trail he'd left behind and was puzzled when my fingers came away covered with a substance that was as cold as water but thicker.

"What is the meaning of this insanity?" The man spoke clearly to the wall of the cabin, his face outraged. "I'll not have you attacking my vessels, or threatening to sink my ship from below me."

I have no idea what was said in response, but his look of outrage grew much, much stronger. I watched him as he was suddenly grabbed by forces unseen and spun back to face his ship where it floated. As I looked away from him, for just an instant I could almost make out the shapes of other men holding him, but when I looked back, they were gone.

"You're a madman, Marsh! What have you done to these people, to this place?"

He froze for a moment, looking out at the galleon in the distance. Then he struggled harder, screaming in protest even as his head was wrenched back and he was forced to watch what happened.

From out of the waters they came, a swarm of the fish men, flowing up the side of the ghost ship in a fury of motion, claws catching the timbers and ripping them away from the ship even as the Deep Ones rose higher. Like the ship and its passengers, the shapes were vague and shadowed, more a hint of a form than an actual image, but there was enough to see, enough to let me know that what attacked was not human.

I stood and watched. I couldn't look away from the sight as the things attacked, but I have to be honest and say the fates of the people on the other ship meant nothing to me. Maybe it was because I knew in my heart that they were already dead and all I was seeing was a memory. I think it was more that I kept thinking of Belle in the hands of those vile things and it crushed a part of me.

Even as vague lumps, they were distinguishable enough to horrify me, not only because of their shapes, but also because of the sheer number of them. There weren't dozens or hundreds, but what seemed like thousands of the things coming from the water and peeling away parts of the ship that they hurled into the water behind them. I saw a documentary on piranha that showed them tearing a cow into confetti inside of a minute. The same thing happened to the nameless ship out there. The people were grabbed and pulled into the water by the creatures surrounding them and the boat was disassembled in a frenzy of activity.

All the while the ghost man on my yacht screamed and struggled against the figures that had done him in sometime in the distant past, and the students on board watched the events as they were revealed to us. They screamed as they were taken down. The people all screamed and struggled and died. I felt my skin goose pimple up as I listened to them and to the croaking calls of their destroyers.

And all I could think about was Belle, lost somewhere out in the water, taken by the very same creatures.

I headed for the controls, ready to get back to the cove and make sure that she was returned to me alive.

For the first time, the ghost being held captive on my yacht by other ghosts who could not be seen, turned and looked me directly in the eyes. "They'll never give her back to you. She's as good as dead, or possibly worse. You will not win this."

"Fuck you!" The words were out before I could even think of stopping them. I didn't want to hear what he said. I never wanted to hear it, because there was a part of me that thought he was right. I would never see Belle again. Not alive, anyway.

I started the yacht forward and heard Jacob protesting.

This was what he was out here for, to witness the ghosts of Golden Cove. I didn't care. My wife was missing and I'd waited too long already to do something about it. If Davey was dead and gone, then I would mourn him later, but whatever slim chance I had of getting Belle back alive was waiting somewhere on the shore and needed to be set free.

The ghost escaped his captors, or maybe they were never there. Maybe they were just memories in a dead man's head and he used them to show me what happened to his ship and crew. Whatever the case, he was in the cabin as I sped us toward the distant cove.

"Do not do this thing, Captain. Do not let one of them free. No good can come from bartering with the demons of the deep."

"She's my wife."

"She's theirs now, and whatever you do to help her will only bring you damnation." His face, faintly transparent now, clear enough that I could see the window behind him, showed nothing but misery. "We stay here to warn others, sir. We stay here to keep others safe."

"She's my wife."

"She's not yours anymore. She's either dead or she belongs to them."

"You go to hell! She's my wife and I'll have her back!" I was screaming at a ghost. I think if I could have I'd have hit him then, just to make him stop telling me my worst fears had already come true.

"I am in hell already, sir." He lowered his head and faded away like a bad dream. I ignored him as best I could and gunned the engine of the *Isabella*, cutting across the water like a maniac until I came close to the docks. Once there, I behaved myself because I had to, and I docked as carefully as ever.

When we were stopped, I called for Ward, telling him it was time to get his fish man.

He nodded and said nothing. I let him lead the way. Golden Cove was dark and wet and colder than I'd expected. The fog that had rolled over the sea had taken home on the streets, turning everything into shadows as vague as the ones on the ghost ship. I tried not to look too closely into the darkness. Every time I did, I saw Belle's face. Not alive and warm and loving, but cold and dead with unseeing eyes staring at me accusingly.

Ward was panting and staggered a bit as he hurried up the steep hillside and headed for the building where the Deep One was being kept. "Not much farther, Captain. We're almost there."

I nodded in response, carrying the tracking device and looking at the wicked barb that had to be put into the monster's hide before he could be let free. I told myself I was doing it for Ward, but in truth I think I wanted to know where they really lived. I wanted to know where they might have taken Belle.

When we finally reached our destination the yacht and docks below were almost half a mile away. I wondered how they'd gotten the damned thing so far away from the shore without ever being seen.

Ward opened the locked door with a key from his pocket and we stepped inside the small warehouse where he'd set up his examination room.

Ward froze at the threshold and stared with wide, wild eyes. "What the hell . . . ?"

I pushed past him, no longer willing to wait patiently before setting the fish man free.

We were too late. Someone had been very busy while we were stuck out in the storm.

I saw the body of Diana's brother, Jan, where he lay on the ground, his head twisted hard enough to let his chin dangle toward his lower back. His leg was still wrapped in bandages, but the rest of him was covered only in shorts and a T-shirt that had been soaked in blood. Judging by the wounds across his arms and chest, I had to guess the blood was his.

Five other people were in the room, all of them just as torn and bloodied. What little furniture the place held—an examination table, complete with straps to hold down the examinee and a few chairs as well as video equipment—was tossed around, scattered and broken by whatever had been in the room with them.

The only thing that was actually missing was the fish man.

Belle's only hope was gone.

You'd think I'd have the good common sense to look around a place where I found a bunch of dead people to make sure everything was safe, wouldn't you?

Well, all I could think about was Belle. Sound a little obsessive? I was. I looked at the bodies scattered around the room, saw the condition they were in, and all I could think of was that the fish man's disappearance basically screwed Belle's chances of surviving.

Something broke inside of me and I started gasping for air. My skin went cold and my vision turned gray around the edges.

Ward was staggering around like a drunk, touching every one of the bodies. I knew what he was doing. He was making sure they were dead. If they were injured, they could be saved. I watched him and felt my knees go weak, rendering me useless.

"Call nine-one-one!" Ward's voice snapped me out of my daze and I looked at him. I knew he'd said something, but it wasn't really registering right then. "Call for an ambulance! Do you hear me?"

"Yeah. Okay." I reached for the phone on the end table

near the front door and I almost touched the receiver when I saw the motion from the corner of my eye.

Oh yes, we should have checked the building out. The fish man might have gotten free, but he had not made it out of the building. He looked at Ward and he looked at me and then he charged, trying to get through the bodies and furniture and then to the door behind me.

The thing was graceful in the water. I knew it had to be, after seeing its relatives swimming. It was nowhere near as dexterous on land. That was the good news. The bad news was it made up for being clumsy by being as strong as a horse.

It let out a croaking roar, and swatted a chair out of the way with enough force to break the frame. Its foot came down on top of a man I'd never seen, who I guessed was a biologist that Ward had hired to look the monster over. The man grunted and twitched as the claws sank into his leg. I heard the knee on that leg popping under the pressure as the fish man pushed itself forward.

Ward had just enough time to look at it and let out a scream before it slapped him across the face with one of its oversized hands. The claws on that enormous paw cut into his hairline. They probably would have ripped his face open if he hadn't flinched. As it was he let out a loud shriek and fell to his knees as the blood started flowing.

The thing ignored him and came for me, determined to get out of the building. I saw the recognition in its bulging eyes, and in the way it tilted its head. We knew each other, and I think maybe we even had a grudging respect for each other. But under that, beneath whatever acknowledgments of strength, there was a deep hatred: I'd wounded it and threatened it. In turn, it was responsible for Belle's disappearance. I stood my ground. Not because I wanted to get ripped in half, but because he was only going to get away after I'd made a few things clear.

Remember what I said about the fish man not being so graceful on land? Well, graceful and fast aren't the same thing. He came on like a freight train and I guess I was supposed to be the poor damsel tied to the tracks.

The good news for me was I wasn't actually tied down. I snapped out of my paralysis and moved as the thing came closer. It took a swipe at me and I ducked it, falling on my ass and breaking the end table under my dropping weight. A hot pain burrowed into my hip where I'd hit, and I rolled over onto my knees as quickly as I could. The fish man had almost made it to the open door and I reached out and grabbed its ankle. When it turned to look at what was holding it back, I pulled up and back as hard as I could and dropped the damned thing into the ground, face-first.

It let out another scream of rage and reached for my face. I pulled on its leg and crawled backward, just managing to miss having my nose ripped off. Adrenaline kicked into my system and gave me false strength. The claw flashed across the very tip and I felt the blood fall at the same time that I closed my eyes against the sudden tearing the strike caused.

Never take your eyes off someone you're fighting. Another of my grandfather's bits of wisdom I should have listened to a little better.

The fish man grabbed at my face and caught it in those freakish hands. I felt the claws slipping through my hair and fully expected to have my scalp peeled away for my mistake. I let out a sound that had nothing to do with rage or bravery and everything to do with desperation and fear.

Then it looked into my eyes again and I knew what was going to happen before it did.

The damned thing communicated again. Showing me images of how badly I would suffer. They weren't pretty. I didn't know how it talked with its mind and I didn't have a clue if it could hear my thoughts, but I tried to make them clear. I wanted Belle back. If I got her alive and intact, I would forgive everything and make sure that the expedition left the area. If I did not...I pushed hard with those images, showing how much devastation I would wish on them if my wife was not returned.

I still couldn't read the facial expressions on the thing. There was no real point of reference and the only thing I could do was note the change in expressions. First it pulled back its head as if I'd slapped it. Then it very quickly bobbed its head from side to side.

I let go of the thing's leg and it stood up quickly, looking at me with an odd tilt to the head. I pointed at the door, and it gave me one last hard look before it moved from the room and down the street.

I watched it go, and looked at the tiny tracker on its leg as it went. Just a little thing, really, once you took off the spear that was supposed to fire it into flesh. All that was there now was the barbed hook and a small cylinder that bounced softly against the moving calf. The hooks were punched into the scales, but I don't think they actually penetrated the meat under the outer layers. If it stayed where it was, it would be something akin to a miracle.

A wave of nausea hit me hard as I stood back up, trembling and disoriented. The adrenaline in my system, the fears for Belle, the close encounter with a demon from hell, all worked to make me violently ill. I bit my tongue and shook my head and made it to my feet without passing out.

I finally started feeling a little better around the same time Ward let out another scream. I looked his way and saw the flow of blood running down his neck. He'd tried to stand up and slipped. I limped my way over to him. I didn't want to help him. I really didn't. But he was a wreck.

"We have to get him back!" His hands clutched at my

shirt and he pulled himself up my body, using me as a brace to help him stand. I looked at him and shook my head.

"He's gone. We need to call an ambulance, remember?"

"I need him!"

"Just calm down. I put the tracker on him."

One of the kids on the ground let out a moan. I looked down and saw one of the presumed corpses twitch. I managed not to scream. Well, not much of a scream at any rate.

Then I went to the phone and dialed for emergency services.

"Nine-one-one, what's the nature of your emergency?"

"There're some dead and injured people here. It looks like an animal attack of some kind." I don't know why I lied, except that I didn't want to be anywhere around the place when the police and emergency techs showed up. I had other things to take care of, like finding Belle.

I looked, and I could just make out the shape of the thing hopping and shuffling toward the shore. Without another word, I took off after it. Let Ward clean up his own damned mess. My body ached and my head was still feeling disjointed from the communication with the fish man but I couldn't let that stop me. I ran faster, my feet slapping the road and sending shock waves through my shins and knees.

Ward didn't come after me. I didn't really expect him to.

SEVENTEEN

I ran down that hill for all I was worth, cursing every cigarette I'd smoked in the last week and hating that my body was getting older and weaker. The ground was slick from condensation and the fog wasn't making it any easier to see.

None of that meant a damned thing. I pushed myself harder, ignoring the stitch in my side that was threatening to rupture. Up ahead I could just make out the thing moving toward the water. There were still a few blocks to go to let me catch up. I ran faster, until I wasn't so much running down the hill as putting my feet forward to stop from falling on my face.

The Deep One was just reaching the water when I got to him. I don't know what was going through my mind. That I would grab him and hold him until they returned Belle? That I would dive with him and somehow manage not to drown? Whatever it was, it didn't work out the way I'd have liked.

The fish man spun around fast and opened its mouth wide. The tongue that came out of its mouth was just as long and nasty as I'd heard and it slapped across my face like a wet slab of meat thrown from a speeding car. My face stayed where it was and the rest of me kept going. I only barely remember hitting the ground near the docks.

By the time I was back up and shaking off the blow to the face, the damned thing was diving into the water. I could just see it as it descended into the depths and swam out toward the reef.

There's an old question that goes with doing the limbo: how low can you go? Gotta be honest, I'd never been lower. I made it back to the yacht on leftover adrenaline alone. I was wiped out. My hands were twitching and my body ached everywhere.

Charlie was there and waiting for me, pacing like a worried hen looking for her chicks. Much as I wanted to be angry with him for everything that had happened, I couldn't be. It wasn't his fault, but he was an available scapegoat.

"Everybody done for the day, Charlie?"

"Uh, yeah, I think so."

"Good. Start 'er up. We're going back out."

"What?"

"We're going back out, Charlie. I'd like to find my wife now."

He didn't question me a second time. I guess the look on my face was enough for him.

That didn't stop Jacob, who came over to me as I was lifting the gangplank and asked what was happening.

"I'm going back out, Jacob. If you and Mary want to get off, that's fine."

"What happened at the studio?"

"Fish man got free and mauled everyone there. I think a couple of them are dead. I called an ambulance." I was doing my very best to stay calm, which I have to admit wasn't very good.

"Jesus, Joe! Who was there?"

"Diana's kid brother, I don't think he made it, and four or five other people. I can't remember." I brushed past him heading toward the diving supplies. I needed Belle back and I aimed to get her, no matter what it took.

"Joe! You can't be serious." He was screaming a bit, but I don't think he knew it.

"Where's your wife, Jacob?"

"What?"

"I said, 'Where's your wife?' "

"She's in the cabin..."

"Now where's my wife?" I did my best to look a few bullets through his head, because I wanted to make my point known and I didn't want to argue with him. I knew my limits well enough to know that I would gleefully pound the crap out of the next person that crossed my path. I didn't know if I should scream, cry or just start swinging, but all of them were looking like good options.

"What are you going to do, Joe? Go diving into that cave and hope they bring her back to you?"

"That was the deal I made when I was down there before. They get their fish man back and I get my wife." I moved past Jacob again—he was very good at becoming an obstacle, which was maybe not the best way for him to stay healthy—and started putting on a dry suit.

"Joe, you keep saying you talked to those things. No one else has talked to them, so I'm wondering if maybe it's all in your head." Now, up until that point, Jacob had never questioned my sanity. Maybe he was just being polite and maybe he thought I was crazier than when I left the yacht an hour earlier. I didn't much care either way.

"It talked to me and I heard it, Jacob."

"But what if you didn't?"

"What? You think I went crazy inside of a couple of

hours?" I actually stopped putting on my suit and looked at him again.

"Charlie called it 'nitrogen narcosis.' He said sometimes divers see things, and you were down there a long time, Joe."

I laughed, but I didn't think it was at all funny. "Yeah, sometimes people get all delusional down there, Jacob. But you know what? The first time one of those fucking things communicated with me it was right here, on the yacht, while I was breathing good old-fashioned surface air. I didn't get stoned on nitro. I had a fish man talk inside my head!"

"Calm down, Joe. I'm just saying you should explore all the possibilities."

I stood up and jabbed Jacob Parsons in the chest with my finger. He flinched but he didn't back down. "Maybe I'm nuts! Maybe I dreamed the whole thing, Jacob. But you answer me this, what would you do if it was your Mary instead of my Belle that had been taken by those monsters?"

He stepped back and shook his head. "Just as long as you're sure you know what you're doing, Joe."

"I don't have any fucking idea what I'm doing." My body was trembling again, the adrenaline was kicking the crap out of me and when it faded I was going to be useless. The only good news was that it didn't seem like it was going to go anywhere for a while. "I'm winging it, Jacob. But I have to have Belle back. That's all that matters to me right now." I looked past him and bellowed for Charlie to get us moving. A few moments later, I felt the yacht lurch gently back away from the docks and I finished putting on my suit.

Jacob was good enough to help me into a new oxygen tank, and after that was all set, I grabbed more supplies. I got the biggest waterproof flashlight on board, and I reloaded my harpoon gun from earlier. I also grabbed my skinning knife and a few extra spears for the gun.

When that was all done, I set up and activated the tracker that was set for the device I'd left on the fish man. I needed to know where he went. I needed to know if he went to the caves, and whether or not that was where I had to start looking for Belle.

The indicator showed that the signal was somewhere near the cave. I took that as a positive sign.

By the time Charlie had set anchor, I was ready for the dive. That fear crept back into my belly and tried to pull away what little courage I had left. For Belle, I would ignore the fear. She was more important to me than any-thing else in the world.

Charlie came out on the deck and told me to wait. "I'll go with you, Joe. Just give me five minutes."

Despite myself, I listened. Those five minutes seemed to crawl on forever, but finally he was ready and we went down. It went faster with Charlie in the lead. I think by that point he probably could have found the cave without even looking.

If I thought the cave was dark before, I was wrong. The two of us kept our lights ahead of us and moved down to the entrance and with every single stroke of my legs, I expected to see Deep Ones coming toward us, claws flash-ing from webbed hands and mouths full of sharp teeth ready to tear into flesh.

Whatever had happened down below over the last few days had riled the hell out of the fish people, and I didn't expect to find the place empty of guards, or at least look-outs keeping a watch for strangers. The thing is, I expected to see them, but I never really took much time to look. I knew where we were going and that was all that mattered to me.

Charlie moved through the water ahead of me and I

kept track of where he was more than I did where we were going. The darkness around us was thick and as foggy as the night above. The earlier storm had stirred the waters and lifted the silt, making it almost impossible to see more than twenty feet ahead.

We made it to the cave entrance and I felt the hairs on my arms stand up. I knew, just knew that there would be something there to greet us.

Instead, there was only the dark cave. Charlie moved quickly, his light scanning everywhere around us, but there was nothing to see but the chamber under the water. It was clearer here, too, because the turbulent waters never made it down this far.

We went for the narrow entrance to the second, deeper chamber and Charlie swam hard enough to leave me winded. He wanted this done as much as I did. The cave went down farther than I would have guessed before it opened up into another, wider area.

It was there that they were waiting. I barely had a chance to realize that the area opened wider before the Deep Ones made themselves known. They came from all directions, a wave of amphibious flesh that blocked our way. The beams from the flashlights ran across the bodies and faces, revealing alien forms that hung suspended in the waters, each of them staring with unblinking eyes.

There were easily fifty of them in the area. They didn't move to attack, but they stopped us from going any farther. Charlie dove low in an effort to get past them and they immediately blocked his path again.

I didn't see much beyond that, because I was trying to make progress myself. I braced my feet on the wall next to the tunnel's entrance and then kicked off, trying to push my way past the living obstacles in front of me.

Pallid, gray flesh blocked my way and one of the more toad-like creatures shook its head in a very human warning

to stop where I was. I didn't listen. Instead, I brandished
the harpoon gun and kept going.

The hands of the creatures grabbed at my arms and my
body and I felt the claws sliding over my suit. Several of the
things let out a thrumming noise, deep and loud, as they
moved around me. While I did my best to focus on saving Belle, I was very, very aware of the creatures and how
deadly they could be. The first thing I noticed aside from
the fact that they weren't tearing me apart was that most of
them were larger than the one that had been on the yacht.

The second thing I noticed was that they didn't look
quite alike. I'd said before that their faces were all a little
different and I saw now how true that really was. Some of
them almost had toad faces, with wide mouths that curled
downward. Others bore a stronger resemblance to sharks,
or catfish. Some of them had tentacles on their faces,
replacing the lower aspects of their mouths. I saw their
faces in quick flashes as they blocked my way—a living
wall of flesh that refused to let me get past them.

God, if only I could explain the rage and frustration. I
wanted my wife, and I wanted to leave the damned area
forever. If I could have made that clear, maybe everything
would have worked out better than it did. I don't know. I
may never know.

One of the things grabbed the harpoon gun and yanked
it away from me hard enough to snap the connector that
held it around my wrist. I felt the skin under the dry suit
scrape and bruise from the sudden, powerful tug.

I let out a scream, but all that came out was a blast of
air from my mouth that spilled from the regulator of my
mask. A second later, one of the clawed hands pulled the
mask away from my face and reminded me that man was
not meant to breathe beneath the sea. Cold water slapped
against my skin and blinded my eyes. I kept the regulator in place, but only out of blind luck. The mask was torn

away from my head and I felt the hair on my scalp ripped loose along with the straps.

It's possible to see under the water without a mask, but it's painful, too. The salt in the water, the impurities of the silt, they all get into your eyes and they burn like mad.

Half blinded by the monsters around us and deprived of my one solid weapon, I grabbed the knives from my belt and prepared to fight them as best I could.

But they didn't attack again. They weren't out to kill us; I believe that. I think they were toying with us, instead. They were showing us the strength of their numbers and letting me know that they could kill us at any time.

Once, when I was a kid, around ten or so, I had a bully a few grades older than me who sat on my chest and slapped me around a few hundred times in the face. Oh, I fought, but he was much bigger and far too strong for me to hurt him. The slaps weren't hard, but they stung. When it was over with, I was humiliated and infuriated. What the Deep Ones did felt a lot like that.

I might have actually fought back, might have even lost my mind a little and killed a few of them, but they did something to stop me without laying a hand on me.

They ripped the tank right off of Charlie's back. It took three of them, but they were fast and strong and had the home field advantage. One of them swam up fast on Charlie and grabbed his face. I thought for sure it would tear his skin wide open with its claws, but instead it just held him.

Another grabbed his right arm and swam hard, pulling his arm straight out, and I heard the sound of his shoulder dislocating and I heard the muffled scream that escaped his mouth when he spit out the regulator and cried out in pain. The third one yanked back on the tank and braced against his back. I swear if the damned tank hadn't come off it would have broken his spine.

Charlie went into spasms. The strap on the left side had

broken and the tank was stuck on his right, freshly dis-
located shoulder. He tried to turn his body but the thing
on his arm wouldn't let him. If the one on his back hadn't
eased off, he would have probably been torn apart by the
pressure.

Charlie did what anyone does after they've screamed.
He tried to breathe. It doesn't work so well underwater. He
bucked and immediately coughed water and oxygen out of
his lungs.

What choice did I have? I couldn't leave one of my best
friends to die in the water, not after all he had done for me. I
dropped my knives and swam for Charlie, and the fish men
let me. They moved out of my way and made more of their
barking sounds as I reached for him and took the regulator
from my tank and slapped it against Charlie's lips.

He took the hint and breathed in, still coughing, until he
could catch his breath. I took it back from him and took a
breath of my own as I headed back the way we had come.

And they let us go.

They parted before us and closed ranks as we passed. A
few of them followed us from a distance as we took turns
breathing from the one remaining tank.

I swam carefully, slowly, needing the oxygen to last for
the entire trip to the surface and having to remember how
deadly rising too fast could be.

By the time we reached the surface we were on the last
few pounds of pressure in the tank. I had to call Jacob over
to help me get Charlie on board.

The moon was rising when we headed for the docks,
with Charlie in a state of shock and my entire body feeling
like someone had worked me over with a baseball bat.

We limped home.

Without Belle.

There was little remaining hope in my heart or mind

that I would ever see her again. The ghostly captain's words came back to haunt me: *"They'll never give her back to you. She's as good as dead, or possibly worse. You will not win this."*

EIGHTEEN

I barely slept after we got into the harbor. Oh, I tossed and turned and did a lot of moaning, but I didn't really sleep. I was exhausted, and I was stressed to the point where going on a random shooting spree didn't seem like a bad idea. My body ached in places I never knew it had and I was soul sick. So, no, I can't say I had a very relaxing night.

Instead, I did what I always do when my life goes to absolute hell: I tried to take care of business.

Certain things have to be done, no matter how shitty you might feel. I was numb and defeated, so I guess you could say I was working on autopilot when I called the Coast Guard to report two missing people. The first was Belle; the second was Davey.

There were questions, of course. Where were we? Why didn't we report the incident earlier? Was there any sign that they might have been wearing safety equipment, etc.

Now, I suppose at this point you're wondering why I called the Coast Guard when I already knew what had happened to my wife. I can answer that easily enough. I needed to take every measure that I could, for one thing. It was also easier to lie to them and ask for help than it was to explain that my wife had been taken by mutant tuna fish with grabby fingers.

"But, Joe, you had evidence, didn't you?"

No. Actually, I had word of mouth and a murder scene being investigated by the Golden Cove PD. Aside from that, I had nothing. And even if I'd had videotaped footage of the entire thing, in this day and age there would have been a hundred people calling the footage a fake and a thousand demanding to see the creature in the pursuit of science. Somewhere along the way, they'd have forgotten about Belle. That wasn't acceptable to me.

So I lied. In the same circumstances, I'd lie again.

But the Coast Guard let me know something I hadn't expected. They told me that they knew all about the storm and that it had been a very isolated event. Though there had been reports of the horrific winds and waves, they stopped about twenty miles up and down the coast.

Jacob and Mary Parsons were right there with me. At least they were after they made sure Charlie wasn't going to die. After a trip to the clinic he was fine, but like me, he spent about twenty minutes in absolute misery after getting out of the water. I hadn't seen him fighting with any of the things under the water, except from the corner of my half-blinded eye, but I'd been a little busy right then.

I appreciated their attempts to make me feel better, but there was nothing that they or anyone else could do for me.

Turned out I was right, by the way. I looked over the radio array and found out it had been knocked loose during the storm. It took me all of five minutes to reattach it. That was five minutes when I wasn't ready to go into a panic attack or try my luck with diving again.

Belle wouldn't have been very proud of me. I should

have been calling Davey's parents and calling my own kids to explain about the missing people. Instead I paced the deck and thought about it, picked up my cell phone a few hundred times and got ready to dial, and then stopped myself. If I made the calls, the problems would be real. I didn't want them to be that concrete.

Jacob came up to me and put a hand on my shoulder. "We're going to take some time off, Joe."

"What?" I have to be honest. I hadn't even thought about their damned expedition.

"You need the break. Martin is getting stitches from whatever happened last night and Charlie isn't up to a dive. So we're taking a few days off."

I nodded my thanks. I couldn't quite make myself talk.

Jacob climbed down the gangplank with his overnight bag and laptop, heading for his rental car.

Mary came up to me next.

"Are you all right, Joe?" She looked at me with wide, concerned eyes. I got the impression, however wrong it might be, that she could read my mind with ease.

That didn't stop me from lying through my teeth. "I'm fine, Mary. Go get yourselves some rest. It's been stressful enough around here; I think we all earned it."

She stared into my eyes for a few seconds, and then slowly nodded her head. A moment later she followed her husband off the *Isabella* and I turned away before I did something incredibly stupid, like collapse on the ground and start crying my eyes out. It's hard to maintain a proper illusion of being a macho sea captain when you're reverting into an infant in front of the people around you.

I finally decided to do the right thing and explain the facts of life to Davey's parents. They were justifiably upset. I took the name-calling and the questions in stride.

I still wussed out on calling my own kids, because, damn it, I was hoping for a miracle.

The phone call came a little after noon. I was giving the entire deck a good swabbing, while Charlie remained out cold in his cabin. As soon as the phone rang, I felt a knot form in my chest. The caller ID told me it was the Golden Cove Police Department. The man on the phone explained he was calling in conjunction with the Coast Guard.

"Hello?" I swear to you, my voice cracked like I was a teenager.

"May I speak to Joseph Bierden, please?" The voice was deep and calm and I hated it.

"You've got him."

"Mr. Bierden, this is John Booth of the Golden Cove PD. Sir, I'm sorry to inform you, but we believe we've found the body of your wife, Isabella Bierden."

Have you ever heard words that absolutely ruined you? I heard the man continuing to speak, but what came through the phone was just noise. My eyes wandered out to the water, to the Devil's Reef off in the distance, and my ability to do more than stare at that damned black rock became a thing of the past. I could hear the wind blowing across the deck, cutting and cold, as it passed me by.

I could see every single glint of light that came down and bounced off the waves as they moved slowly toward the shore.

I could smell the ocean and the cleaning solution I used to swab the decks.

My eyes caught the seagulls as they drifted lazily in the wind, effortlessly skimming the water as they looked for something to eat.

I saw and heard and tasted everything as clearly as I ever have in my entire life.

And not a goddamned bit of it mattered to me.

Belle was dead.

That was all that I cared about in the entire universe.

My wife, my reason for getting up every day and going

through whatever life might throw my way, was gone; killed by the damned things that crouched in their vile caves and watched the surface world with more than passing curiosity.

"Sir? Are you still there?"

"Yes. I'm here."

"Sir, we'll need you to identify... to make sure that we've made a proper identification. Do you need someone to pick you up? We can arrange for transportation."

"No. No, it's all right. I know where you are. I'll be there as soon as I can."

"Sir, I wish that I could make this easier for you..."

"I'll be there soon." I ended the call and folded my cell phone closed.

I didn't wake Charlie. I just started walking, every step a beat of the funeral drum as I headed for the Golden Cove police station.

I don't remember much of the long walk over to the station. The whole trip just blurred until I actually got to the morgue on the basement level. The officer that helped me was very calm and very polite. I remember his eyes were brown, but I'll be damned if I can remember anything else about him.

They slid the sheet-covered body out of a cooler and I looked at that draped white cloth as if it were the most horrible thing I had ever seen.

As bad as the phone call was, it was nothing in comparison to looking at Belle's lifeless face. She was as beautiful as ever, as calm as I had ever seen her, and yet her body was a cold, dead thing.

I would never know her touch again, or hear her laughter, or feel her breath on my neck while we hugged. Or look into her eyes and marvel at the way she looked when she smiled. Or kiss her again. Or hear her gripe about the fucking Red Sox when they blew a game. Or taste her cooking, or hear her gripe good-naturedly about the fact that she'd married a slob. She would never surprise me with breakfast in bed again, or pretend to be surprised herself after I'd made a mess of the kitchen while trying to return the favor. She would never wake me from a doze and lead me to the bedroom on a cold winter's night when I sat too damned close to the fire and I was going stir-crazy from a month of not working every single day for three or more months. She would never again keep me at bay and fend off a much-needed hug because she was still frying another pan of potatoes and ham. She would never, ever kiss me awake again.

Dear Lord, the list of things she would never do again was endless, almost as vast as the gulf that separated us as I stared down at her refrigerated corpse, unmarked but still so very, very dead.

I know I talked, eventually. I know I did things. I took care of matters, because, really, that's what you're supposed to do. I made arrangements to have her body transported back to our little town, and I called the priest at our church and the insurance company, and a hundred other numbers. I know I spoke to my kids and listened to them cry, listened to their slow realization that it wasn't just a social call because I missed them.

I remember all of it in a distant way, like it happened to somebody else. Because for all the world, the only thing that mattered to me was that Belle was dead.

Belle was dead.

Murdered.

Stolen from me for all time.

NINETEEN

There are things we do in our lives that we regret. For every single thing I got right in my life, I suppose there is at least one action or idea I had that I would gladly do over. That's the way the world works.

I never regretted any part of my time with Belle. I was ashamed of certain things I did, and if I could have changed those things, I probably would have, but none of them involved her, not directly at least.

I thought about that a lot as I sat in my empty home and stared at the water. The funeral was over, and my children who had come to say their last goodbyes were gone again, made smaller and more fragile by the loss of their mother.

I was made smaller, too, and emptied of something vital. I sat on the deck and drank to her memory, fully aware that something inside of me was dead. Not dying, but already dead.

There was no silver lining to the cloud over me, just more bleak days and cold misery.

I probably would have sat on that porch for a week or

two and seen if I could drink myself to death, but there was something I had to do before I let that happen.

I had to kill some fish men.

Now I expect a few people would think I was a little crazy at that point. Gotta say, there's a good chance those people would be right. But when there's nothing else going in your life, revenge can seem like a damned fine alternative to suicide. Besides, there was always a chance I'd get lucky and manage to get myself killed in the process. What can I say? Being raised a Catholic lapsed or not, suicide in and of itself wasn't really much of an option.

Still, one man against an army of fish-faced froggy things with big claws? Absolutely insane. Let's not kid about this. They'd already taken me out twice with a few quick maneuvers, and I couldn't go down after them with a machine gun and just go all Rambo on their asses.

So, again, I wasn't really feeling like a poster child for mental and emotional health. But I also wasn't quite as suicidal as a lot of people would have thought if they'd known what was on my agenda.

We've all done things that we're not proud of. Yes, I know I'm repeating myself, but there's a reason for that. If you've been reading all of this you might remember that I did some things when I was getting started that I felt very uncomfortable with.

What I haven't mentioned before is who I did those things for. Isabella was raised with enough money to live comfortably. She was given a decent allowance and taught to appreciate the value of a dollar. She was given her first car when she went off to college and her education was paid for, all by the man I delivered drugs for.

How do you think I got in the business and then got back out in one piece? I ran the drugs for her father.

Demetrius Edward Sloan was a short man, with shoulders broader than mine and a temper that had caused him trouble in the past. He took anger management courses to make himself more presentable to the world at large. He and I shared more than a few drinks when I asked for his daughter's hand in marriage. We drank and we told stories and we became, if not truly friends, at least very good acquaintances. Convincing him to let me marry his only daughter had taken a lot of work and part of that work had been proving that I was going to be a good provider for her. In addition to a very lucrative chain of restaurants, he also did some work on the side, the sort that never gets declared on taxes and can cause a man to spend a lot of his life in jail. Demetrius never went anywhere near a prison. He was far enough removed from the actual work that the chances of him ever getting caught were less than the chances of Coca Cola giving away their secret recipes.

He knew I needed money to make my dreams come true. He knew I wanted to make his daughter happy more than I wanted almost anything else in the world. He was willing to make that happen, but nothing in this world comes without a cost. I had to do a few deliveries in exchange for the loan that let me buy my second boat. That was the one that let me earn enough to take out a legitimate loan on the *Isabella's Dream*. So I got the money, and he got a son-in-law he knew was loyal.

We were never friends, but we were partners in crime.

I drank myself stupid for two days after the funeral. I drank as hard as I ever have and I cried my tears and cursed myself with every breath I took and got all of the grief I could out of my system.

And then I paid my father-in-law a visit.

Belle's family lived in the same house the family had owned for years, a swank little affair up in Black Stone

Bay. Let me emphasize this for you: they were well off, as in filthy, stinking rich.

The place was as big as a palace and I would have never felt comfortable in there. Still, I'd grown used to the idea of visiting now and then after the first decade of married life.

It wasn't that the place was huge; it was just so damned perfect. I don't think a blade of grass would have had the nerve to grow too long in that lawn. I never felt like I was in a house when I visited. I felt like I was in a museum.

I didn't call to tell them I was coming, so Marie, Belle's mom, was a bit surprised to see me. We hugged and she cried a little, and I cried a little too, because looking at her was like looking at Belle the way I was supposed to see her in another thirty years. Marie was very old school; when I told her I needed to speak to Demetrius, she simply nodded and sent me to him.

He was out on his back porch, staring out at the ocean in the distance, with a snifter of brandy in one hand and a cigar in the other. I can't say that he looked happy to see me. I knew even then that he, like me, believed I was to blame for her death in some way. Why? Because he gave me his only child with the understanding that I would always protect her, and consider her life more important than mine. At least the second part of that was right. He still smiled when he saw me, but there was a distance in his eyes that hadn't been there in a very long time.

We didn't sit and chew the fat for a while, that had never been our style together. Instead, I sat down and got right to business.

"I need a few things, Demetrius."

"What sort of things?"

"The sort that you can get me."

"I figured that, Joe." His dark eyes looked at me for only an instant, but it was long enough to know that he'd taken my measure. Unfortunately, he was another man I found unreadable. He only ever let what he wanted to be seen show on his face. In all the time I'd known him, he'd never once given away anything unless it suited his needs.

"I have unfinished business to take care of. Back in Golden Cove."

"This have to do with Isabella?"

"Yeah." For maybe the third time in my life, I had trouble meeting my father-in-law's gaze. Shame will do that to you. "It does."

"You let something happen to my little girl, Joe." He didn't raise his voice. He never raised his voice when he was angry. "And now you want to come to me for help?"

"They took her from me. I was down belowdecks and she was just looking out over the water and they stole her from the yacht, damn it. In the middle of the fucking water. Do you understand me, Demetrius? They took her when she should have been safe and they promised they'd return her, and they took her from me."

"Who took her?" His voice didn't sound right, and I finally looked back up at the man and saw the fury on his face, a rage that made him not just intimidating anymore, but terrifying.

I told him everything I knew. He listened and never once asked me any questions. At least not until I was done.

"You know what Golden Cove used to be called, Joe?"

"Oh yeah. I know."

"But you went anyway. And you took my daughter with you."

"She came up to surprise me. I know the reputation, Demetrius. Everyone knows the rep that place has, but I had a deal signed and delivered before I even knew where we were going." I looked down at the boards under my feet, trying not to scream. "And she came to me."

The old man nodded his head and looked back out at

the water in the distance again. He didn't speak for almost ten minutes and I knew better than to talk to him. I was making a request, and when it came to Belle's father, you learned to wait if you wanted an answer.

"So what do you need, Joe?"

I knew what I needed. I also knew that some things you don't ask for out loud. So I'd taken the liberty of writing down everything I thought I might need. I gave him the list.

He looked at the single slip of paper for a long time and then he nodded his head.

"Thanks."

"I'll have it for you tomorrow night."

I nodded and stood up.

"Joe?"

"Yeah?"

"You don't do this the right way, don't bother coming back. Understood?"

I nodded my head and turned away. There were times in my life where if I'd heard that sort of comment from Belle's father I would have been terrified. Just lately, nothing much scared me. I'd already had the worst happen to me. And, frankly, I wasn't so sure I'd be coming back either way. I wasn't going on a pleasure cruise. I was going hunting for some very deadly game.

I didn't do much for the next day. I spent my time cleaning the house, leaving everything in order. I didn't sleep much. My mind wouldn't let me. It kept trying to tell me that I was being a whiny asshole.

I didn't much feel like listening to that crap, so I ignored it.

The next night, just as the sun was setting, a truck pulled up to my house. The thing was as nondescript as they come, with white sides and a cab that was the same musty shade of non-color.

The man that came out of the cab was completely unknown to me, but I recognized his type. He looked like any of a hundred men I'd dealt with in the past who worked for Demetrius: tall, lean, a little older than I expected, and with a slick way about him. If I were a cop, I'd have him pegged as a crook in five seconds. Then again, most cops had no reason to deal with the sort of man who was in front of me. Most cops probably wouldn't have known anything about how dangerous that sort could be. He had dark brown hair cut very short and a face that was just about as plain as vanilla ice cream.

"You Joe Bierden?"

"That's me."

"Your father-in-law sent me." He walked toward me and I saw the way he looked the entire area over with a quick glance. If there had been anyone in the neighborhood who didn't belong, I knew he'd have spotted him or her.

"What's in the truck?"

"Supplies you requested."

I pointed at my piece of crap boat, the *Marianne Winston,* and started following my own finger. *Isabella's Dream* was still in Golden Cove, and I didn't know if I was going to be coming back, so I left the other yacht where it was as something for the kids to remember me by.

"You want to pull up over here? I can get it unloaded in no time." What can I say? I was in a hurry to get where I needed to be, and I figured if I pushed it, I could get there well before dawn and be done with everything.

He moved the truck in as close as he could to the dock and parked it. Before I even reached the back of his vehicle, he was unloading the packages from the rear of the truck. The muscles in his arms corded with the weight, but he hauled the bulky cases with nearly manic speed. After

I joined in on the process we were done in just under five minutes.

"Well, thanks for your help." I looked at the man and smiled. Were you supposed to tip hired muscle? I didn't know but I was willing to find out if it got him off the boat a little faster.

The man just stood there, looking back at my street and my house and finally looked over at me. "I'm sensing you might not have all the details. I'm going with you."

"Excuse me?"

"Demetrius said I was to bring you your supplies and go with you. Said you would need backup."

"Yeah? Well, he's wrong." I walked toward the captain's deck and nodded in the direction of the gangplank. "I appreciate the offer but I've got everything under control."

"How long have you known Demetrius, Joe?" I knew where this was going and pretty much resigned myself to it.

"Little over twenty years."

"Ever known him to like it when he asks you to do something and you don't do it?"

"Can't say as it's a wise thing to do."

"So you can understand when I tell you to just start going. I'm not here to report to him or any of that shit. I'm here to make sure his son-in-law comes back in one piece."

"Fine. You can lift the gangplank."

He did and I did. Not much later, we were on our way back to Golden Cove and I was trying to talk myself out of pushing the stranger who worked for my father-in-law off the side of the *Marianne Winston*. He would have probably made me into chum for the fish before I'd managed to push him over, so I let it go.

We didn't become friends. I was too busy piloting my crab boat and he was too busy looking at the water like it was a foreign thing. Maybe he was looking for Deep Ones. I don't doubt Demetrius told him everything that I had said.

As it turns out my new bodyguard's name was Buddy Fisk. I can't imagine that Buddy was his real name, but it was good enough for me. He didn't smoke, he didn't drink and he didn't talk, so the travel time was smooth and easy.

I pulled into the docks and took care of getting myself a second spot to park one of my vessels. I didn't think I'd be there for very long, but I went ahead and rented space for a week.

The guy who took my money expressed his condolences, but he did it with a look on his face that made me think I was supposed to be a local celebrity of some kind. I guess it's not every day you find a corpse on the shore, even in Golden Cove.

Once business was taken care of I looked out toward the reef and saw my yacht sitting in the same place where it had been for the last two weeks. Two weeks to completely turn my life into shit. It didn't take long to knock the foundations out from under my world.

I took the *Marianne* out to the reef myself, with Buddy along for the ride. He still wasn't much of a talker and that suited me just fine. I didn't feel much like chitchat to pass the time. The only people on deck when I dropped anchor were Jacob and Mary Parsons. They seemed a little surprised to see me, but helped me climb from one boat to the other anyway.

I had to climb the ladder on the port side, as the starboard was being left for the divers to come back on board. Damnedest thing: climbing aboard that yacht felt like coming home. Even with everything that had gone to hell lately and with everything I was planning, it was nice to set my foot on the *Isabella*.

The heart almost never makes as much sense as it should. I guess that's the only way I can put it.

"Joe, I wish I knew what to say to make it better." Jacob looked positively miserable. I knew the feeling very well.

"Not much you could say, Jacob, but thanks."

He shook my hand and nodded his head. Mary was a little more straightforward. She moved over and hugged herself to me, looking at me with tears in her eyes. "She was a special lady, Joe. I barely had a chance to meet her, but she was something special."

Damn, but I didn't want to cry. I felt like that was all I'd been doing.

"So, why don't you guys catch me up on what's been going on around here." I didn't want to talk about Belle. I didn't want to hear any condolences. I wanted to know what I might be facing.

"Well, Martin filled us in on what happened when you and he got to the lab." Jacob didn't look at me as he spoke. "That was after he went to the emergency room. He got lucky. He only needed around forty stitches to sew up his head from where that thing got him."

"Yeah, well, we weren't really expecting it to already be loose." I felt bad about what had happened to him. Not bad enough to let him off the hook for what he'd done, but a little guilty for not being more prepared when the damned thing charged.

"He said you saved his life."

"'Scuse me?"

"Seriously. He said if you hadn't distracted that beast it would have taken his head off his shoulders."

"That wasn't the way I saw it, but okay. What did the police do?"

"What could they do? They took the bodies and took their pictures and now there's an ongoing investigation."

I didn't think the cops would have much luck finding the fish man and said as much.

"They'll never solve the case, but I don't think they'll try very hard, either."

"Why's that?" It was Buddy who asked the question this time.

Jacob eyed him for a second, taking his measure, maybe, and then answered anyway. "Because a lot of the officers in this area bear the 'Innsmouth Look.'"

"Bullshit." I couldn't stop my mouth from opening. My protest had as much to do with shock at the notion as the thought that he was wrong.

"Is it, Joe? You saw the police officers that were on the docks, pulling out their paperwork. You dealt with a few more of them when you went to the station. I'm not saying that they're monsters. I'm saying there's a chance that they are more than they seem and that they were placed there by their relatives."

The very notion made me seethe. I had reported people missing to the police in town, reported my wife missing, hoping and praying that she would be returned to me safely. Instead, I got a call from the police—who according to Jacob were part of a much bigger problem—saying they'd found her body.

"Okay. What else is going on? I thought you guys were going to take a few days off."

"We did, Joe. But, with everything that happened, with poor Belle..." He stopped talking and looked to his wife.

Mary spoke softly, but I heard her. "Martin had some tests run on the samples while you were gone."

"Samples?"

"DNA tests, genetic profiles, everything he could think of. He went to a couple of different labs and told them he needed to identify a species. The results were sort of cloudy."

I kept looking at her, trying to absorb what she said. When I didn't stop her, she continued. "Martin says the results proved what he expected. He said the Deep Ones are genetic chimeras."

"Which means?"

"They can breed with other species, Joe. They can mate with a human being or with an octopus and still produce viable offspring. There's evidence in the DNA from that one specimen that shows dormant genetic information from several different species, including human DNA and I think even some shark."

"How very nice for them, I'm sure." I knew it was a big thing. Like I've said before, I'm a reader, not a scientist, but I knew enough to understand that what she was talking about was the sort of thing that would make genetic scientists go bug-shit crazy.

"I know it isn't exactly what you want to hear about, Joe. But it is significant."

"I get that they're a big deal. Unexplained phenomena and genetic chimera and all sorts of new studies will come from them. I get that, Mary. But all I care about is that those things down there killed my wife and they're dangerous."

It was Jacob that answered me. "Martin also said he'd managed to break the code of how they speak."

"Excuse me?"

"He said he could communicate with them."

"Yeah? How about he passes a few messages on for me?" I felt my temper rising and tried to bite it back.

"You never can tell, Joe. He's down there right now, trying to work out a way to have a meaningful conversation with at least one or two of them."

"I don't believe this." I stopped myself from saying anything else.

The Parsonses looked away from me, at a loss for words. I looked away from them, too. I looked down at the water where it lapped against the side of the Devil's Reef. Martin Ward was trying to talk with monsters somewhere down below that rock. He wanted to have a meaningful conversation with them. He wanted to learn from them, and who knows, maybe learn the secrets of the universe from the damned things.

I hoped it was a good conversation. I really hoped he had a wonderful time learning what they could teach him, because as far as I was concerned, it would be his last chance to talk with the things.

I meant to see them ruined for what they had done, and I wasn't going to wait to make sure he got what he wanted.

As far as I was concerned, Ward was talking to dead things. They just didn't know it yet.

TWENTY

I was in my cabin asleep when the divers came back on board. I stayed that way for most of the night. Buddy took one of the other cabins. What he did I do not want or need to know.

When I woke up it was just after three in the morning. I'd slept for close to eighteen hours.

What woke me was the sound of people arguing. Well, that and maybe the crick I'd developed in my neck from sleeping too damned much.

I recognized the voices. Charlie was having it out with Diana. I stood up and walked to the door of my cabin, having no trouble at all hearing every word they said.

"It's not like that Diana. This was your project, your dream. I was trying to help you."

"It was never my idea to try talking to those goddamned things. They're monsters!" Her voice sounded like she'd been crying. Charlie's sounded like he was trying to calm her down.

"Well then why were you out here? What made you come back here if it wasn't to learn about them?" Okay, maybe he wasn't trying to calm her down, but he was certainly trying to stay calm himself.

"Because Martin asked me to come back. He needed a diver."

"Divers aren't that hard to find, Diana. Lots of divers come around when you're near the ocean."

Instead of listening to any more of their talk, I slipped my pants back on, put on my loafers and walked out of the door, heading for the galley. Both of them shut up while I was in the hallway and I pointedly ignored them. I didn't want to deal with any of their romance problems and they definitely didn't want to hear my opinion about Ward or his scientific plans.

There was coffee already made, and I poured myself a mug as I looked out the galley window. We were docked again, which suited me fine. I have no idea who piloted the yacht and the crab boat back to the harbor, but they were both where they were supposed to be.

Out in the water, I saw lights flickering along the edge of the Devil's Reef. There were a lot of lights, moving along the top of the reef and sliding in and out of the water. I didn't bother ordering anyone to fire up the engines. I knew what was out there. But I still wanted to see. It only took me a couple of minutes to find my binoculars.

Charlie and Diana were still going at each other as I passed them. Neither of them came up for air this time around; they just kept arguing.

The lights were still on the reef when I looked out again. There had to be a good fifteen or twenty shapes up on the rock, and from what little I could see, they were all Deep Ones.

I took a few deep breaths and watched them. Whatever they were doing, it looked like a ceremony of some kind. I saw a lot of weird-looking things they brought with them, chains and headpieces made of shiny metal—gold most likely—and an oddly shaped bell that they lowered into the water on a chain.

I was seriously thinking about going out there and messing up their little church service, or wedding or whatever. It would have offended them, it would have ruined their special time and I would have loved to get them all pissy. But I wasn't ready yet. I had the supplies, but I didn't have them ready for use. I probably would have gone out anyway, if I hadn't looked beyond the reef and seen the fog coming in.

Instead of starting the *Isabella* and cruising the distance out there, I interrupted Charlie's argument with his girl. Diana had reached the screaming stage: "I buried my brother two days ago! Two fucking days ago, Charlie! They had to keep the casket closed, because they couldn't make him look good enough for people to see! How do you think I feel?" Her eyes were teary and red and streaks of moisture ran down her face. I felt for her. I did.

I just couldn't let it show.

"Charlie. Get the video equipment for me. Get any long-range lenses, too."

"What?" He looked at me like I'd just interrupted an important and life-altering conversation, which, of course, I had. But I also knew Charlie well enough to know that if I didn't break them up for a minute or two, he would say something stupid.

"Before you answer any more of Diana's comments, get me the video equipment and a long-range lens."

Charlie muttered to himself and stomped down the hallway toward wherever that sort of crap was being held.

Diana looked at me out of the corner of her eye and cried.

I knew what she was going through. She knew what I was feeling.

So I looked at her and asked something I could only ask

when Charlie and the rest of them were away. "You want to kill them, don't you? The fish men."

She nodded and wiped at her eyes.

"Yeah. Me, too."

"You gonna do something about it?" Her voice was scratchy from crying, but there was a strength to it that came from hatred.

"Maybe. We'll see."

"If you do, I want to help."

"Maybe. We'll see."

She looked hard at me, trying to see what I was hiding, I guess. And finally she just nodded. "Okay. That's good enough."

"Good. We'll talk later."

No sooner had I finished telling her that than Charlie came up with the video camera, a tripod and a lens. He cast a grateful look my way. I'd given him enough time to calm down from fucking up his relationship. Charlie's a good man, but sometimes he likes to fight a little too much. Not fistfight—he'll do that if he has to—but argue. He loves to argue.

I took the stuff and heard him apologizing to Diana at the same time. That was probably his best choice. I went out on deck, cursing myself for not remembering a coat, and set up the video equipment. It wasn't long before I was capturing all of the action on the camera and recording it on a tape.

At least until that fog came in and obscured everything.

But I got enough.

I got enough.

By the time I was done playing cinematographer, Charlie and Diana were busy having make-up sex in his cabin. Any chance I'd had of going back to sleep was shot to hell right then and there. So instead, I prepared for the coming day. First I set up the tape in the main deck and hooked everything up to the TV I have bolted to the wall. It doesn't get used much, but it's there for when people get tired of fishing. Then I started the coffee and started making breakfast for the small army that would be coming along soon enough. Nothing fancy. They got eggs, fried potatoes, and bacon.

Around the time I was finished, Ward and his school of scientists made themselves known. Ward looked at me, his every gesture saying how much he wanted to say something to me. I didn't make it any easier. He wasn't completely at fault for my wife dying, but he had his hand in it. What can I say? I'm not the most forgiving man. Want to know how out of it I was? I never even realized that the Parsonses were still on board. Either they slept through the screaming match the night before or they just ignored it.

Anyway, I waited until everyone had finished breakfast before I told Jacob what I had filmed.

Just like I expected, he told Ward. Next thing I knew, everyone was sitting down in the main cabin and watching what I'd filmed.

There wasn't really that much to see for most of it. The Deep Ones were definitely doing something. They had their little lamps burning, and they rang their bell and they lowered it into the water and chanted something. There was more gesticulation than at a traditional Catholic wedding: they stood up; they bowed; they waved their arms; they croaked and chanted—though it was too far away to hear what they said. Understand me, you could tell they were saying things, but the ocean is always noisy and they were almost a mile away. Telephoto lenses can't give you better sound quality, no matter how much you wish for it. I guess with enough work and the right equipment, Ward could figure out what was being said, but it would take time.

The highlights came toward the end of the footage, but it was worth waiting for them. First off, my earlier estimation was wrong. It wasn't a dozen of the damned things. It was closer to a hundred. They were in the water all along the reef, and even though I only filmed one part of the land there, you could count the fucking things with ease. The moon was up and bright when I taped them. You could actually see a decent amount of detail on the tape. There was enough to make Ward gasp, and I could almost hear his heartbeat get faster. Why? Because the Deep Ones were revealed for the first time, revealed well enough to see that his little "chimera" theory was absolutely correct. I don't know how or why they would mate with different things from the sea, but they had. Seems like most of the ones we'd run across looked more human than some of the ones that took place in the ceremony. A xeno-biologist's wet dream was what I'd filmed. Some of the fish men had full dorsal fins, the sort you see on sharks. Some had tentacles in place of limbs, or in addition. Most of them still looked like they were at least related to humans, but now and then there was a flash of things that just didn't belong in the world, or at least not above the surface of the water.

Hundreds of them. Ward was the only one who didn't seem unsettled by that. He was too busy being all excited about the visual record of his discovery.

The only other person who looked as hyped about it was Buddy, who never said a word but watched the entire thing like a hawk looking for tender prey.

He walked over to me when it was all done and the scientists were all chattering at once.

"Those are the things?" His voice sounded a little less confident than before. He was whispering, because without bothering to ask me, he knew the people on the *Isabella* wouldn't approve of what was going on.

"Yeah."

"Now I understand the equipment."

"Thought you might."

Before we could discuss the matter any more, Jacob came up to me, smiling.

"That was amazing, Joe."

"I sort of thought you wouldn't want to miss it."

"Did you see the fog? Did you look at it carefully?"

"No. I went to get more coffee."

"Look at it again. We're going to watch it a second time. Look at the fog, Joe."

I nodded and they started the damned tape a second time. I was drawn to watching it, repulsed by the things on there and also fascinated by them. Mostly, I watched because I needed to know everything I could learn about them before I sent them to hell.

You know, I watched that film a dozen times that day and I looked at every aberration from the shapes I'd come to expect, and studied them. The one that unsettled me the most looked almost human. She was as naked as the rest, and she had a face only a mother could love, but she also had a body that would have shamed most Playmates. She bothered me the most I think, because it put paid to any doubts I had about whether they could mate with humans. She was too much like a human for my comfort. Most of them were thick-limbed and scaly to the point where they could have been completely alien and just lucky enough to walk on two legs, but her? She looked more human than she did alien and it messed with me. One of the college boys pointed her out. He made comments about how hot she looked. Most everyone else made sounds of disgust. I hoped he was kidding. Like I said, she just made me sick.

When the fog rolled in this time, everyone shut up. The white clouds rolled over the Devil's Reef, swallowing it completely, except for the lanterns and torches that the fish men carried.

You had to look carefully, but there were ships in that fog. Ghost ships. I recognized the shape of a couple of them, including the one I'd seen disappear before.

They moved around the reef, circling it like they were trying to find the best way to keep the Deep Ones stuck there.

I could see why they would fascinate Jacob. Ghosts were his thing, after all, but all they did this time was piss me off. The ghost captain that had warned me before—and I'd damn him for being right if he wasn't already damned—could do nothing but watch and try to warn others. What good is a warning that comes too late?

Ward kept looking at the tape. Eventually he turned it off and started lecturing his students about what they had just seen. The scary thing to me was that they listened. After everything that had happened, after seeing those damned fish men up close and having a few of their friends mauled or killed by the monsters Ward had introduced them to, they still listened. I used to wonder how things like the Reverend Jim Jones wiping out a whole cult with poisoned Kool-Aid could happen, but I looked at those kids while he was talking to them and I stopped wondering. I took the tape from the recorder and headed to my room.

I didn't make it fifteen feet before Ward was in my face. "What are you doing?" It wasn't really a request for information; it was more like a demand to explain myself.

"I figured I'd make you a copy of the tape."

That took all the wind out of his sails. He was all ready to start another fight with me—and I would have let him, because then I'd have an excuse for beating the little shit to death—and I went and said something sensible.

He nodded impatiently and then went back to his classroom. I was good. I didn't punch him in the back of his head.

I made four copies of the tape. I kept the original for myself and an extra one, too.

The rest of them I gave to Parsons. He could decide if Ward needed one, but I wasn't going to do a goddamned thing to help that little bastard.

A little before noon, the divers got all dressed in their gear and went into the water. I stayed behind and then changed my mind. I didn't go diving. I went out to the reef proper and took a walk. I didn't go alone. I brought a nice .45-caliber pistol with me. I made sure it was loaded.

You'd think there'd be something, some sort of evidence that the creatures had crawled all over the black stone reef, but there wasn't any. All that proved anything ever happened there was a sort of negative vibe and that might have just been my imagination. The rock was just rock, and the ocean was just the ocean. It was a little weird to realize that there were caves under my feet and, at the very least, there were people swimming somewhere below me. I wished I had a nuclear bomb. I would have happily shot one down into the depths and watched everything around me vaporize if it meant I could kill all of the monsters I'd watched doing their religious dance and shuffle where I was standing right then.

I was merrily envisioning the flesh and bones of the Deep Ones boiling away in a radioactive firestorm when I heard the sound of the waves splashing around me change.

I turned and looked and saw one of them climbing out of the water. It was looking right at me, and I recognized it by the healing slit on its throat.

Live and learn: I reached into my shirt pocket and slipped on a pair of reflective sunglasses. I didn't know if it could talk to me if I was unwilling, but I knew it had to look into my eyes to do it. Can't see my eyes, can't start a dialogue, that's what I figured.

The thing stood looking at me, water dripping from its scaly hide, and made low croaking noises in its throat. My hand slid over to the pistol grip. I looked down at its leg and saw the small tracking device was still dangling from the scales at the back of its calf. Imagine my surprise.

Meanwhile, the bulging eyes on the thing's face looked directly at my hand near the pistol in my waistband, and it let out a warning hiss.

"What the fuck do you want?"

It bobbed its head a few times and dropped something on the shore. Whatever it was, it flashed a brilliant golden shade as it fell. I thought hard about pulling the pistol and firing into that sick thing's chest until it fell over dead. I ached to kill it.

And while I was thinking about taking it out, it turned and took two steps before it dove into the water again.

I waited a minute or two before going to see what it had dropped on the shore. It wasn't hard to find, not too much was gold and shiny on that black rock.

When I looked at Belle's dead body I only looked as far as her face. I didn't bother with her fingers, so I didn't notice that her wedding ring was gone. That was what I found waiting for me, hand delivered by the fish man that was supposed to be exchanged for her.

Just a simple piece of gold with a very fine engraving of our initials and the date we got married on the inside of it. I could still see the marks, but they'd been distorted. I guess one of the fish men had decided they liked the look of her ring and tried to wear it after they took it from her. The metal was stretched thin in a few spots.

I held the ring for several seconds, looking it over and feeling my rage grow hotter again.

Maybe the thing was teasing me; maybe it was trying to

tell me something. Maybe it was simply doing what it could to honor its part of the bargain we'd struck. I didn't care.

All it did by showing me what I'd missed was make me angrier than I had been. I went back over to the *Isabella*. I had things to plan and prepare for.

I spent the earlier part of the afternoon on the *Marianne* with Buddy. The instructions for what I wanted him to do were easy enough to follow, and he had no problem handling them. Then I had to get back to the *Isabella* in time to make lunch.

I went the easy route and made hot dogs with all the fixings.

While I was serving everything up, Charlie kept looking at my old crabbing boat and the obvious physical changes that were taking place. He shot me several questioning looks and I ignored them. If he wanted to know what was going on, he'd have to ask me out loud and when there was no one else around.

So he waited, and when the situation looked right, he pulled me aside. "What the hell is going on, Joe?"

"I'm serving lunch."

"Don't fuck with me. What are you doing to the *Marianne?*"

"Getting her set up."

"For what?" He was trying to be patient.

I looked at him for a few moments and covered by taking a bite of a chili dog with extra onions. Here's the thing: Charlie was one of my best friends in the world, but just lately it hadn't really seemed that way. He was too busy hanging with his new pal, Martin, a lot of the time. Charlie I trusted. Martin Ward I did not. So the problem I had was trying to figure out where his loyalties lay. Does that sound harsh? Maybe, but considering he hadn't even expressed his condolences on Belle getting murdered, I had my doubts.

Finally, I gave him an answer that was partially the truth. "Not sure if you remember this part, Charlie, but I had to bury my wife a couple of days ago." Did he flinch? Yeah, like I'd slapped him with a jellyfish. "So I figure if I'm gonna be out here, I'm going to have a few defenses in place on my boat. Things to stop those fuckers from just climbing on board and doing whatever they want."

Charlie looked back at me the same way I guess I'd been staring at him. "You don't trust me anymore, Joe?"

"Not that I don't trust you, just that I don't like all of your new friends."

"What the hell is that supposed to mean?"

"Do the fucking math, Charlie." I dropped my lunch in the trash can. Suddenly, I wasn't all that hungry.

Charlie looked away first, his face flushed red and his hands clenching into loose fists. Was I worried about him hitting me? No. I knew him better than that.

"He's a good man, Joe."

"I'm sure he is." I shook my head. "He still got Belle killed. So we're not going to be friends."

"He didn't get Belle killed."

"Really? How do you figure? His pet fish got caught and then my wife got taken so he'd let it go."

Charlie shook his head and looked at me, his face made miserable with grief. "No, Joe. I was the one that caught the fish man, remember? It was me. So it's my fault."

Charlie isn't one to cry in public. He never was. When his parents died, he showed nothing but the proper New England stoicism. He didn't cry out loud and collapse at the funeral. Instead, he stood still and thanked everyone for their concern and then he got a little sloppy at the wake, but he never broke down in tears, not until most everyone else was gone.

So he didn't quite start crying when he said those words, but he came very close.

Me? I was too busy reeling from the comment. It never occurred to me that he might feel partially responsible for Belle's murder.

I looked around at the group of exhausted divers who were eating dogs and drinking sodas and then I pulled him away from the main group and into the hallway.

"Listen to me, Charlie. Are you listening? Because I don't want to discuss this with you again." He nodded, still too hurt or ashamed to look me in the eyes for more than a second. "You might have caught it, but Ward was the one that took it off this boat and locked it in a lab for study. You might have helped keep it here, but he's the one who took it inland. He's the one who started taking his blood tests and his skin samples. I said my wife was missing and all he cared about was keeping his pet fish."

"I was still there, Joe. I should have done something."

Now it was my turn. I wasn't completely innocent in this myself and I knew it. "I should have never let you bring that goddamned thing on the *Isabella*. I should have made you let it go. I should have stopped Belle from coming here, or sent her on her way. There's plenty of blame to go around, Charlie, but in the long run, it was Ward. He's the one that's been trying to talk to these fucking things. He's the one who's been hiding things since this started."

"What do you mean he's been hiding things?"

"You can check with Diana, but I'm betting he knew those Deep Ones of his were in this area and still alive. He's supposed to be an anthropologist, but he has all sorts of doctors and labs waiting in the wings, including his own people ready to rush genetic tests. Tell me he didn't know what he was getting us into."

He wanted to say something. I know he did. He wanted to defend Ward, or maybe just put more of the blame on himself or less on me, but it wasn't an easy thing for him. I'd made my points very clearly. So, instead he tried to get back to the original subject.

"What's going on with the *Marianne?*"

"I'm not taking any chances with those fuckers, Charlie. I know Ward wants to have a meaningful dialogue with them but I don't trust them to keep their word and I just plain don't trust them. So I'll sit back and be prepared. When the *Isabella* docks tonight, I'll be staying out here on the *Marianne.*"

"Fine. Then I'll stay with you."

"Nothing doing." I shook my head. Did I like the idea of Charlie with me? Yes, because I knew if there was ever a problem, he'd have my back. But as far as I knew this was a one-way trip I was taking later that night.

"Why not?"

"Because if those things decide they want to get bitchy, I need someone to take care of the *Isabella* and finish this job."

"Screw the job, Joe! You should leave here and so should everyone on this rig."

"We got paid to do the job, Charlie. We're going to do it. But I want to make sure there's nothing coming up at night that shouldn't be. You dig?"

"What makes you think—"

"You saw the same tape I did today, Charlie. What do you think it means, them coming out of the water in that kind of number? That they're planning a picnic?"

"I don't know what it means, Joe. I just don't like the idea of you being out here by yourself."

"Don't sweat it. I have a few things to defend myself with. And then there's the changes Buddy is making."

"That's another thing. Where do you know him from?"

"Buddy? He came with the equipment."

"Yeah? I hope the price wasn't too high."

"What do you mean?"

"I know him, Joe. I've seen him before."

"Where?"

"Back when I was active in the Navy. There was a problem with a couple of guys getting themselves in trouble with a loan shark."

I didn't like the way this was going and I nodded for him to continue.

"I'm not saying he was the one that did anything, but I'm good with faces and he looks an awful lot like the picture that ran for a while in the local papers up that way. After the two guys wound up dead with bullets in their heads."

"I don't think that's a problem here, Charlie." I walked and he followed and soon we were outside and looking down at the *Marianne* and Buddy, who was wrapping barbed wire along the railing on the smaller boat.

"No?"

"No. He's pretty much here to make sure I don't get myself hurt."

"Then I hope he's really good at his job."

I nodded and then I looked over at Jacob Parsons who was standing only a few feet away. He was good to me and threw me a cigarette. If he heard any of what Charlie and I said, he gave no indication. Like I said before, not a man I'd play poker with.

Ten minutes later Charlie was getting his gear back in order and preparing for another dive.

Jacob was leaning against the railing and looking at Buddy as he worked, and I was cleaning up from lunch.

After that was done I took a nap until the divers came back up a second time. It was cold and the weather was quickly heading toward ugly storms. I advised that the divers call it a day and Ward was smart enough not to argue with me.

I was sort of surprised by that. Seems like he'd had some

luck on his latest dive; they'd run across one of the fish men that was willing to listen to the recordings the professor had made the night before and then was even good enough to talk into his microphone and let itself be recorded.

The good professor couldn't have been happier.

Good for him.

If everything worked according to my plans, it would be the last recording ever made of one of the Deep Ones.

Everybody else on board was going to sleep in Golden Cove that night. Me? I was going to war.

TWENTY-ONE

I watched the *Isabella's Dream* coast back to shore at a lei-surely pace and felt my heart tremble a few times. I fully expected I was saying goodbye to a part of my life. Maybe even all of my life.

The *Marianne* was just fine for what I needed. I looked around at the alterations Buddy had spent most of the day work-ing on. No doubt about the fact that he was a professional.

Aside from the barbed wire, there were a few subtler changes that had been made. The biggest of them was the hot wires that ran around the railing. They were there, but harder to see, and he'd had to work carefully to make sure they wouldn't get tangled into the new decorations.

The hot wires ran a quarter inch under the barbed wire additions, and they were stopped from touching the metal railings by small rubber squibs that he'd glued into place. There were three separate lines running near one another, each hooked into a separate generator. They weren't hot yet, but as soon as I gave him the word, they'd be turned on and send enough voltage into anyone touching them to deep-fry a salmon in around three seconds.

Next up, I had to check over the rest of the packages. The biggest surprise had already been set in place. When the time came, I didn't think I'd have any problem at all pushing the button. There were guns aplenty and that suited me fine. Buddy had taken the time to load each one and had several spare clips for each carefully set in a sling sack that draped from the stocks.

Anyone boarding the boat right then would have been in for an ugly surprise.

So the time had come and I still didn't want to do it. Not all of me, at any rate. I have to be honest and say I didn't much expect to survive whatever went down. I just intended to take as many of them with me as I could.

The sky was darkening nicely, and we puttered around a little before moving the *Marianne* over to where I knew the entrance of the cave was waiting below the surface.

I looked over at Buddy. He looked back, his face as calm as could be, but a little paler than he'd looked the last time I checked. "You don't have to do this, Buddy."

"Yeah, I do." He shrugged his shoulders in a way that said this was all just business as usual for him.

"No. I mean it. I know you watched the tape and I know it wasn't superclear footage, but it's enough to let you know what's going down here, and I don't much like the idea of you staying here and dealing with what's coming."

"Listen, I appreciate the sentiment, but this is what I do. Demetrius says jump, I jump. Demetrius says go watch over my suicidal son-in-law and make sure he doesn't fuck up, that's what I do."

"There's going to be a lot of those things if this goes the way I want it to."

"There are a lot of bullets here and a few more surprises, too."

I stared at the man, completely without any idea how to respond. He knew what he was getting into, and I'd given

him an out to make sure he could survive it, but he didn't
even blink.

"You really think you can pull me out of this in one
piece?"

Buddy shook his head. "Fuck no. But I've been in tighter
places."

"My ass you have."

He chuckled. "Believe it, Joe. Working for Demetrius
means you work in some very sharky waters."

"All right then. Don't say I didn't give you an out."

"Not in a million years." He pointed back toward Golden
Cove and shook his head. "But what about them?"

I turned and saw the *Isabella* coming our way and
groaned. "I told Charlie to leave the fucking boat in the
dock. One little goddamned order and he can't follow it."

"Yeah, well, maybe we should wait until you've told him
again before we do anything." He sounded amused.

I stood in plain view as the *Isabella* came around and
coasted up next to us. Charlie came out a few moments
later after dropping the anchor.

"What the hell are you doing out here, Charlie? I told
you to go to port."

"Yeah. I heard you. What are you doing out here tonight,
Joe?"

"None of your goddamned business. Go back to the cove
and park for the night. We can discuss it in the morning."

"Not gonna happen."

"Then get down here so I can kick your fucking ass!"

"Diana wanted to talk to you and your radio isn't on."

I let loose the sort of profanities that would have had
Belle ready to wash my mouth out with soap, while Diana
and Charlie climbed down from the *Isabella* and boarded
the *Marianne*.

Diana didn't waste any time with pleasantries. "You
gonna kill those things?"

"Maybe."

"I want in."

"No."

"They owe me." She spoke in a low hiss, her eyes slitted and her teeth bared.

"I'll tell them to send you a payment. I got everything taken care of."

"I'll trade you information for the right to be here when it all goes down."

"Now just a fucking minute here!" Charlie stepped up and got in my personal space. He's one of the few people I'd let do that. "What the hell are you planning to do, Joe? Take them all on?"

"First, get the fuck out of my face. Second, yes. That's exactly what I plan to do."

"You've lost your fucking mind."

"One thing at a time, Charlie. Let's hear what Diana has to say and then you can try to talk me out of it." He wouldn't be able to, of course. I had no intention of backing down now.

Diana looked at me. "We have a deal or not?" I looked at her eyes, looked hard, because I wanted to know what she was thinking. All I saw was the same sort of rage I was feeling. She was as good as dead inside; I could see that well enough to know that even if I said no, she'd still find a way to be here.

"Fine. Deal. Let me have it."

"So I was looking over Martin's notes. Not the normal ones he leaves out, but the ones he keeps in his personal notebook, and I saw some of the things he'd translated."

She paused and waited for a response. I nodded my head and told her to go on. I got a feeling in the pit of my stomach that told me I wasn't going to like what I was about to hear.

"Charlie said the other day that you heard Martin say something to the Deep One on your boat."

"Yeah. Don't ask me to say it though, because it isn't gonna happen."

"No way in hell I could say it either. Martin's been practicing. Look, I don't know for sure, but there's one phrase written out and then about five pages of notes before there's another phrase in their language." The more she spoke, the more hesitant she seemed to be about finishing. I crossed my arms and waited for her to finish. No way was I going to make it easier on her. She wanted to buy the right to her death; I was going to make her work for it. I already had enough pre-battle guilt on my shoulders thanks to Buddy.

"He writes translations of what he's trying to say. That first entry—the one that was by itself—said 'pick the one you would have as your sacrifice.'"

What can you say to something like that? I could barely even think, let alone answer the comment. But I could feel. I felt it when the tendons in my hands started screaming because I made fists harder than I think I ever had in my life. I felt my blood pressure surge like high tide coming in. Oh, I felt that and more.

"Really?" One word. That was all, but I guess I made my feelings pretty clear with that simple phrase, because Diana got a different look on her face. Maybe it was satisfaction; maybe it was something else. I can't say for sure. She nodded her head and I nodded mine. "Welcome aboard the *Marianne Winston*."

"Wait a minute." Charlie was sounding a bit weak and looking like a strong breeze would have knocked his ass into the drink. "Wait a goddamned minute. You mean he told them to pick a victim?"

Diana nodded and so did I. "More than that, Charlie. He told them to choose their own sacrifice and they chose Belle."

Charlie's hands went into his short hair and he started shaking his head. "That's crazy talk."

"Yeah. I'm not really thinking Ward is all there right now, Charlie. Go get back on the *Isabella* and get out of here." I didn't want him hurt, but I also didn't want to be the one who hurt him. Charlie was currently in my way and I had things to do.

"There's no way he would have done that!" Charlie was sounding a bit stressed out, and I was just plain not in the mood for him.

"Diana's known him a lot longer, Charlie. Why don't you take the *Isabella* back to shore and you can ask him in person."

Before he could answer me, I saw the floodlights on the *Isabella* light up the darkening water. As I'd thought only Charlie and Diana were on board, I was a little surprised.

So were Charlie and Diana.

"Who the hell is up there?" Charlie was frowning.

Diana talked at the exact same time, frowning as she spoke. "We were the only people on board, weren't we?"

Buddy stepped back from us and his hand reached for the holster he had draped under his shoulder, mostly hidden by the jacket he was wearing.

I looked up at my ship and waited. I figured someone had just announced his or her presence. It was just a matter of waiting.

Martin Ward stepped forward until he was looking down at us. I couldn't have missed him on a bet.

"Ahoy there." He was sounding awfully smug.

"What are you doing on my yacht, Dr. Ward?"

"Well, I was just listening to your conversation." He looked down and placed his hands on the railing. "I guess you'd like some answers." His voice carried down to us easily, because the storm that had been threatening still hadn't shown itself. The air was still and so was the water.

"Just one. Did you tell the fish men to pick a sacrifice?" I did my best to keep my voice calm.

"I wasn't really sure what I'd said at first, Captain. I just quoted writings from Obed Marsh's personal journals." His face was heavily shadowed and backlit by the floodlights, but I could see genuine regret on his features.

And I didn't care at all.

"You told them to pick a sacrifice and they took my wife!"

"Yes, I'm afraid so."

I started toward the yacht and had my hands on the ladder to hoist myself up before I even thought about his answer. I was looking at the reason Belle was dead as surely as if I'd been looking at one of his Deep Ones. I'd been thinking he was responsible all along, but more as a side effect of his obsessions than because he'd told the damned things to do what they pleased. Before he'd just annoyed me, but now? Well, I have to be honest. Right then when I was looking up at him, I didn't even think about the fish men. I wanted to kill him with my bare hands.

"They said you'd react like this. They were right." His head looked away from me and down toward Diana. "And you. How could you betray me?" The thing that really knocked my logic circuits crazy was that he actually sounded hurt.

"They killed Jan!"

"Jan was there and the Deep One wanted to escape, Diana. I told you it was dangerous to bring your little brother along but you didn't want to listen to me." He was so sure of himself. I guess that should have been the first sign of trouble.

I guess I should have known that a snake like Ward would bring backup with him. Or have it nearby, like in waiting just below the surface.

As I started up the ladder on the side of the *Isabella,* he let out a loud, rattling call and lit a fuse on something he held in his hand. I dropped back down to the *Marianne* and got ready for whatever sort of fireworks he had with him.

What I didn't expect was for him to throw whatever it was high into the air above the reef.

When it detonated it let out a brilliant green flash of light—so strong that it left everyone stupid enough to keep their eyes on it, like me, half blinded for a moment—like looking at a flashbulb only much more powerful.

"I've made a deal with the Deep Ones, Captain. Do you really think I'd let my new associates be attacked without warning them?" I heard Ward's smug words as I blinked away the spots in front of my eyes and caught a whiff of whatever residue came from his homemade flair.

All around the Devil's Reef, the water seethed, and a moment later the Deep Ones came out of the water, hundreds of the demons rising up and treading surf as they looked from one boat to the next. They made their choice and one or two of them let out heavy croaks, then turned toward the *Marianne* and came for us.

TWENTY-TWO

Well, it wasn't exactly what I'd wanted to happen, but the added adrenaline surge was a blessing. I looked at Buddy and he looked at me and then ran like the devil himself was trying to bite his ass off.

Then I ran, too. Not for the generator switches, because I knew that was where Demetrius's sidekick was heading, but for the artillery.

I barely bothered to look, but scooped up what I hoped were all loaded weapons and put them on the deck as Diana and Charlie screamed at Ward. For his part, the professor was looking down on us with a calm, slightly insane smile. I'm guessing on the crazy part, of course, but I had my suspicions.

The first of the Deep Ones cleared the water and landed at the guardrail, holding on with thick, wet paws. It looked over at us with bulging eyes and bared a formidable mouthful of teeth as it hissed.

Charlie was a little faster on the uptake than Diana. He grabbed a weapon for himself and one for her.

As for me, I looked at the fish man, then grabbed my

own weapon and spun around, taking careful aim at Ward's face.

He was answering whatever the hell the other two had said to him, and he was looking back at Diana when he spoke. "It's about immortality, Diana. Not for me, but for the human race. If we don't change, if we don't become more like the Deep Ones, we're all doomed by our own stupidity."

"Hey, Ward!"

His head snapped around as I yelled for him and he looked at me like I'd just interrupted one of his class lectures. He was in preach-mode and as the only member of the Church of Martin Ward, Scientist, I guess he wasn't used to getting interrupted. For one second he looked outraged, but seeing the business end of my assault rifle aimed in his direction, he changed his tune fast.

"Wait! You can't do this!"

I shot him. It would have been so perfect to see his head explode all over the place and to see him die right then and there. I wanted him to pay for what he'd done. I didn't care about his beliefs. There are freaks like him all over the planet but, oh, how I cared about Belle. So I shot him.

Sad to say my aim wasn't perfect. Instead of watching his head explode, I got to watch his right ear vanish in a quick red spray.

Martin Ward's eyes bugged even wider than a Deep One's and he let out a wail of pain and dropped from sight, screaming in agony.

I didn't have the time to finish the job. The first of the Deep Ones was almost on board my crab boat.

God love him, Charlie had the situation under control. His face was set like a statue, angry and determined. He fired his weapon and three bullets blew out the back of the fish man that was just setting foot on the deck of the *Marianne*.

The thing let out a wet sounding howl and fell back into the water, bouncing against a couple of its relatives before splashing down.

By that time around fifteen of the things were all over the guardrails and doing their best to overrun us. At least two of them were dumb enough to get caught in the barbed wire and were roaring and bucking as they tried to get untangled.

Before I could do anything to end their suffering with a bullet or two, the hot wires activated. The air was filled with a series of little popping noises and a very clear electrical hum, and every last one of the fish men who was scaling the sides of the *Marianne* jerked violently as live current cooked their bodies. Diana let out a scream, and I think I did, too. Charlie just calmly took aim and fired again, blowing holes in the face and chest of another target.

The ones still there, the army of the damned things that was surrounding us, they went a little crazy, screaming and barking as they backed away from the boat. Quite a few of them ducked back under the water, but not nearly all of them. I stepped closer to the railing and opened fire, spraying the damned things with ammo. The ones hit by the bullets discovered that I had claws, too, only mine were longer.

Diana finally figured out how to get the safety switched off and put a couple of bullets in the deck before she got a better aim and fired on the fish men.

By the time Buddy made it back to the deck, the Deep Ones had moved out of easy targeting range and were making lots of noises while they stared at the boats.

"So, I thought about what you said earlier, Joe. I think you're right. You can handle this by yourself." That was Buddy. His voice was tense, but he had a thin smile on his face and his eyes were hard.

"Might be a little late."

"Yeah. I figured as much. Same luck I always have with the lottery."

Several of the Deep Ones had fallen away from the electrified wires—or burned away—and a few of them actually caught fire. I trusted the rest of them to watch my back and grabbed a wooden pole I usually saved for pushing away from shallow spots. I used it to knock the burning corpses off the side of the *Marianne*. Each one that fell was already dead, but hissed anyway as it hit the water.

All around the *Marianne*, the Deep Ones were treading the surface and making their odd croaking noises, like a million frogs singing in a choir. When I was done with my grisly task, I put the pole down against the cabin wall and got a few more weapons from inside. Like I said, we brought an arsenal. One of the nice surprises that my father-in-law added to the list of supplies, aside from Buddy, was body armor. Unfortunately he only brought two sets. One of them went on Buddy. The other one I made Diana wear. What can I say? I was raised to be a gentleman.

"Why aren't they doing anything?" Diana's voice was shaky. I could understand the reasons well enough.

"They are doing something. They're thinking about how they should continue." That was Buddy. He looked around at the things out there and shook his head. "Damn me if they aren't smart."

Turns out they were smarter than we thought. The next wave came from the air, not from the sea. While I was busy pushing corpses aside and the rest of my group was watching for unexpected attacks from below, the Deep Ones that had disappeared were scaling the far side of the *Isabella*. They didn't actually fly, but I have to tell you I let loose with a very unmanly scream when I saw them come over the railing of my yacht and drop down on the deck of the *Marianne*.

They were strong and they were fast, but like I said before the Deep Ones didn't seem really built for land attacks. A couple of them fell back against the railings and got themselves hooked into the barbed wire. One of them tried to twist around and in the process managed to make contact with the hot wire and immediately fried.

That only left twenty or so to safely land on the deck and come at us in a wave. The first one I fired on took a few bullets to the guts and fell down, but the one after that jumped when I was expecting it to run and it cleared the distance before I knew what was happening.

It landed on my chest and knocked me flat to the deck. What had to be easily two hundred pounds of fish man slammed me to the ground and immediately swatted the gun out of my hand. I'd have been dead right then and there, but Buddy was watching my back and blew the damned thing into bloody pieces with a full clip of bullets.

Let me tell you something, and I say this with conviction. I would have died ten times over if Buddy hadn't been along for the ride. I have never in my life seen anyone outside of a Hollywood action movie who could do what he could with a firearm. It was more like watching a ballet than seeing a man fighting for his life. As I lay there trying to get over the fact that I was alive, Buddy cut down four of the Deep Ones. The one on me was so much dead meat and bones, but at the same damned time he was saving my hide, Buddy was firing a pistol with his left hand and punching holes in three more of the things.

Charlie was damned good—he mowed down three of his own—and Diana was a surprise. Once she figured out the kick on the weapon and how to control it, she tore through them, firing steadily until her clip was emptied. Diana watched Charlie as he pushed out the spent clip and dug a full one from the small bag of extras on the stock. She mimicked him and had her weapon reloaded only a few seconds later. Neither of them would have lived through the assault either, except for Buddy. While they were reloading, he was firing his pistol and either killing or maiming with every shot he spent.

The last three able-bodied Deep Ones tried to make a run for it. One of them was smart enough to clear the railing. The other two fried themselves for their efforts.

It was all over by the time I stood up, wincing because the fish man's toes had sharp claws, too, and they'd ripped through my jacket and shirt and finally skin before they stopped.

It was fully dark out now, and the light of the moon wasn't shining through the clouds. All I could see of the Deep Ones in the water was what light came from the *Isabella*'s floodlights.

Yeah, that was working fine until that bastard Ward shut them off. Maybe he wasn't as ignorant of the sea as I thought he was. A second later, I saw the *Isabella* pulling smoothly away from us, leaving the *Marianne* surrounded on all sides by the fish demons.

Despite the danger, I spent a moment looking at the *Isabella* instead of at the monsters all around us, and I saw Ward still standing on the deck. He was only a silhouette, but both of the hands on the hunched over shape were clutching the right side of the head. Someone else was actually piloting my yacht as he moved toward the distant shoreline.

All of us were shaken—well, except maybe for Buddy—and none of us spoke as the *Isabella* moved away. The Deep Ones were watching, too, and probably not thrilled about losing their diving board.

"What are they going to do now?" That was Charlie, who had missed the show a few nights ago when the ghost ship showed us how it had been torn apart.

"They're going to *kill* us, Charlie. I fucking told you to stay in the cove! You should have listened!" My voice was just as shaky as Diana's. Like I said, I could understand her nervousness. I was also very angry, because

I didn't want him here, I didn't want Diana here. I fully expected to die tonight, but I didn't want to take anyone else with me.

Meanwhile, Buddy calmly reloaded his small arsenal of weapons, several of which hung by the straps around his shoulders. Almost calmly, really. I could see the slight shake in his hands from the adrenaline rush.

"Not really a good time to lecture me, Joe!"

"Fine. I'll save it for them." I pointed out to the now dark waters and the forms that could just be seen moving around in the waves. Unlike the *Isabella,* the *Marianne Winston* didn't have floodlights. It was my piece of shit boat for going crabbing, for God's sake. I never expected to be using it in a battle against sea monsters.

Diana was trying to look everywhere at once, her face set in hard lines and her eyes rolling wildly from point to point as she studied how badly screwed we were.

She took a step toward the railing, only one because she didn't want to fry, and started firing at anything that moved. I thought about telling her to stop but decided against it: if she could hit a few more of the things before they rallied for another attack, all the better.

The Deep Ones took poorly to it. They backed away some more and made a lot more noises. It was really the only way we could figure out where they were.

"You think they'll try again?" Charlie was looking at the darkness out there, and getting jittery.

"Oh yeah, but we have a few surprises in store for them."

"Like what?"

"Buddy, you think you can get out a few of the surprises?"

Buddy stepped back into the cabin and came out with a small canvas bag. He opened it and pulled out three avocado-sized grenades. Without waiting around to see what anyone would say, he pulled the pins on two of them and hurled them as far as he could out into the water. They let out tiny little splashes, and then a few seconds later the water lit up to the north of us and to the west.

"Concussion grenades. Only have a few, but they might make this more interesting."

They'd fallen deeper than I expected them to before they detonated. It took a few seconds for the explosion to break the surface. By then the light was already gone. The spray from the explosions washed over the sides of the *Marianne* and soaked us, sending sparks across the hot wires.

The Deep Ones didn't take well to the surprise. While they were all thinking about the noise, I went into the captain's deck and found my one decent flashlight, still cursing myself for not even considering the darkness that would make it impossible for us to see.

I had just managed to get a decent beam of light out of it when the Deep Ones attacked again. They tried to clear the guardrail by jumping hard, but it wasn't going to happen. So instead, when one of them hooked the hot wire and started bucking, two more came out of the water and pulled down as hard as they could. I don't know if they were trying to help the one stuck up there or not, but what they managed to do instead was rip the hot wire free from its moorings and drag it down with him. They got shocked to hell and back in the process, but they managed to ruin our defense in that one spot. I could see the three of them, either dead or stunned, floating on the water as the circuit broke. That was all the invitation they needed and the Deep Ones came flowing out of the water along the spot where the electricity was gone. One of them grabbed the barbed wires and savaged the metal strands until they snapped, its hands bleeding all over the place in the process.

I put a few bullets into the damned thing, but the damage was done. Even as it fell back into the water seven more took its place. When they came for us before, they were like soldiers doing what had to be done. I say that because the second wave that hit us moved like rabid dogs. They were angry now and they wanted to rip us apart.

Buddy wasn't angry, he was just determined. He moved in front of us all and started cutting loose, firing his weapons with deadly accuracy and blasting the fish men all around him. A lot of them fell back, but just as many fell forward, building a gathering layer of bodies that not only made a shield for their fallen brethren, but also put a terrifying amount of weight on one side of the boat. I could feel the deck shifting from the change in distribution.

I also felt something else, something that really had me worried. There was a vibration coming from below my feet that had nothing to do with waves or even the bodies hitting the deck.

"Oh shit! They're trying to come in from below!" The words were out of my mouth and I was moving, running toward the far side of the deck as fast as I could. I almost got stupid and touched the railing, but I wised up. Diana was right next to me and the both of us watched as the Deep Ones at the lower edge pounded their claws into the bottom of the *Marianne*, breaking wood and then tearing it free from the level that was normally underwater.

"Go get that bag of grenades." I spoke to Diana as we both watched, and then I opened fire. The angle was wrong; I could see them down there, but I couldn't get a bead on any of the ones actually doing the damage. The closest I could come was the ones moving behind them, and even then it was literally hit or miss. Several of the things let out barks of pain and wheeled away from the rapidly growing hole in the *Marianne*. More of them came closer to take their place. I emptied two clips of ammo before Diana made it back with the bag; the tilt of the boat was getting more pronounced and she almost had to crawl to get up the wet deck.

I risked a look back at the opened area and felt my heart stop. The fish men were falling fast but their numbers were almost endless and Charlie and Buddy were going to run out of ammo eventually, assuming the ship didn't sink first.

I grabbed the bag from Diana and fished out a grenade with absolutely no idea of what I was doing, except what I'd seen in movies. The pin was tighter than I expected and for a second I thought I'd never get it out. I let out a scream of frustration and almost broke my finger pulling, but finally it came free.

I pushed the grip down and took aim, then dropped the bomb down toward the fish men below. It landed in the water and sank fast. I didn't wait around to see how long it would take to detonate. I didn't want to be too close when the moment came.

Remember how I said Buddy threw the grenades as far as he could? I should have followed his example. The side of the *Marianne* where Diana and I were standing went up by a good five feet and then dropped down hard into the water.

The boat dropped faster than we did. Both of us were catapulted forward and rolled as we landed, smashing into the cabin wall.

I heard Diana's screams mingling with my own, through the incredible ringing that dwarfed every noise I'd ever encountered.

Off on the far end of the *Marianne,* Charlie and Buddy were hanging on to the railings, caught in the barbed wire. It was probably the only thing that saved them from falling into the sea when the boat almost capsized because of my stupidity. Most of the dead fish men had been washed off the deck and for the moment at least the *Marianne* was almost righted.

Buddy ripped himself away from the guardrail and

reached for another weapon. I guess the blast had made him drop whatever he'd had in his hands.

Charlie opened his mouth, looking at me with a furious expression that told me whatever was about to be said wouldn't be a pleasant thing to hear. That was the expression I remember on Charlie. His anger and pain, defined for a moment just before the first of the Deep Ones rose out of the water and sank powerful claws into his shoulders. Charlie never made a sound. The thing ripped the meat from his arms and chest and he never made a noise. I guess the pain of dying was just too big.

I was still trying to right myself as my first mate, one of my dearest friends, got hauled away from the side of the *Marianne* and thrown into the water.

TWENTY-THREE

Want to know what's right up there on the list of things that will fuck you up? Try watching a man who is almost like a brother getting torn to pieces before your eyes.

I didn't have any choice in the matter. I was looking right at Charlie when the Deep Ones ripped into him, tearing and clawing and biting. For almost a full minute they forgot about the rest of us and ripped Charlie apart.

Did Charlie scream? No. He never made a sound, or if he did, I couldn't hear it over the noises coming from the frenzied demons. As much as I wish I could say I ran to his aid, I was frozen while it happened. I couldn't have moved if I wanted to. I'd never been that horrified in my entire life.

Buddy wasn't involved personally. Maybe that's why he didn't have the issues that I had or Diana for that matter. While the two of us remained in our frozen stages, he cut loose with both barrels, successfully stopping the Deep Ones from taking the *Marianne*.

"Get your fucking asses in gear!" His voice was hoarse and furious, but his face remained unsettlingly serene as he kept firing away.

It was enough to motivate me. I picked up my automatic and started firing again, hitting more than I missed. I'd like to say that I was a damned fine shot, but the truth is, there were just too many of them to make it hard to find a target and hit it.

I moved closer to Buddy and yelled to be heard over the sounds of the Deep Ones and the automatic fire from the assault rifles. "They're tearing us apart from below!"

He nodded and looked away for a moment, grabbing clips and replacing the emptied cartridges with new ammunition. The air was cold enough for us to see our breath, but the weapons he was using were hot enough to let off steam.

"It's rigged up to go whenever you want it to, but the button is in the main cabin."

"I push that button and we're dead, you know that."

"Don't be a dumb fuck. We're dead either way."

I wish I could have argued the point with him, but, really, as far as I could tell we were toast. As I backed away from him and moved toward the cabin, I could see Diana taking shots at the Deep Ones daring the electrified barrier. It was only a matter of time before one or more of them decided to get all suicidal and sacrifice life and limb to the cause of ripping down the rest of the hot wires and then adding us to the menu of dead people.

I went inside and flipped the switch that Buddy had added to the control panel. The only thing it did for now was turn on another red light, this one hidden under the panel.

It also armed the explosives belowdecks. At a guess, it was somewhere close to five hundred pounds of plastic explosives, but what the hell did I know? I hadn't taken the time to weigh the stuff when we were carrying it on board.

I don't know how much it cost Demetrius to load me up, but I knew before I asked that he'd have no trouble at all footing the bill. I was doing this for Belle, after all, and what man wouldn't want payback against the bastards that took his daughter's life?

I grabbed a few more assault rifles on the way back out to the deck, and the transmitter that would detonate everything wired into the bottom of the boat.

Things had gotten worse by the time I made it outside again. True to my predictions, the Deep Ones had decided to pull down more of the hot wires and now they were climbing all over the place. Far in the distance, I saw the bank of fog that seemed to be the only sure sign that the ghosts were around the area, and grimaced. What good were they if all they ever did was watch? A few hundred ghostly sailors coming in to kick the crap out of the fish men would have been nice, but instead I got a spectral cheering squad.

Diana was about to get overrun and I moved in her direction. I waited until I was next to her to begin firing. She grabbed one of the rifles from my left shoulder and started shooting without bothering to check if I'd turned off the safety. I hadn't and that mistake cost her. One of the things let out a roar that was loud enough to rattle my bones, and swatted her across the chest. If she hadn't been wearing armor she'd have died right then. Instead she just staggered back and dropped her new weapon.

I killed the thing, spraying half a clip of bullets into its body, and then I killed the two behind it. Then another of them got past my defenses and scraped its claws into my chest as it pushed me. If it had managed to catch me properly it would have torn through my rib cage, but instead it only added to the multiple cuts I was already suffering.

Buddy was there a second later. I don't know if he was trying to save me, or trying to get away from the swelling tide of the things that had finally overtaken the *Marianne*,

but he was there and he was firing. Contrary to what anyone believes or what Hollywood portrays, firing a weapon
is hard work. One or two bullets and you're fine, but a con-
tinuous flow of automatic fire is like doing push-ups for at
least the same amount of time and he'd been shooting at
the damned tide of fish men for what seemed like an eter-
nity. Every muscle that showed past his armor was corded
and straining, and the blank expression was gone from his
face, replaced by the pain he had to be feeling.

"Hit the switch! Hit the goddamned switch and then
dive for it!" His voice was strained and desperate. He didn't
want to die on that boat and I didn't either to be perfectly
honest. I had unfinished business to take care of.

Diana was back with us again and firing in a constant
sweeping arc that lasted maybe seven seconds. The clip
in her rifle was emptied in that amount of time, and she'd
cut a path into the Deep Ones' ranks. It would have meant
more to me if they weren't already filling in the gaps,
swarming over their fallen brethren. I remembered what
Ward said about them not caring for their own kind except
in a peripheral way and I had to wonder if that was true,
because sure as hell, they seemed to want us dead more
than they wanted to live.

I felt the same way about them, so I listened to Buddy
and hit the switch on the detonator.

I looked at Diana and hollered "MOVE!" right before
I opened fire again, using her example to try blasting a
path through the fish men. Then I ran as hard as I could,
screaming the entire way, and dove over the side of the
Marianne.

What I fully expected to do was dive right into a whole
bunch of the bastards below, and that is exactly what happened. The only good news was that they weren't really
expecting a frontal assault. I guess they panicked, because
when they saw me coming down with Diana on one

side and Buddy on the other, the ones directly below us scattered.

They tried to scatter at least. I wound up landing on a few of them, and instead of splashing into water deep enough to dive into, I bounced off of them and then into the shallow water of the Devil's Reef.

I didn't have time to think about the fact that I'd parked the *Marianne* right above their cave entrance, right against the edge of the stone outcropping. For that matter, I couldn't even see the reef through the Deep Ones standing on it. So it was blind luck that I'd landed on a piece of ground and almost bashed myself senseless in the process. I got to my feet and ran as hard as I could, shivering in the cold.

You know what the biggest problem with chivalry is? You can't really turn it off. I headed back the other way when I heard Diana screaming and spent precious seconds pulling her from the water. She was an athletic woman, but she was also wearing a lot of now waterlogged body armor. As soon as we were both up, we started running again. I knew what we were running from, but I have no idea what was going through her head.

I looked back at the *Marianne* and saw her floundering. She was sinking at a decent pace and the Deep Ones crawling over her were adding to the damage, ripping parts of the hull away and trashing anything they could get their hands on.

Buddy was right behind me, staggered and winded, but still letting out an occasional burst of gunfire at the fish men who had noticed us in all the chaos.

We ran. It was all that was left to do.

And then the night exploded behind us and took the *Marianne* and at least a hundred of the water demons with it. The charges Buddy had set and that I had detonated blew my crabbing boat into a ton of driftwood and sent a shock wave powerful enough to knock all three of us through the air. I know people talk about how life and death moments seem to grow longer in recollection, but I was too busy curling myself into a ball and screaming bloody murder to notice much of anything. I was thrown around and bounced across the Devil's Reef, the impacts so powerful that they rolled me end over end and it was all I could do to keep my wits about me. When I came to a stop I didn't try to move or open my eyes for several seconds. My head was ringing like a church bell, and even though I knew I wasn't moving, everything around me was trying to spin.

When I finally moved, everything spun faster, but I knew I couldn't sit still for long. There were too many of the Deep Ones around for me to risk that. I opened my eyes and crawled to my hands and knees as I looked around.

There wasn't much to see; the fog was too thick. It hadn't been there only a moment before, but now it was as thick as the skin on cold pea soup. My head had stopped ringing; the high humming tone came from my ears alone. Still, I managed to stand up. Every weapon I'd been carrying was gone, lost as I was thrown across the black rock. I saw Buddy lying facedown on the ground, and heard him moan as he started to come to.

Then I heard Diana scream, a wild, panicked yelp that was quickly lost in a wave of the fish men's vile voices. I knew it had to be too late, even as I moved toward her voice, but I had to try. The damned fog was so thick I couldn't see more than shadows from five feet away. By the time I finally made it to where I thought I'd heard her voice, all I found was the remains of her body armor. The flack vest and matching leggings were heavily shredded and torn from her body.

Diana was gone, and I never saw her again.

As I stood there trying to absorb everything that had happened the Deep Ones kept up their infernal croaking, the sounds growing louder and more frenzied. I moved toward the edge of the reef, barely aware of anything. Somewhere behind me, Buddy coughed a few times and then called out to me.

I didn't respond. I was too busy watching what should have been impossible. The galleon I'd seen torn apart in a ghostly replay was right at the edge of the reef, and I stared as the dead sailors from another era climbed down the sides and set foot on solid ground. They did not pay me the least bit of attention as they moved across the land. Instead, they moved toward the Deep Ones and drew their weapons, muskets and swords alike, and engaged the enemy that had killed them in the distant past.

I heard the sounds of the renewed combat, but saw nothing through the fog. Pity, really. I would have liked to watch as the fish demons were slaughtered.

I was still thinking about them when I fell flat on my face against the rocks and the water. I guessed I was hurt a little more than I first thought.

Have you ever been whacked so hard that you could think but couldn't do much else? Well, I have. I was conscious enough to know that things were happening, but I couldn't move, and all the wishing in the world was not enough to open my eyes.

I know I was carried up the side of the ghostly ship. I know I was set down on the deck. I heard the sounds of the returning sailors. They moved grimly, with little or no celebration for any victories they might have had in their battle.

Still too dazed to do much of anything, I felt the ship move and turn against the tide, and was aware that we were going somewhere, but couldn't have guessed where.

Was I afraid? No. I think I was too surprised to be alive for that.

I did not see the captain of the ghost ship, but I heard him as he spoke and felt his hand on my chest. "You've done well, Captain. Better than I would have hoped. The Devil Reef has long been a bane on us. The water devils prevented our coming closer with their magic. Their sorceries have been our curse for over a hundred years. We could not pass the Devil Reef, nor even touch its stone. Deep below the waters, where you and yours have traveled, the land was marked by their spells. Whatever sorcery you used to destroy your vessel has ruined that for them."

I tried to speak but couldn't, and I think it was then I began to suspect my paralysis was from something other than my injuries. I couldn't open my eyes or even lift one finger, but there wasn't enough pain for me to believe that I was physically unable to react.

"Sleep, if you would, Captain. We'll have you to shore soon enough. We have had our fill of the sea demons and their constant interferences. We shall do what we can to guard against them in the future."

I slept. I really don't think I was given a choice.

When I woke up I was on the *Isabella,* in my bed. The sun wasn't up yet, but I could see the dawn's light creeping from the edge of the ocean in the distance. Between that light and the edge of the yacht, I could see what was left of the Devil's Reef—or I guess more properly the Devil Reef—and that the shape of it had been changed by the explosion.

I didn't think for even a second that anything that had happened to me was a dream. My body hurt too much and I was still covered in the foul stink from the fish men.

If anything, I thought my still being alive was a dream.

I moved with all the speed of a geriatric paraplegic. I don't think I've ever hurt that much in my entire life, physically anyway.

I had a thousand questions I wanted answered, but didn't

have the initiative to get up yet. Diana was gone, I was sure of that, and I hoped for her sake that she was dead. I didn't much want to think of the alternative.

Charlie was dead. That knowledge sapped me of strength, and left me almost as cold and empty as the knowledge that Belle was gone forever.

Buddy. I had no idea where he was.

That was what finally got me to move. I stood up and walked from my cabin, slowly working the stiffness from my shoulders and legs. The face I saw in the mirror looked only a little familiar. My reflection had more lines and wrinkles than I wanted to think about, even if they were hidden under some serious bruises and scratches.

I found Buddy unconscious on Charlie's bed and left him there. Then I went to my cabin again, stripped out of my clothes and took a long shower, careful to examine the deep cuts in my chest from the claws that had torn my clothes and skin alike.

When I was done I dressed as calmly as I could and made breakfast. I knew the divers would be around soon enough. I really, really hoped Ward would be with them.

The professor and me needed to have a long talk or maybe a short one. I guess that depended on him.

Buddy woke up by the time breakfast was finished. The way he moved made me feel better about my own aches and pains. His hands were swollen from all the weapons he'd fired the night before and despite his normally calm exterior, I could see that he was still shaken by what had happened.

Neither of us said a word about it at first. After a few minutes of eating and drinking coffee, he was the one who broke the silence. "Why are we still alive?"

"Dumb luck, apparently." I told him what I remembered from the night before and he confirmed my own beliefs. He'd been up and moving before the ghosts came along and dropped him in the same way they'd put me down.

I got out a set of binoculars to look over the Devil's Reef, trying to find any signs of what had happened the night before. I found plenty of them. Though the *Marianne* was properly scuttled, there were fragments of wood and bits of debris still floating in the water.

The part that actually threw me was when I realized there were no police vessels out there. Even that early in the day I'd have expected some sort of response from the noise of the explosion alone.

The college kids didn't show up to distract me from my thoughts. Neither did Ward. But the Parsonses did. Jacob and Mary climbed the gangplank and called out to let us know they were there.

One look at our faces was all it took for them to know that something was wrong, but I learned soon enough that they'd already guessed that.

"Martin is in the hospital," Jacob explained. "He said one of the Deep Ones bit his ear off."

"He's lying." I poured them each a cup of coffee and repressed the urge to head straight for the hospital. "I shot his ear off."

"What in the name of God happened last night, Joe?"

It took about twenty minutes for Buddy and I to fill them in, and fifteen more to answer all of their questions. They were horrified, of course, but both of them listened as calmly as they could. I guess when you've done the sort of work they do you get used to things not being what they seem at first.

"I checked Martin's room this morning, Joe. I found all of the notes he's made and I'm taking them with me."

"Not worried about breaking and entering laws, Jacob?"

"It's hard to prove, especially since all of the rooms are in my name and the contracts we signed before this started give me full rights to all research." He smiled, but it wasn't a happy expression. Jacob was bitter, and I suppose he had every right to be. He was especially shocked by the news that Ward had given the Deep One that had been his "guest" permission to choose a sacrifice from the people aboard the *Isabella*. I imagine he figured it was the luck of the draw that had ended Belle's life instead of Mary's. Or maybe the thing that had been in the shower had somehow told the other fish men who to grab. I don't think I'll ever really know the answer to that.

For her part Mary sipped at her coffee and listened to us talking, her eyes moving from one speaker to the next as she absorbed every word that was spoken.

She finally spoke up after the conversation died down. "Obviously the expedition is done." Her words were strictly business, but her tone also carried a hint of apology and maybe regret. "We never meant for any of this to happen, Joe. Please believe that."

I looked at Jacob and then at Mary and nodded. "I know. I don't hold you accountable for anything that happened here, guys. Not one bit of it."

"Maybe you should." I looked over at Mary as she said that, puzzled by her response. "We were the ones that agreed to this. We were the ones that funded it."

"You've been friends with Ward for years, right? Did he ever come across as a fanatic?"

Mary shook her head. "Eccentric, maybe, but he never really talked much about the studies he did until he came to us for funding. We thought he was looking for signs of a dead race, and it was a good excuse to get out here and see if we could find any truth behind all the rumors about ghosts."

Jacob nodded his head in agreement.

"So why would I blame you? The way I figure it, as far as he was concerned everyone on the yacht was a potential sacrifice. I've been thinking about it a lot, too, believe me.

The man came on at least two expeditions out here and the only person who survived both of them was him. That tells me he's either very lucky or he was up to something. After what happened last night, there's really not much doubt about which answer is right."

"What are you going to do about it, Joe?" Mary's voice was small and weak, barely even a whisper.

Buddy answered before I could. "He's not going to do a thing." I looked at him and he shrugged. "All he has to work with are allegations and guesses. All that could happen to him is he could get himself in a lot of trouble with the law, and one of the reasons I'm here is to make sure that doesn't happen."

I stared at him for what had to be half a minute and he stared back. Finally I nodded my head. "What he said." I wasn't happy about it, but what else was there for me to do?

We talked for a while longer and Jacob came up with a theory about the ghosts. He mentioned it out loud after we left the docks to take one last look at the Devil's Reef. Not so much because we wanted to see how much damage was done, but because I wanted to pay my last respects to Charlie, who I was certain would never be found.

The damage was much more impressive than I'd expected. While I could see what had happened to the reef with binoculars when I was onshore, most of the real impact had happened on the far side, facing the ocean, not Golden Cove. A good fifty feet of the black rock had been shattered in the explosion, and the crater was easily fifteen feet in from where the edge had been before. If there were any bullet casings or firearms out there we couldn't see them and I have to be honest here—I wasn't willing to look around for very long.

While the ghosts had apparently done one hell of a job slaughtering the fish men, I wasn't exactly willing to bet my life on all of them being gone.

We left after I spent a couple of minutes looking over the damage.

Around an hour later, the Parsonses had gathered all of their belongings from the hotel and told the college kids that it was finished. I didn't bother leaving the *Isabella* or trying to file a police report. Let's be honest here, I had every reason to believe that Jacob was right about the police in that town. I didn't see any reason to push any buttons with the locals.

How did I feel as I left Golden Cove? I don't really know. Numb, I guess. After everything that I'd been through, I just didn't have it in me to care about the damned place. I was alive, which was more than I expected, and I hurt in both my body and my soul.

I went home. I piloted the *Isabella* back to her proper place at Bowden's Point, and I said my goodbyes to the Parsonses. They promised to keep in touch and I promised the same. Maybe we will, but I think we all have a lot to recover from.

Buddy said he'd let Demetrius know what had happened and I thanked him for that.

I cleaned up the *Isabella* as best I could, washing her down and shutting her down. It was late enough in autumn that if anyone had wanted to go out on the water I'd have just laughed at them. If I'd been starving and desperate, I still wouldn't have considered taking her out. Of course, after what I'd been through that wasn't even a possibility.

I went home. To my empty house, my empty life, and I started the process of mourning properly.

Did I ever think about the Deep Ones and Golden Cove? Yes, every day. Mostly I locked myself away in my house and stayed there like a hermit and let myself think about Belle and Charlie and everyone else.

And I let myself heal as best I could.

By the spring thaw I was mostly myself again. When

the weather finally started getting warmer, I went back to the docks and cleaned up my girl, grateful for the chance to escape from the house I'd made a prison for a while.

I was on the *Isabella* and polishing the brass railings when I spotted Davey. He looked remarkably fit for a dead man.

In all the confusion from those days I'd never found out what happened to him, but he told me. The waves had taken him down and into the water during that sudden storm and he fought hard to stay afloat. According to what he had to say, the Coast Guard picked him up early the next morning, and he wound up in a hospital, with no recollection of who he was or how he got there.

His parents found him after almost a month, and while it had taken a while, he'd eventually gotten most of his memories back.

It's plausible enough, I know that. There's no reason to doubt him, but I still do. We parted company on that spring day and haven't talked except to nod at each other when we cross on the street.

I wish I could give a reason, but the only one I really have is that I know he's lying through his teeth. I don't know what he's hiding, but I do know the Coast Guard didn't pick him up. I checked with them when he disappeared, and even with my memory being less than perfect, I remembered them saying that the storm was incredibly isolated and they found no one.

Davey is alive and I guess that's a blessing, but there's just something about his story that doesn't fit and I can't make myself let it go. I guess maybe I'm getting a little less trusting in my old age.

It wasn't much after spring came around that I got the letter from Demetrius. It was short and to the point. Inside the envelope there was an article from a Boston newspaper and three lines from my father-in-law. His words were simple: "I hope you're well. Come see us when you have a chance. Thought this might interest you."

The article talked about the unusual circumstances surrounding the death of one Martin Edward Ward, a college professor who was found dead in his home. The man managed to drown in six inches of water in his tub. According to the paper, he apparently slipped and cracked his head open on the edge of the tub and then just choked to death on the water he sucked into his lungs.

I've still got the paper folded in my wallet. When I think of Belle and the weight of her loss becomes enough to crush me, it makes me feel a little better to read that piece.

I guess I'll have to thank Buddy if I ever see him again.

In the meantime, the busy season is getting ready to start and I have a new crew to hire. There are plenty of prospects and it shouldn't be hard to come up with a few competent people to help me.

Local charters only from now on, of course. I won't be taking anyone fishing up the coast for a long, long time if ever again. I can't just stay at home, a man has to make a living, and like my father and my grandfather before me, I'm a fisherman first and foremost.

Besides, I think Belle might actually come back to haunt me if I sulked around the house for too long, and I've had enough of ghosts to last me a lifetime. I prefer to think she's in heaven if there really is such a place.

But what about Golden Cove? What happened to it? Will I ever go back?

Golden Cove is still in the same place, and the tourist business is getting a little better, I suppose. Not so many claims that the place is haunted. Who knows, maybe the police there have gotten a little more caring. I can't say, as I haven't been back. Will I ever go there again? Maybe. I just don't know yet. Part of me wants to, I can tell you that much. Part of me wants to check everything out again and see if there are still lights late at night on the Devil's Reef, or strange fogs that come and go at their own whim.

Most of me just wants to do what I have always done and to try to put the pieces of my life back together.

My grandfather used to tell me that the oceans knew all the secrets the world had to offer. I've learned how to listen for them and these days, I keep a few surprises hidden on board, just in case those secrets come back to bother me again.

Don't miss the page-turning suspense, intriguing characters, and unstoppable action that keep readers coming back for more from these bestselling authors...

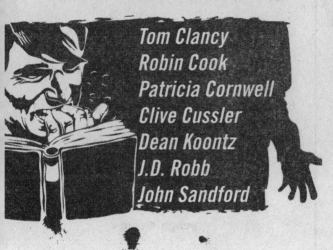

Tom Clancy

Robin Cook

Patricia Cornwell

Clive Cussler

Dean Koontz

J.D. Robb

John Sandford

Your favorite thrillers and suspense novels come from Berkley.

penguin.com

M14G0907

Penguin Group (USA) Online

What will you be reading tomorrow?

Tom Clancy, Patricia Cornwell, W.E.B. Griffin,
Nora Roberts, William Gibson, Robin Cook,
Brian Jacques, Catherine Coulter, Stephen King,
Dean Koontz, Ken Follett, Clive Cussler,
Eric Jerome Dickey, John Sandford,
Terry McMillan, Sue Monk Kidd, Amy Tan,
John Berendt…

You'll find them all at
penguin.com

Read excerpts and newsletters,
find tour schedules and reading group guides,
and enter contests.

Subscribe to Penguin Group (USA) newsletters
and get an exclusive inside look
at exciting new titles and the authors you love
long before everyone else does.

PENGUIN GROUP (USA)
us.penguingroup.com

M224G1107